Bayou Curse

Riley McKissack

About the Author

Riley McKissack is an award-winning journalist. Cornered gunmen, cop killers, a bomb going off in a domestic terrorism incident, Riley's covered them all. Riley spent years chasing stories involving every type of bad guy and cop imaginable, including FBI, Homeland Security, homicide detectives and arson investigators.

Riley sponged up the drama, tension and danger on SWAT operations, hostage negotiations, drug busts and countless other dangerous situations.
That passion and drama spills out onto the pages of Riley's novels, along with the personal stories behind the men and women who stand between danger and the people they love.
Riley has spent a lot of time in small Georgia towns and enjoys writing about them.

Riley can be found at:
https://facebook.com/riley.mckissack
http://rileymckissack.com
https://twitter.com/RileyMckissack

i

Danger lurks in the bayou for a reporter who follows a story deep into the swamps of Cajun country.

Has a curse called Jenna Lejeune to southern Louisiana to rendezvous with her lover from centuries ago?

Whether a curse or superstition, the powerful attraction between Jenna and Eddie Devereaux feels like a memory echoing through time, bringing them together in life after life.

Whatever the reality, someone wants Jenna Lejeune dead.

CHAPTER ONE

Syrupy fog flowed off the Mississippi River as it curled around New Orleans. The mist licked hungrily, greedily along the cobblestones of the French Quarter.

The deep fog cloaked the buildings, misting the area with a softening gray that swallowed sound.

Jenna Lejeune peered through the dark, swampy air at almost midnight, trying to get her bearings. Which way to the hotel? Everything blended together in this mist.

She'd been so deep in thought about the articles she needed to write that she'd become a bit distracted.

Muffled footsteps echoed along the dark street. She looked back over her shoulder, for the first time processing that someone might be following her. Those feet seemed to have deliberately turned left as she had twice now.

She stared into the darkness, attempting to decipher the various shades of charcoal. Was that someone darting in and out of the shadows? Had they sidestepped into the shadows, like a black cat on a dark night, slipping along the corners of buildings?

It was probably just some drunk guy behind her, thinking he was following his girlfriend back to the hotel, after a fight maybe. Lots of heavy partying going on tonight in the Quarter.

Still, she started moving forward with purpose, determined to get back to the heavily trafficked tourist areas. She shouldn't have tried a shortcut. A brushing of footsteps along the brick pavers echoed loudly in the dark night. It sounded like the person was gaining on her.

The sound of the closing footsteps whispered to her that someone was coming for her.

Her heart rate accelerated, beating the warning into her blood - don't question it, just believe it.

The mist swirled along behind her, a ghost following, whispering her name. She strained to see through the fog. *Oh, God, please let nothing be there*.

A skittering to her left sounded loud in the night. What was that? A cat scuttled across the ancient paving stones.

Her breath caught, then she released the air held hostage in her lungs. It was only a feline inhabitant of the Quarter slinking deeper into the shadows.

Then, the phantom gray mist behind her floated free of the image of a man before closing back around to dissolve him again.

She almost screamed, but pulled the sound back in, somehow sensing it might result in an all out race to evade whoever was behind her. She continued walking, heading toward help.

Still, her pulse bolted into a flat out sprint. Run, run, run, her blood urged.

A noisy ruckus echoed distantly from the direction of Bourbon Street. If she yelled, would anyone notice? If they did, would they mistake her for just another reveler?

Calm down, you've been in worse situations than this, that little voice that had kept her alive so many times before coaxed. She'd headed into pounding hurricane-driven rains to cover storms, and stared into the barrel of a gun on a particularly hairy story.

Yeah, a drunk in the French Quarter was nothing. Still, all the spooky things that had happened since she'd come to Louisiana haunted her mind, and she kept glancing over her shoulder.

She inhaled a long steadying breath, then determinedly placed one foot in front of the other just short of a run. The mist closed in front of her like a cloud, and she pushed into it, swimming through it as much as walking, droplets sprinkling on her skin, wetting her hair, blinding her.

The tapping footsteps sounded close, as if the man could lurch forward and grab her.

She broke into a run. With a shuffling gait and her hands extended in front of her, she fled. Her blood pulsed through her veins so loud she no longer knew what she heard and what she imagined.

She rounded a corner and the mist cleared as quickly as it had come. A well-lit street with strolling tourists materialized out of the mist, with the accompanying normality of the tourist area.

She ran toward the nearest crowd, dodging into their midst, their wonderful, stumbling and joking midst. "Hey, baby," one half-drunk man said jovially, wrapping his arm around her waist.

Never had a drunken man's embrace felt so comforting. She inhaled the odor of beer that drifted off him as she gulped in air.

She didn't care that he was leaning unsteadily into her. Her chest heaved and her heart pounded with relief for the company.

"You okay, darlin'?" The big man listed to the side as he looked into her face with a genial, good old boy smile.

"I think some man was following me," she pushed out the words from her constricted lungs.

"Where?" He looked back, suddenly seeming much less drunk. "Hey, guys," he called after his buddies. "Some jerk's giving this lady trouble."

"I'm okay. He probably just wanted my purse," she said.

"Well, I'll go kick his ass, thinking he can rob some woman. Let him mess with me." The man took a step forward, but Jenna grabbed onto his shirt. "He might have a gun," she said.

The man stopped and nodded.

The shadowy figure had felt menacing, terrifying even, the way he'd clicked along after her so steadily. As if calculating, waiting for just the right moment to strike.

Jenna looked over her shoulder, straining to see. Who would round that corner behind her?

Seconds passed, slowly counting themselves into minutes, until finally she realized no one was going to show himself. No harmless, innocent looking person would appear so she could laugh at her ridiculous fear.

The eerie feeling she'd experienced in the last few days of being watched intensified. She glanced around at overhead balconies, side alleys and then back at the corner.

Only a trailing finger of mist crawled around the corner, slowly dissipating.

"Thanks so much, guys," Jenna said, with a smile that she hoped didn't look like a grimace. She glanced around, and without the mist, she suddenly realized she was very close to where she was staying. "I think he's gone." She waved at them and headed toward her hotel.

The streets surrounding Jackson Square were wet, the old paving stones glistening in the dark. Beyond them, a wave of mist flowed off the river, rolling along like a living thing, obscuring the ground, heading straight for her.

Her hotel at the corner of Jackson Square beckoned to her, lit from within with heat-filled light that beat back the mist. She gave one final wave back to the watching group and hurried toward the hotel.

She pushed open the front door. The lobby was abandoned, the front desk empty with a note and a bell. She padded through the quietly echoing room to the elevator, entered and pulled the antique cage door closed, punching in her floor. The metal contraption clanged its way heavily and slowly toward the fourth floor.

*****

Deep in the heart of Cajun country, in the swampy Louisiana bayous a hundred miles west of New Orleans, mist swirled around the front porch of an old, low-slung cabin.

Two women, past their eightieth birthdays, huddled together around a kerosene lamp sitting on a battered wooden table. Shadows flickered across their faces, emphasizing the grooves time had etched in their skin.

A line of smoke from the flame curled into the air, twining around them, tying them seemingly into one being, their heads close together.

"The babies are dying. Something must be done," a quivery, old woman's voice whispered in the dark night.

Deep in the dark, beyond the meager light thrown from the front porch, an owl hooted with a haunting sound that echoed through the moss-laden trees. Both women looked away into the woods surrounding the cabin, then turned back to each other, their eyes narrowed, their mouths taut.

"I have issued the call," said the elder, though only the two of them remembered anymore who was the oldest. "If she is the right one, we will know soon enough."

The other old woman's eyes watered, her face crinkling even further, an apple doll's face after a hundred years. She'd been young once, beautiful, and men had desired her. She'd married and lost her first child, so she knew the pain facing her granddaughter if she lost the child she was carrying.

"The woman must come soon. My great grandbaby is due in a month. I will not see the beautiful face of my granddaughter covered with tears."

"Aah," answered the eldest, her eyes looking into the distance. Seeing the future or the past? "It has begun. Three babies dead in as many weeks. There's no doubt the curse is back and must be answered."

Mist curled around the edges of the porch, then crept into the night and into the darkness to join all that lived at the edges of civilization.

Then, it trailed off toward the east looking to meet the fog that flowed off the Mississippi River as it curled around New Orleans.

CHAPTER TWO

Spanish moss trailed from ancient trees along the country road as Eddie Devereaux steered his old truck toward his mama's house on the outskirts of Eufaula, Louisiana. Only about a hundred miles west of New Orleans, it might as well have been another world.

Heavy Cajun accents rang out whenever Eddie hung with his family. The accents and the food were some of the reasons he loved this part of southern Louisiana so much.

It was still early when he pulled his pickup truck into the front driveway of his mama's low-slung house with its wrap-around porch - the old home place. He walked around back and in through the kitchen door.

"Hey, Mama." His mother's kitchen smelled the same as it had when he was six years old - of cinnamon, coffee and hot sauce.

"Hey, sugar, how are you?" she said in her heavy Cajun accent as she rose on her tiptoes to kiss him on the cheek.

Soft and round, Margeaux Devereaux was still pretty. Her olive colored skin was unlined, and the woman wore lipstick and makeup even just around the house. Her dark brunette hair always looked like she'd just been to the beauty parlor, courtesy of the pink foam rollers she slept with at night.

Pride filled him every time he saw her. He'd drawn the lucky straw for mamas.

She wiped away the lipstick mark she'd left on his cheek and pointed at a chair in the living room, visible through the open archway separating the two rooms. "Can you help me shift that over a bit, sweet pea?"

"Sure, Mama. Where do you want it?"

She pointed to a window. "I want Celia to be able to sit over here by the window and look out, then maybe your sister won't get cabin fever so bad." She followed him into the living room and reached for a side of the armchair. "I'll get this side."

He waved her away. "I got it. Don't want you throwing your back out again."

He was Margeaux Devereaux's baby, her firstborn. That's how she'd always think of him though he towered over her. He was really lucky to have a mama like her who lavished love on everyone in her family and he repaid her every chance he got, even if it was just moving some furniture.

"That Celia." Eddie grinned. "She's getting bigger every day. Are you sure her due date is still a few months off?"

"She's carrying big." His mother pointed to the spot by the window. Eddie hefted the chair over his head and hauled it across the room. "That doctor really wants her off her feet as much as possible. I thought maybe I'd teach her to knit. Something to keep her occupied."

Eddie thunked down the chair.

Then, he parroted back his mama's often repeated words, even raising his voice higher in an imitation of her voice, "Probably gonna want her on bed rest, if she doesn't start taking it easy."

Margeaux arched an eyebrow at her son's teasing. "I tell you what, she's like a treed coon, all agitated." She tutted and tsked for a moment. "That doctor, he don't

want her sitting at home alone while Larry's
in town at work. If she goes into early
labor and starts bleeding a lot, she could
pass out, all alone out there in the
country."

Eddie sobered at the thought. Everyone
was talking about the recent deaths of
babies born prematurely over in Saint
Thomasville.

His mother looked at him as if she'd
just read his thoughts and bobbed her head,
as if agreeing with herself. "She's best off
here with her mama. Ain't nobody like Mama
when you're pregnant."

"She's lucky to have you looking after
her, Mama."

She beamed with pride, but the nervous
energy still thrummed beneath the surface of
her skin.

"She's gonna be fine, Mama. She's a
healthy, young woman, no reason to worry."

A dark shadow passed through her eyes.

"What aren't you telling me? Has the
doctor told you more about what's going on
with her?"

She shrugged.

"And what's with all those babies dying
over in Saint Thomasville? Is there some
tainted food or something? I'll check the
Internet and see if there's anything we're
missing."

"It's nothing like that," she muttered,
almost to herself, then she seemed to
realize she'd said the words out loud and
laughed with a false ring to her voice.
"Everything will be fine."

"Where is Celia?" He looked around.

"Oh, she's in the potty right now."

"Should'a guessed." Eddie nodded.

"Every time I come over here, she's coming or going from there. When I was driving her home last week, we had to stop halfway so she could use the restroom at the gas station."

His mama laughed. "Oh gawd, not that nasty one on the way to her house. I would get out and go on the side of the road afore I'd go in there."

"But, yeah, seems every five minutes, the girl is getting up to use the bathroom," his mama agreed. "Got TB, tiny bladder. Last trimester baby bladder."

"So, everything's normal, then."

Margeaux glanced away, her eyes scanning the surrounding woods outside the window.

"The doctor, he say everything going okay, eeh?" He heard himself slipping into the Cajun pattern he fell back into whenever he spent time with other Cajuns.

"Oh, yeah," his mother answered. But a glimmer of worry skimmed across her face.

"What?" He stepped closer.

"Oh, it be nothing. Just a mama worrying about her girl having her firstborn."

But that wasn't all. Her face hid very little from him. As her firstborn, he'd seen her as a young woman. They'd almost grown up together, so he knew her.

What wasn't she telling him? She turned away, straightened a pillow on the sofa, then headed toward the kitchen. "Back in a flash."

Just then, Celia came out of the bathroom.

"Hey, bro. What brings you by?" His sister waddled, ungainly, across the floor.

"You sure they got that due date right?" She looked ready to pop.

"Thanks for the reminder. I know I'm as big as a house." She tilted her mouth down accusingly. "Actually, I think I'm about to give birth to a gallon of ice cream."

Warmth bubbled up inside him, seeing his baby sister about to be a mama.

"I been overdoing it a bit while I've been sitting around watching soap operas." She smiled, self-deprecatingly. "The young and the restless is me."

"Oh, you look great. Glowing with pregnancy and all that." She did look good, despite the waddling. Her long auburn hair was glossy, and her coffee colored eyes shone with health.

Celia smiled. "Thanks." She leaned in to whisper. "I think Mama and Grandma got the doctor to tell me to take it easy."

She raised an eyebrow. "I don't think he believes there's anything wrong with me. Just kept saying I need to take off work and put my feet up, and sending glances Mama's way, as if checking to see if he was saying what she'd told him to say."

"Yeah, you know those two went to high school together. I think he was sweet on Mama back in the day," he added.

Celia whispered, "Well, who wasn't sweet on Mama back in the day?" They both smiled, knowing Margeaux Devereaux could still turn a head. Celia put both hands on her lower back, as if an ache was coming on that sometimes bothered her as the day wore on.

Eddie patted the big armchair, and Celia settled down into it, using both arms to support her heavy descent. "I miss work."

"What with all your running to the bathroom, I don't know if you could have kept up the waitressing." Celia laughed a bit. "Besides," he added, "Larry's making enough money and you were going to quit anyway as soon as the baby came."

"Oh, I know. But then, I'll have my darling baby to occupy my every thought." She rubbed her belly, a look of pure love on her face. She was going to make the best mama ever.

"I miss seeing everybody more than my tips and paycheck." She pulled a rueful face. "I'm out of the loop out here. Don't get to hear the gossip firsthand. It's always so much juicier in first person." Eddie brought a footstool over and she propped up her feet.

"I'll run you in for lunch one day this week," he promised. "I'll catch up on the gossip with you."

She laughed. "Yeah, you listening to gossip will be the day. But, thanks, Eddie. I'm marooned out here when Larry takes the car to work." She pointed out the window. "I'd take Mama's car into town, but suddenly, it's *unreliable*." She blew out a gust of air. "It's like she's trying to keep me cooped up here."

"Mama hen," he made an excuse for his mother. "She's always been overprotective of you."

"I know." She threw a look over her shoulder toward the kitchen and lowered her voice. "All those babies dying over in Saint Thomasville has got everybody freaked out. Is there something in the water over there?"

He shrugged. "I've heard about it. I'm gonna check to see if there's anything about it online."

"Insane! Whoever heard of that many stillborns and babies born in distress and dying all in a row like that?" She shivered. "Horrible! Thank God there's been nothing like that over here."

Then, she seemed to deliberately place a smile on her face. "So, Eddie what's up with you?"

"Nothing," he answered honestly. "Nothing at all."

"No love life, still? That girl up in Baton Rouge your college roommate fixed you up with didn't take?"

He shook his head. "Nah." He plopped down on the couch. "She was pretty and all that. Smart." He waggled his hand in the air.

Celia grinned, naughtiness playing in her eyes. "Not even good enough for one night?"

A laugh burst from his mouth and he leaned forward. "I wouldn't be talking about it to you, if she had been."

"Since when?"

He glanced back toward the kitchen. "Since you've been spending so much time out here with Mama. No telling what girls will get to talking about when they're as bored as you obviously are."

Celia put her hand over her mouth, holding back a laugh so their mother wouldn't come out to see what was so funny.

"You ought to take up knitting or something to keep you occupied. Mama said she's willing to teach you. Make some booties for the baby." Eddie pushed up from the sofa. He patted his sister's stomach. "See you, kiddo," he said to her belly.

Celia smiled back at him, a bit of the *little sister* showing around her eyes.

"I'm gone, Mama. Got to get to court."

Margeaux walked out of the kitchen, grabbed his shirtfront and pulled him down to her level, then bussed a big kiss on his cheek. "You need a haircut."

"I know, Mama, just been too busy to get that done. Take care of little sis." He escaped out the door.

As he got in his truck and drove away, Margeaux watched her firstborn from the window.

"He ought to get himself something better to drive than that old truck," Celia said, peering out the window from her big armchair. "How are people gonna know he's a big, successful judge?"

"The only people who don't know that aren't from round here," Margeaux answered. "And he don't need to be having nothing to do with those people no how."

Celia looked back at her knowingly. "You're talking about that Lejeune woman."

Margeaux squinted her eyes at Celia. "What have you heard?"

"Only what you told me, Mama. That Cousin Mike saw him reading those newspaper articles written by her."

Margeaux looked intently at her daughter. "Eddie hasn't said anything about her to you? Does he know her somehow? Are they dating?"

"How would he even know her?" Celia leaned for the remote control on the side table.

"He did go down to New Orleans last week."

Celia looked up. "You told me that

woman lives in Atlanta, not New Orleans. I don't know why you're so fixated on that Lejeune woman." She shot her mother a look. "It's not like she's the real *Lejeune Woman*," she said in a spooky voice.

Margeaux shook her head. "We don't need no Lejeune women coming round here!"

Celia's eyes rounded and she stared at her mother for a long moment before shaking her head. "I'm not a little girl you need to scare with tales about how the Lejeune Woman's gonna get me if I go into the woods. Though, I admit, she did do the job of keeping me from getting down by that lake where the gator lived."

Her mother narrowed her eyes, as if she thought Celia was keeping information from her.

"I don't think he's got anything going with any woman, so don't worry about him getting involved with The Lejeune Woman."

"Well, that's alright." Her mother nodded, her warm brown eyes narrowing with satisfaction. "Me and some ladies from the church are gonna fix him up with a nice girl from round here."

"Right," Celia blew out in a burst of amused disbelief. "You and the church ladies got it all set. Who?"

"Never you mind. We're gonna find him somebody. Somebody better than that ex-wife of his from up in Baton Rouge." She uhm-hummed. "He needs to stick with local girls. Not them outsiders."

Celia nodded. "You never did like Lidia."

Margeaux sniffed disdainfully. "I liked her fine till she cheated on my boy and broke his heart."

Celia smiled sadly. On the subject of Eddie's ex-wife, they were in perfect agreement.

CHAPTER THREE

Jenna walked into the courthouse of Eufaula, Louisiana, deep in the heart of Cajun country. A welcoming wagon in the form of a motorcycle cop had given her a ticket for running a stop sign.

She'd told him there was no way she could be blamed for not seeing that sign with the foliage growing over it and that she would definitely fight the ticket.

He'd glanced at her out of state driver's license, then assigned her to a court appearance on the same day, saying he had to show up then, and wouldn't be back in court again for weeks. If she wanted to fight it, today was apparently the day to do it.

The bailiff at the courthouse front door glanced at her name on the ticket, then did a double take up to look at her face. "Magistrate court will be officiated by Judge Edward Devereaux in Courtroom Two." He pointed down the hall.

"Really! A Devereaux? They seem to be everywhere over here."

He nodded. "We're full up with Devereaux over here. Your people, the Lejeunes, mostly stay over in Saint Thomasville. They don't come over here."

"What?" The way he'd said her last name was as if he'd personally known some Lejeunes, and they obviously hadn't been nice people. She'd gotten that double take a lot since she'd been in town, when people heard her last name.

She'd have to check out what type of people those Saint Thomasville Lejeunes were.

She headed toward the courtroom. The old courthouse was incredibly beautiful. Her heels clicked on the wide, heart-of-pine floors worn to a soft sheen by years of use.

The high ceilings, bead board walls, and oversized, heavy, antique doors were lovely, but her growing anticipation of encountering Judge Edward Devereaux distracted her. The traffic ticket had been a speed bump, slowing her from covering her story, but since she had to deal with it, at least she'd get to meet a real live member of the Devereaux family.

She needed to work her hurricane survival stories.

But, Devereaux, that name kept haunting her mind.

She'd asked around after the traffic stop about Jean Claude Devereaux, the man whose journal pages and a copy of whose portrait had been slipped under her New Orleans hotel room door. Funny how hardly anyone had information to offer on the subject.

Finally the local librarian, a relative newcomer, her parents having moved to the area only forty years ago, said the Devereaux family had been here for generations.

That wasn't surprising. When she'd done an Internet search, countless Devereaux appeared for the area. She'd found so many of them that she wasn't sure where to start in her quest to get answers about the Cajun's fate.

Eufaula, Louisiana, about two hours

west of New Orleans, and deep in Cajun country, was a hotbed of Devereauxs.

She stopped and shuffled in her shoulder bag, looking for her tablet, with the photos she'd taken of the overgrown stop sign. Had to make sure she had her evidence.

But the manila envelope in her bag called her to look at its contents once again. She pulled it out, and slid the papers out, as she'd done so many times since someone had slid this under the door of her New Orleans hotel room for some weird reason.

It was just another of the strange things that had happened over the week. She and her photographer, Zoom, had been doing their story of the follow up to last year's massive hurricane evacuation from the low-lying areas around New Orleans. Rafael's winds had wreaked havoc. Would that area ever be safe from the flooding of hurricanes?

She looked at Jean Claude's handwriting, feeling a personal connection to the man. The journal excerpts in the archaic handwriting were heart wrenching, with Jean Claude's longings for his Genevieve. But, it was the photo of the portrait of Jean Claude that haunted her the most.

Those black eyes stared out at her, connecting with her, as if she actually had known the man. It was crazy. She shuffled the papers back into the envelope and headed toward the courtroom.

As Jenna neared the courtroom door, her pulse accelerated. It was as if she was opening the door for a long anticipated first date with a guy with whom she shared incredible chemistry. A guy with whom it was only a matter of time.

But this judge wasn't Jean Claude. Jean Claude had to have been dead for three hundred years although she had yet to find an exact date. If she got this excited over every Devereaux she met down here, she'd be out of adrenaline quickly, with exhausted hormones.

As she raised her hand to the courtroom door, something stopped her from touching it. An edgy, almost electric sense came from the wood. She moved her hand closer and the humming grew stronger in her fingertips, as if a charge were passing between her body and the door.

Tentatively, she made the connection with the door handle, and as if the energy passed through her and on down into the floor, the sensation faded. She pulled on the handle and the door swung open.

Judge Edward Devereaux sat on the bench. Her breath caught in her chest and her stomach twisted with a wrenching pulse.

The judge looked so much like the portrait of Jean Claude Devereaux. Not an exact likeness, but as if someone had painted a portrait that hadn't quite captured the true image of the man - the unbelievably sexy man.

As if two dimensions couldn't show the way this judge looked. Intelligence and vitality flashed from his eyes, and a wave of masculinity rolled off him.

A man like him could inspire you to search endlessly, if you felt you held his heart.

There was no denying his heritage as a descendant of Jean Claude Devereaux. The family resemblance was too great.

This guy was a judge?

His dark brown hair seemed a bit too long for a judge, more like the rustic image in her dreams, and his shoulders stretched wide under the judicial robe, which seemed designed to disguise his attractiveness. Big fail.

The heavy wooden door slipped out of her grasp and closed with a resounding thud.

The judge looked up and their gazes locked, with an instant connection of awareness, his gaze holding hers with that unmistakable male assessment of her as a woman.

And something more.

Or rather, her sensible side said, as though he knew she was staring avidly at him. Finally, he broke the connection, glancing down at the papers in his hand before quickly looking back at her as she still gaped at him.

Get a grip, girl. You've met serial killers and acted less foolish.

The sense of knowing him, and of being known by him, was powerful. It had been too long since she'd felt this instant connection to a man.

How crazy.

She'd probably killed any credibility she had for fighting this ticket. Acting like a loon, coming into court and staring at the judge.

But, suddenly, the ticket seemed so unimportant.

It felt as if she'd met Jean Claude. No matter how absurd it sounded to search for a dead man, something deep inside her pushed her on with a driving desire to find him.

She tore her gaze away and searched for
an empty seat. The courtroom was packed with
a full listing of people on the docket for
traffic offenses. Was the area some type of
a speed trap? Once she was settled, she
chanced a glance back at the judge.

He seemed to be in his mid-thirties. As
he'd looked at her, his deep brown eyes had
sparkled with vitality and masculinity, and
maybe it had been her imagination, but
virility also. That thick, dark hair could
use a trim, but it wasn't too bad, just like
a guy who'd gotten too busy to get a
haircut. She kind of liked the unpolished
look. Especially on him.

Jenna glanced down at her hands,
finding it hard not to stare at this man.

"Lacroix," the bailiff called loudly.
"Lacroix!"

A man raised his hand. "I'm a friend of
his. He'd mentioned he had to be in traffic
court today. But, I knew he wouldn't be
remembering nothing 'bout no ticket, after
what happened. So, I came down here for
him."

The bailiff motioned him to stand.

"What happened?" the judge asked.

"His baby died last night."

The judge's eyes narrowed and someone
behind Jenna gasped. She glanced back at two
young women with their heads together. One
whispered, "Three babies died in three weeks
over in Saint Thomasville. Now one over
here."

"Oh lord," her friend whispered back.
"I hope it's not moved over here; whatever
they've got." The woman placed her hand over
her extended stomach. She was probably in
her sixth month.

So many babies dying in such a short period? Perhaps caused by something in the water or air or food, or who knows? Now, that was a story.

One that really mattered.

"It's that *Lejeune Woman* thing," an old woman sitting beside them muttered, as if to herself, but her words had been loud enough for Jenna to hear them.

Lejeune woman? Jenna was tempted to turn and look at the woman to see if she recognized her, but decided not to, considering how her name had been said.

"I didn't realize that was his baby that died," the bailiff said, with a sharp glance at the judge.

Judge Devereaux shook his head sadly. "Dismiss that ticket. He called in to my clerk and said he'd been hurrying his wife to the hospital over in Lafayette when the cop stopped him, afraid she was going into early labor two weeks ago when he got that ticket. Shouldn't have ever been issued in the first place. Some newbie cop, probably. Is the cop even here?"

The bailiff shook his head and handed the ticket to the courtroom clerk, looked down at his clipboard then called, "Lejeune. Jenna Lejeune."

An audible gasp came from the courtroom crowd. She stood and all heads whipped toward her.

A mixed reaction showed in their eyes: fear, surprise, curiosity, even anger. Still, there was interest in every face. Whoever that *Lejeune Woman* was that they all seemed to know must be something.

Feeling like she was on a stage, Jenna approached the podium as the cop who'd written her ticket appeared across the courtroom.

The judge nodded in acknowledgement of the cop, who smirked as if he couldn't quite hide a smile.

What the hell? Did he have that much invested in getting the money from her ticket?

"So, *officer*," the judge said. "This is your case?"

"Yes, your honor."

The judge just shook his head. "I think I'll hear from the lady first, if you don't mind."

"It's your courtroom." The officer nodded. There was definitely some undercurrent running between the judge and the cop. Was he known for stopping tourist women, or something? The whole thing had felt funny from the beginning. The judge nodded at Jenna.

"Your honor," she said.

His deep brown eyes surveyed her, waiting expectantly, a shadow of the same reaction as the crowd showing in his eyes, as if he knew her or something.

Nervous energy thrummed through her body as his dark brown eyes skimmed across her, seeming to look into her very soul, intense, probing. His tanned skin looked good with those eyes and his dark brown hair.

She cleared her throat. This was about a ticket, nothing else. Not about that man who came to her in her dreams, with the wicked hands and the knowing mouth. She swallowed, her mouth dry, wishing for a glass of water.

The judge motioned to his bailiff

toward a pitcher of water sitting on a nearby desk. The bailiff took the hint, poured a glass of water, and brought it to Jenna.

How had the judge known? As if he could read her thoughts. As if he'd read her journal.

She gulped down a swallow of water, then began her defense, describing the situation with the traffic ticket and the shrubbery. "The sign was not visible," she concluded.

The judge accepted the tablet she handed to the bailiff, his eyes still connecting with Jenna's. Finally, he glanced at the tablet, then at the cop and shook his head, his expression grim. The cop smiled slightly, then looked back at her as he seemed to struggle to tamp down a smile.

What was so damn funny?

"I know that intersection," the judge said, his face serious. It was all professional on the surface. But his deep voice, masculine in timbre, skimmed across her skin, activating pheromones and nervous energy.

She tried to concentrate on his words.

"You should have been looking for a stop sign on some corner, yours or theirs, and wondering why you didn't see one." He looked at the cop. "*However*, the county needs to keep the shrubbery trimmed. So, I'm going to dismiss this ticket."

The cop didn't protest, but just waited. His eyes glinted with amusement as he fixed them on the judge.

The judge stared at him with no expression, as if this were just business.

Which of course it was. But, what had

been with that cop's grin?

The judge shook his head at the cop.

Jenna pulled a sense of professionalism from somewhere in her psyche, somewhere underneath all the hormones this judge evoked and the curiosity the cop's smile had sparked. She kept her tongue in check and just nodded.

She'd beat the cop's ticket.

And, as irritating as the time suck of having to come to court had been, and as much as she suspected the judge also thought the cop writing the ticket had been wrong, she'd still met this judge, who was a Jean Claude look alike.

So, there was that.

The judge signed off on her ticket and handed it to the bailiff.

She stood there for a moment, wanting the judge to look up, to meet her gaze again, to connect with her. She didn't want to leave, but the bailiff nodded for her to move over to the clerk's desk, so she had to leave.

Something in her wanted to stay in the judge's presence all day, wanted those coffee-colored eyes to turn her way again. Still wanted it, felt slightly bereft without his gaze on her.

The judge motioned the cop to approach the bench and shifted the microphone away so that his words wouldn't be projected to the courtroom audience. His eyes narrowed as he spoke to the cop. "If you ever …" His next words were unintelligible since the judge dropped his voice even further.

Jenna walked to the clerk, a little gray-haired lady dressed as if for Easter Sunday: wearing a pale pink suit with a fresh flower pinned to her lapel and pink lipstick and nail polish that coordinated with her outfit.

The clerk finished with the person in front of Jenna then took Jenna's paperwork. "Lejeune?" She read the name, then sat back quickly, the papers fluttering out of her hands to the floor.

The bailiff picked them up and handed them to the clerk. The woman shot a secretive glance at him but his expression remained noncommittal.

"I didn't see your name on the calendar, dear," the woman whispered, leaning in to catch Jenna's words as if she were hard of hearing, obviously having missed the whole courtroom drama her name had invoked.

"I was added at the last minute."

"Lejeune? Jenna Lejeuene? Would Jenna be short for Genevieve?" the woman almost whispered. Said under her breath that way, it sounded wistful.

Genevieve? A dart of awareness shot through Jenna.

Genevieve, the name of Jean Claude's long lost lover.

She remembered some talk when she was little about her own name being a derivation of Genevieve. But her parents had chosen the more modern Jenna.

"No, it's just Jenna."

"Oh," the clerk said softly with a trace of disappointment, then she smiled as her gaze darted between Jenna and her paperwork. "Your family must be from down here in Louisiana with a name like Lejeune."

Jenna shook her head. "No, ma'am. We've always been from Georgia for as long as I've known."

"Hmm," the little lady purred to herself. "Hmm." She glanced furtively up at the judge then leaned forward. "Did the judge say anything about your name?"

Jenna shook her head. "He must get Cajun sounding names all the time. I'm sure he thought nothing of it."

"Hmm," the lady murmured again.

What the hell was it with her name? It was getting a bit tiresome. "Who is this Lejeune woman that everyone seems so fixated on?" Jenna blurted out. "Everybody looks at me all crazy like when they hear my last name? Does she look like me?"

"No one knows, dear." The woman shook her hand in the air, as if shaking away Jenna's question and she wrote something on Jenna's ticket and handed it back to her. "Hang onto that copy in case *that officer*," she tilted her head toward the cop who'd written the ticket, "or any other officer questions the disposition of the ticket, dear."

The bailiff motioned Jenna to move on. She took a few steps then looked back at the judge as he handled another case.

Her cop was also on that case. What crazy ass ticket had he written that driver? Was this how they kept down the property taxes? By writing tickets left and right?

The Honorable Judge Devereaux didn't look her way.

But she sensed he was as aware of her presence as she was of his.

And the feelings he evoked were as powerful as her dreams. She wanted his gaze to meet hers, and more, wanted to feel what it would be like to kiss those lips.

To have his body over hers in bed. His hands on her.

Stupid, stupid, stupid.

Every adult part of her knew this was inappropriate.

But it was still true. The man evoked a powerful response. An instantaneous, combustible reaction.

CHAPTER FOUR

Jenna parked her car in the New Orleans parking garage about two blocks from her hotel. The heat of the day had faded as night closed in on the Quarter, a wisp of mist already beginning to sweep in from the river.

The smell of a thousand different seafood dishes simmered in the air, and the riverboat horn blew as it prepared to take tourists on a night run up the river. The steamboat carousel tinkled out a tune, an invitation to take a ride on the old lady.

New Orleans felt like home after the backwater town of Eufaula, Louisiana, the small town near Lafayette, where she'd had to appear in court. A comfortable hotel, with a room that she was accustomed to, sounded good. Amazing how humans could so quickly claim a space, even if it was just a rented room in a hotel.

She'd wanted to wait for the judge after court hours to ask him about Jean Claude, so convinced she was just from looking at him, that he had to be a descendent. But, she'd had to return to New Orleans for an appointment she'd made days ago to interview a government official about her hurricane aftermath story. She locked her car then walked through the French Quarter to her hotel.

It was late, and darkness with the usual evening revelers was replacing the daytime family-flavored tourists.

As she neared her hotel, she noticed blue police lights flashing along the brick walls, with a staccato rhythm that could only belong to a crime scene.

Jenna picked up her pace, drawn in so quickly, with a building excitement. This wasn't her town and crime wasn't her beat anymore but she still couldn't help the instinctive reaction, like a shark drawn in by blood.

They'd chummed the waters with cops and blue lights and she needed to know what had happened. She'd been born with that innate curiosity that made for a good reporter.

News cameras lined up behind the yellow tape that had probably been pulled just to keep the news people from getting too close.

Reporters buzzed around with microphones and notepads, gathering what information locals and beat cops might tell them.

Jenna edged through the crowd of onlookers that had gathered behind the TV cameras.

Down a small alleyway leading to a private garden, Jenna could see cops milling inside the primary crime scene. A second yellow tape indicated where the action had happened and where only those closest to the investigation were allowed.

A white cloth covered a form. It appeared to be quite large, a man probably.

She looked around and realized the alley led to the private garden of her hotel. Beyond the body, a fire escape crawled up the side of the building. She hadn't noticed it before because it connected to the end windows, a place she'd never passed by since the elevator was in the middle of the floor.

The young clerk who had manned the desk this morning, his face pale in the darkness, stood by the cloth-shrouded figure. A cop leaned down to pull back the sheet revealing the body.

The boy nodded affirmatively, seeming to gag at the sight. He staggered back and leaned against the alley wall, his eyes wide with shock.

The detective took him by the shoulder, shaking him slightly, as if to bring him back to himself. They talked for a few minutes, the clerk's mouth running nonstop.

The cop began walking the clerk away from the scene and back toward a side entrance to the hotel. As they got closer, the clerk glanced at Jenna, apparently only just noting her presence. He reached out a wraithlike arm, pointing at her.

Why was he pointing at her?

In unison, two cops turned toward Jenna. One spoke into a radio and a uniformed cop near the yellow tape motioned to her.

Every camera and the eye of every newsperson instantly trained on her.

But, she wasn't involved in this crime in any way. She couldn't be. Then a powerful pulse shot through her. She hadn't seen or heard from Zoom all day.

That couldn't be him underneath the sheet. She moved forward quickly, ducking under the yellow tape, closing the space between her and the body until a cop placed his hand on her shoulder, stopping her.

"Is it my friend, the photographer?" Her heart pulsed so loudly in her ears she could hardly hear over its din as she waited for the desk clerk's response.

"No." He shook his head.

Thank God. Tension snapped loose in her body, all her muscles going limp, and she stepped back half a step and leaned against the brick wall of the nearest building.

"It's that guy who tried to enter your room this morning, the fill-in maintenance man," the clerk said, his voice raspy and hoarse. The clerk definitely remembered Jenna going down and raising a bit of hell because it had been so strange.

"What happened to the guy?" She looked around at the cops but their faces were unreadable, almost purposefully so. "Was it an accident?"

The desk clerk bleated out, "No. He was murdered."

A detective raised his hand. "We don't know that. Take the clerk back inside and we'll finish up his report in there." He waved toward the hotel's side entrance and a uniformed cop led the kid away. The boy's choked breathing faded away.

The detective's face wasn't giving anything away. But he was taking in everything about her, studying her reactions and facial expressions.

"I never even saw the guy who was outside my door this morning," she offered. Even though it had been frightening when someone almost entered her room while she was showering. Luckily, she'd had the safety lock latched. "It was bizarre how he tried to come into my room."

The cop nodded, his face impassive. "And you're in New Orleans why?"

"I'm a reporter, doing a story." She pulled out a newspaper credential.

He glanced at it then half-laughed. "You find yourself at the center of the action wherever you go, huh?"

"Not by choice, detective. Sometimes

the action just finds me."

This time he gave her a real smile
back. "Look, I hate to do this to you. But
could you look at this guy and see if you
recognize him. Maybe you saw him on the
street earlier or something . . . Maybe he
flirted with you at some bar or something
then found out where you were staying." He
lifted a shoulder.

Seeing the actual body? Man that was
something she always tried to spare herself.

At least she didn't have to see the
crying relatives. That was the worst.

Suddenly, the memory of someone
following her and of being watched clicked.
Could the cop's theory be right? Had someone
seen a woman and fixated on her, and
followed her to her hotel?

Finally, she nodded. The detective led
her underneath the second yellow crime tape,
leaned over and lifted the edge of the
sheet.

A white male, about sixty years old, in
a jump suit like a maintenance guy might
wear, lay face up on the pavement. Jenna
studied his face, trying to ignore the fact
that he was dead, just thinking of how he
might have looked passing her on the street
or in the hotel hallway.

Finally, she shook her head. "Never saw
the guy before in my life."

The detective eyed her carefully,
waiting. For what, the truth?

"Is this where the attack happened?"
She tried to look innocent. Well, because
she was.

The detective shook his head,
apparently deciding to believe her. "No. It
happened back there by the fire escape. A

blood trail leads here where he collapsed."

She nodded.

"He doesn't actually work for the hotel, turns out," the detective said with a lifted eyebrow.

A shiver coursed through her. "He tried to get into my room while I was still in it, even though I yelled to come back later. When I went down to complain at the desk, they said he'd *gone out,* to get something from the hardware store or something."

The detective just listened.

"He doesn't actually work for the hotel?" She lifted her shoulders. "Just some pervert, a sex criminal? A thief? A drug addict who needs money desperately? I guess he could have been there for lots of reasons."

The detective smiled darkly. "Yeah, just fill in the blank." He looked back over his shoulder. "That kid just took the dead guy's word for the fact that he was filling in for his *nephew,* when he showed up here this morning. Gave him a universal keycard. Makes you feel real safe letting your women and children stay here."

"Jeez, guess now we have to go looking for the *nephew,* see if he's dead," he added as an afterthought.

Jenna felt the blood fall away from her face. "It couldn't be as organized as that, could it?"

The detective's mouth turned down at the corners. "Seen more unbelievable stuff. Who knows, maybe the guy knew the other guy worked here and killed him so he could fill in and rob every room in the place."

"And then someone killed him?"

The detective shrugged sagely. "Haven't

got it all worked out yet."

Jenna gave him a card with her cell phone number on it. "Can you call me if you get a better handle on this guy and what happened here? I'm getting out of town tomorrow."

"Had your fill of the Big Easy?"

"Big Uneasy is more like it this visit."

The detective laughed obligingly. "I'll let you know when we get this figured out."

If they got it figured out would have been her guess. One for the unsolved case files, more likely.

The detective gave her a card, too, and pointed her toward the side door where the desk clerk had gone. Then as if as an afterthought, he asked, "What you doing a story on? One of our esteemed politicians or the cops?"

People who'd have a reason to kill her?

She shook her head. "Hurricane recovery."

He shrugged. "Fasten the safety chain on your door."

A chill shivered through her, though this probably didn't have anything to do with her, personally.

She walked inside the hotel's side entrance. The desk clerk sat with another detective who murmured quietly to him. The twenty-something clerk's face was pale, with a stunned look, his eyes just staring. A dead body would put that look on your face. She remembered her first murder scene and how nauseous she'd felt upon seeing the victim. The guy probably had never experienced anything like this before.

She wished she could say the same.

Weaving through cops and crime scene
technicians in the lobby, she got on the
elevator. When it reached her floor, she
couldn't help but scan the hallway.

Everything looked normal but her heart
rate accelerated, and a nervous pulse ran
along her skin. When she entered her room,
she did the same scanning procedure, peering
around the door and into the room, almost
expecting someone to jump out at her.
Inching in, she pushed open the bathroom
door, leaned forward as her stomach turned
and yanked the shower curtain back.

Empty. She inched toward the bed,
grabbed the dust ruffle, and flipped it up
to peek underneath the bed.

Nothing. A deep burst of air released
from her chest. Looking around her room, she
checked for anything out of place. Then
finally, she shut the door, bolted it and
put a chair against it.

Tomorrow, she was getting the hell out
of town.

A curling weasel of anticipation gnawed
at her stomach. Tomorrow, she'd look up the
judge.

See if he knew anything more about his
Cajun ancestor.

It would be a professional visit. For
the story she was going to pitch to her
managing editor.

That's all.
                *****

Edward leaned into the desk, eating up
the articles that felt as if they'd been
written especially for him. To him. He loved
the way this woman thought.

Jenna Lejeune.

She had a way of taking a subject and

twisting it just a bit so he got a new angle on the matter.

He liked to end his days reading her articles, or rereading old articles if the paper hadn't put up new ones on their website. His favorite ones had been when she'd covered Rafael, the biggest hurricane after Katrina, the storm known locally as the Second Big One.

So bold, the way she'd gone into devastated areas and covered the day-to-day struggle of the survivors to get food and water, and other basic necessities of life. She'd reached many areas even before FEMA, Red Cross or the National Guard had gotten there.

In the comments section of the online reports, one mother had written about how Jenna and her photographer, Zoom, as the woman had called him, had given the family the first food and water they'd had in a day. Their entire house had been destroyed and the family's car wouldn't start.

Jenna and Zoom had driven them out of the backwoods devastation their property had become.

You had to admire a woman like that.

He'd already known she was on hiatus, even before he saw her in his courtroom. When she was absent from the daily stories, he liked it, because he knew from experience that meant she was out working on a special.

He'd be rewarded for the wait, with a bounty of new articles, day after day, until she'd completely explored the new subject matter.

What was she doing in his parish? What story was she working on? That had been what he'd really wanted to ask her today when she'd walked into his courtroom.

Damn his cousin Mike, giving her that ticket. He ought to call his supervisor.

What a shock when she'd entered his courtroom, looking so much like the photo topping her column.

He'd followed her online articles for so long that he felt as if he already knew her.

"Damn, I'm an idiot." He barked out a laugh tinged with embarrassment, as if someone could see him. Could know just how obsessed he'd become with the woman. *Her ideas*, he corrected himself. *Not her.*

He leaned in, closing the gap between himself and the computer, with that photo and those eyes that stared out at him. What man wouldn't be fascinated with a woman who looked like that, with that expression on her face?

"Jenna Lejeune, how many male cyber stalkers you got? I bet men who live in Atlanta go to great lengths to meet you."

And she'd just walked into his courtroom. Looking the way she looked.

That long, honey blonde hair and those blue eyes. She'd worn a skirt that had hit just above the knee, showcasing those long, slender legs. It was almost as if he'd taken a photo of her when she'd stood by the courtroom door, because he could remember everything about her.

That creamy, white skin and those full lips with the rosy lipstick.

He stared at the photo. It didn't really do justice to just how attractive she was in person, the way fire had flashed in her eyes when Mike had grinned at her. She'd sensed something was off with that. He ought to kick his cousin's ass for that stunt.

He looked back at her online photo and it was like those eyes gazed back at him, as if she knew him. Their seductiveness, their intelligence called to him, luring him in. The woman in the photo looked like the woman who would write the words that had initially drawn him in.

But, the photo still didn't have the hot factor of Jenna Lejeune in the flesh. It had been the hardest thing he'd ever done, resisting the urge to call her back into chambers for a *consultation*.

With a remembered frustration, he pushed away from the desk and leaned back in his chair, propping his feet on the desk, swirling a golden inch of Scotch around in a short glass.

Then, reluctantly, he pulled the laptop off the desk and read the last article she'd written before she'd gone on hiatus, inhaling her essence.

It went down as easily as the single malt whiskey.

He'd need the alcohol to help him unwind from the feelings this woman unleashed in him.

The way she'd looked standing there in his courtroom …

CHAPTER FIVE

Jenna slid between the soft sheets in her New Orleans hotel bed, willing the present away and expecting to drift quickly into the dreams that had seemed so much more enticing than her ordinary, everyday reality.

Until she'd met Judge Edward Devereaux today, that was. The sensations coursed back through her body the same as when their eyes had met in his courtroom.

The look of recognition in his eye couldn't be mistaken. The same as she'd felt, an old, deep connection, like that of former lovers seeing each other after a long separation.

Sleep moved in on her, softening the line between possibility and her heart's desire. Then, the dream began, and she sighed, languidly, luxuriating in the sensual images and sensations.

Slowly, he approached her, sure of his welcome, his wicked brown eyes flashing with sexual fire.

Her pulse rate answered with a quickening. His arms slipped around her waist at the same moment that her hands rose to caress his face.

He was beautiful in a wild and devilish way, ebony hair hanging around his shoulders, a soft cotton shirt loose, revealing his chest.

Jenna slipped her hands inside the fabric and caressed his body, his skin as warm as café au lait, as deliciously enticing.

"I've waited so long for you," he murmured in a low, husky voice. Her

heartbeat accelerated and her hands found
their way to his back just as he pulled her
close. Jenna gasped at the hardness of his
male body. His searching mouth found the
pulse point in her neck. A low cry slipped
from her lips just before she took his face,
pulling that wicked mouth to hers, wanting
all the passion that mouth knew how to
elicit.

His lips met hers, softly at first,
then demandingly insistent, parting her
lips, plundering her mouth with his tongue,
taking all that she wanted to give.

His hands slipped down, sliding
underneath her gown, pushing it up over her
head, until finally he pulled her to his
naked chest and it was flesh against flesh.

With a jolt, Jenna awoke, opened her
eyes and sat up, alone in her bed. A
feverish haze glistened along her skin, her
body heated and wanting. She glanced around
the room, looking for her midnight lover.
Wanting him back in her arms, wanting the
dream to continue.

The room's chill brushed her skin and
she ached for the warmth of his skin against
hers. A deep shuddering sigh pushed from her
chest. It was only a dream.

A vivid dream. Almost like a memory.

Her body called out for him and all the
things they'd shared in the night.

But the dream wasn't real.

Wasn't real?

It felt more like a memory than a
dream. It felt like a night she'd shared
with the man she'd met today in that
courtroom. Felt as if she and Judge Edward
Devereaoux had been lovers before.

*****

The next morning, Zoom came to her hotel to go to breakfast with her, and catch up on what she'd been doing on the story as he'd gone his own way, taking photos for the article.

They'd only been able to get one room in the historic hotel. But Zoom had been happier with the fancy, modern hotel on the outskirts of the French Quarter.

Zoom stretched lazily, hitching his camera bag from one shoulder to the next as they left Jenna's hotel. He looked like he'd gained weight in just the short time they'd been in the New Orleans area. "So many restaurants, so little time," had become his catch phrase for the trip. His clothes never really fit, always loosely hanging on his large frame, and he often had a food stain on his shirt from eating so enthusiastically. Some people might have referred to Zoom as a slob.

Jenna preferred to think of him as relaxed casual. His sandy blond hair always needed cutting, and he didn't shave every day. But you couldn't ask for a more cheerful colleague, one who never shirked work, always ready to get one more photograph, and loved his camera almost as much as he loved his wife and two kids.

As they left the hotel, Jackson Square was waking up, mist curling in from the river. Ambience seeped up from the cobble stone street in front of the hotel. A warm smell curled from the Café Du Monde, only a block away, and her stomach grumbled. A man covered in gold lame paint lugged a block into the middle of the sidewalk to use as a stage.

A woman in a colorful, gypsy skirt set

up a card table, then threw a blue cloth
over it. In another life, Jenna was going to
move to New Orleans and do something on this
square. Anything that would allow her to
linger here all day long.

She loved this spot on the planet, with
all the artistic energy flowing. A guitar
player strummed lightly, tuning his
instrument, humming softly.

Then, something caught her attention.

A lone figure on the other side of the
square stood out because of his stillness,
his quiet intensity. Seeming to stare at
Jenna and Zoom.

A shiver ran down Jenna's spine. He was
so out of place. Maybe he was just waiting
for his wife, or girlfriend. Silently,
patiently, waiting for someone.

And staring intently at her. Why was he
staring at her? A chill ran through her
body, remembering last night's murder and
the man who'd followed her through the mist
the night before.

She was done being stalked. She'd turn
that man into prey before she ran from him
again.

"Hey." Jenna lifted an arm into the
air. The man looked at her for another long
moment, then turned and walked away quickly.
Had she seen him before?

Zoom, a step ahead of her, glanced
back. "What?" he asked, "See your mystery
Cajun man?"

Jenna looked after the retreating form.
Then, on impulse, she ran toward the corner
he disappeared around. It couldn't have been
more than sixty seconds, but when she
reached the corner, she saw nothing.

"Damn it. This is insane," she said,

blowing out a burst of air in exasperation. "He was definitely staring at me." He couldn't have gotten far.

She dashed forward, again, pelting along the cobblestones until she reached the next corner, where she stopped, looking all around. "Nooo." There was no one even resembling the man in any direction.

Her heart racketed against the insides of her ribs with such force that her whole body shook. She sucked in air, willing the panic to leave her once and for all. She'd never been such a baby before. Panicking, running after strangers, acting so dramatic and insane. But she hadn't imagined the dead body.

That was as real as it gets.

"Okay, let's go face the music with Zoom. He's gonna want some explanation." Because she sure as heck would if a colleague was acting like her.

She slowly walked back to where Zoom stood at the first turn staring in confusion at her. All the way, she searched for words that would make her seem less a nut.

"Did you get a look at that guy?" She pointed at the far corner, deciding to act like this was all normal.

Zoom's expression told her he was starting to question her sanity but he smiled to cover it. "You got a bad case of the heebie jeebies?"

She couldn't help but laugh. "I'm about ready to leave this town." Something she never would have expected herself to say.

"I thought you loved New Orleans," Zoom said with a laugh.

Not this time. Everything felt out of control, like being in the middle of the

Mississippi River after a tumultuous rainstorm, tossed around with the flotsam and jetsam that washed free from upstream. Trees. Industrial waste. Bodies?

Zoom patted her on the shoulder and began walking, so she followed. She still hadn't filled him in on the dead maintenance guy. That was a whole long discussion in itself.

She also hadn't told him that the same man had apparently tried to enter her room while she was still inside. A shiver coursed through her at the memory and just how frightening it had been at the moment.

Maybe with cause. Because the same man had ended up dead later in the alley behind her hotel.

It was just a short distance to the famous Café Du Monde, where a covey of small Vietnamese women flitted about with strong coffee and heavily powdered beignets. Their sugary scent filled the air.

She and Zoom grabbed an outdoor table, with no one within earshot. Most people had taken the inside tables, or were still sleeping in.

Within moments, there was a plate of the hot French doughnuts in front of them and rich cups of café au lait with its hickory scented flavor. Jenna took a long sip before biting into a crispy, hot beignet, the sweet fried flavor exploding in her mouth.

Outside the wrought iron fence surrounding the Café Du Monde patio, horse and mule driven carriages rumbled by with the few tourists who had already made their way to the Quarter, carriage drivers announcing the history of the area as they passed.

A stooped old white man wearing a worn cowboy hat walked an equally ancient dog to the corner, bought a newspaper and then proceeded to a bench to read the morning news. It all looked so normal.

But was it?

Her cell phone rang and Jenna pulled it out of her pocket.

"It's Richard," she said to Zoom after seeing the number of the newspaper's managing editor.

Zoom held up a finger. "Just so you know, he's getting tired of this story. I heard he wants us back in Atlanta."

She rounded her eyes and grabbed the call before it went to voice mail. "Hey, Richard. What's up?"

Jenna took another bite of beignet, savoring the crunchy exterior with the soft interior. No telling how long Richard could talk once he started expounding on all he had to do, making sure everyone knew he ran the show and the paper was nothing without him.

She looked around them, making sure no one had sat down near them in the last few minutes, then she punched the button to put him on speakerphone. She turned the sound to a low level but even so, Zoom rolled his eyes. She rolled her eyes back at him and smothered a laugh. Why should she be alone, listening to the boss' boring, pedantic diatribe?

Besides, if Zoom's shots didn't properly capture the essence of her story subjects, her reporting suffered. That was something she didn't have to worry about. Zoom was the best, always sensing just where to position his camera to capture the most emotion, to let the reader connect with the subject.

"So, have you guys gotten anywhere," Richard's voice boomed out of the small phone, "finding those people you did the original pieces on?"

Jenna swallowed her bite of beignet quickly, choking to get it down. Richard never got down to business this quickly.

"I found some and have leads on several others," she mumbled, the sugary doughnut still caught in her throat. She took a quick swallow of coffee.

Zoom arched an eyebrow, a laugh just wanting to escape his lips.

She frowned at him and concentrated on salvaging her story. "Seems most of the first neighborhood we covered went up around Lafayette. They had ties there and just about the whole neighborhood was somehow related to each other."

"Just like those Cajuns," Richard said dismissively, his tone acid and as dry as Jenna's throat had been before the coffee. "Never want to venture far from home or if they do, they take home with them in the form of cousins and cousins of cousins."

Zoom's eyebrows shot up. He started imitating an airplane, sending the clear message that they were going back to Atlanta soon.

"Surveys say people are so over hurricane stories," Richard said dismissively.

After this last hurricane, Rafael, the uncle of Katrina people called it, nothing was as it had been before it and Katrina. And might never be again, people said.

Southern Louisiana had just suffered too many hard blows. The thought shook Jenna to her core.

Richard cleared his throat. "Unless you can come up with some new twist, I need you back in Atlanta. You're way over budget."

The first thing that flashed through her mind came out of her mouth. "I found this journal."

Zoom's eyes got big. He sat back in his chair almost like, *I gotta hear this.*

She narrowed hers. Don't start, her expression warned.

This wasn't about Jean Claude, it really wasn't. It would be insane to think she had a crush on a dead guy. Really crazy.

Except, it seemed she might have transferred that crush to Judge Edward Devereaux yesterday. Which was equally ridiculous.

"The journal is about the exodus of the Cajuns . . . when they left Nova Scotia and came to Louisiana."

Richard umhummed, like of course he knew the history. Even if he didn't, he would have pretended he did. That was one of the reasons she'd never wanted to date him, his know-it-all-ness.

Aside from the fact that dating her boss wasn't a good career move, she wasn't attracted to him at all.

He'd hinted often about them going out. Once even placing his hand on her shoulder in an uncomfortable moment, before she'd subtly pulled away.

"Maybe we could do a comparison about then and now," she elaborated, "that the post-hurricane displacement of Katrina and Rafael is just the next wave of Cajun wandering and the next change in New Orleans and this whole area. Make it about the future and the past." She'd already formulated it in her head, planning to pitch it to him.

"Sounds good, Jenna," another voice chimed in from Richard's line. They were on speakerphone on his side, too? "You just come up with that?" Walton, the editorial director asked.

He was one step up the management chain from Richard and usually didn't get involved at this stage of her articles. But, thankfully this time he had and could overrule Richard, if necessary.

"I've done a little preliminary research but I need to do some more to find out how things turned out. I need to spend some time up in Lafayette where the trail of the Cajun lovers leads, to follow up on my families from the hurricane, anyway."

"Good, that's good." Richard's enthusiasm sounded forced. "Maybe we could do the first piece about what you found in New Orleans. Then tease 'em about what you found in the journal. Get people's curiosity going. Make 'em want to read the second part."

"Like the old serial shows they used to have on Saturday mornings at the movies when my mom was a kid," Zoom piped up.

"Zoom, I didn't realize you were on the line," Richard said with a sharp laugh. He didn't like surprises, liked to be in control. But that probably just went with the territory of being the boss.

Then a sudden prickly feeling caused Jenna to turn and look behind her. She sensed someone watching.

She scanned the street and the plaza, searching the faces of the artists and tourists. There was a lot of shrubbery landscaping the area, enough to provide coverage for anyone not wanting to be seen. A sick feeling wrenched her stomach. She felt like prey.

And she didn't like the feeling, had never experienced it before this trip. As though someone were setting her up for something. Stalking her.

CHAPTER SIX

Late that afternoon, Jenna positioned herself outside Judge Edward Devereaux's chambers door in order to catch him on his way out. A thousand invisible insects bit at her skin, licked at her nerve endings and generally harassed her as she waited.

They ran through her mind also, whispering all the things she already knew.

He wasn't Jean Claude. He wasn't the man from her dreams. Still, as if an unseen being had attached a harness to her, pulling her toward him, ever toward him, she'd come to find him.

She watched the door, willing it to open, willing him to come out.

Then he did. And she did a double take. "Damn," she muttered under her breath. Jeans, formfitting, slightly worn in all the right places jeans, that didn't fit her image of a judge. A navy blue T-shirt covered a hard male body. He looked more like an outdoorsman than someone who spent his time poring over legal briefs.

The memory of her dream shivered through her, along with a flash of desire. This man, or a photocopy of him, had held her in his arms, and his mouth had found sensitive spots she didn't know she possessed.

She was in deep trouble.

She attempted to shake off those secret night thoughts and tell herself this man had nothing to do with her dreams. Her subconscious had taken liberties with his image.

It wasn't his fault he looked sinfully delicious.

As he drew nearer, Jenna stood and plastered what she hoped passed for a professional smile on her face. He couldn't read the very unprofessional feelings that ran through her body. Or at least, she prayed he couldn't.

"Your honor," she ventured.

"Yes." His eyes crinkled, curiosity embedded in the laugh lines. Such nice chocolate brown eyes, the type of eyes that could coax a woman to bed without saying a word.

Heat flushed from her chest to her face, and she worried about the telltale red that could give her away.

Silently, he waited to hear what she had to say.

Judge Edward Devereaux - even more imposing in person than he'd been behind the judge's bench. Then, she had not been at eye level with his chest, in that T-shirt that conformed to his body, and those jeans that made her want to let her eyes drop to the worn spots.

This man didn't have those same memories of her dreams. He'd never shared a lover's kiss with her. This man didn't know her from the next stranger sitting in his courtroom.

Though some subconscious niggling kept telling her he had recognized her when he'd first seen her. She had to shake that, that swamp fever craziness that urged her to push herself up against him.

The judge coughed slightly. It was only a cough, still, the deep masculinity of the sound evoked a response.

Get a grip, girl. Get a grip.

Taking a deep breath, she dragged her

mind to business and launched into journalistic mode. "I'm Jenna Lejeune . . . from the traffic ticket, yesterday."

He smiled slightly, a hint of wryness lapping around his eyes. So much implied with just that little expression. *I remember what goes on in my courtroom,* he seemed to say without words.

"The ticket's not why I'm here, though." She waved her hands around the corridor. Like a crazy lady. Damn, everything felt so awkward with him. "I'm here as a journalist, doing a story on hurricane recovery."

He arched an eyebrow. He sure didn't talk much outside the courtroom.

"I'm trying to weave another element into my story, about the wanderings and relocations of the ancient Cajuns." He just kept looking at her, with those eyes that were the color of pecan pie, sweet and tempting. *Just damn.*

"Like the big hurricane exodus that happened after both Katrina and Rafael are just new phases of the Cajun story," she added. *Just keep talking.*

He raised a shoulder. And with that gesture, raised her estrogen level. It was like his testosterone called out to the woman in her, making her feel more like a woman every moment she was in his presence.

"I was wondering if you might be a descendant of a Jean Claude Devereaux."

He shrugged like he wasn't surprised, as if he knew she were here for that reason.

"I take it that's a yes?" She gazed intently at him.

He raised a shoulder again. She wished he'd quit doing that. It made his chest flex and emphasized his whole upper body underneath that soft T-shirt.

Testosterone rolled off him in waves she could almost smell. She wanted to lean in to catch his scent, to nose into his neck and bury herself in his smell, that wonderfully attractive aroma that she could barely detect from here.

"There are lots of Devereaux folks around," he answered, with a normality that mocked her crazy impulses. "Why would I think you were looking for me specifically?" Right to business. Nothing distracted him, making it impossible to come up with the right words.

Right. Business. The reason she'd searched him out today. The presumed reason.

"Because," she reached into the file folder she'd brought for this very type of reason and pulled out the portrait of his near double, the last item that had been sent to her at the hotel, "you look just like him."

The judge looked down at the portrait, taking it from her, his fingers brushing hers. She wasn't sure if the touch made her want to move closer to him or step back as she ought to if she ever hoped to regain her professional footing. Which she was no longer sure she wanted to do.

Throw the pretense aside, just go with this attraction to the man. How often did someone find this raw, hot need to be near a man?

"You think he looks like me?"

They were both hot. She swallowed hard and nodded. "He's your twin."

"People have always said that." He shook his head and handed the photo back to

her. "I don't see it. We have the same black
hair and brown eyes." He grinned with the
devil's own mouth, that mouth that had
driven her crazy in her dreams. "We both
have a nose and a mouth. But I look like me
and he looks like him."

And they both looked like sex
incarnate. Standing probably about six foot,
two inches, the judge oozed masculinity in
his well-worn jeans.

Every female impulse she had perked up
its dangerous head. Your mate, her estrogen
whispered, a man worth your time and
trouble.

The photograph. He said he didn't look
like it.

Jenna had heard about identical twins
who didn't think they looked like their twin
though everyone else struggled to tell them
apart. It was hard to believe there could be
another one of him in the whole world. But
the resonance of character that flowed off
him was the same as emanated from the
portrait of Jean Claude.

The sense of knowing him was so strong.

"I have something else, part of his
journal, if you haven't already seen it,"
she offered as an enticement to cooperate in
her story, pulling the papers out of her
shoulder bag.

He reached for the handwritten journal
as if she'd handed him the first copy of the
bible he'd ever seen, awe struck, eyeing it
avidly, scanning each page. As if he'd heard
about bibles but …

"It's Jean Claude's journal, of his
search for his long lost love Genevieve,"
she explained.

"How much of this do you have?" He

glanced at her, his gaze connecting with hers, intensity simmering in his eyes, all humor gone.

"That's all," she forced herself to respond past the knot in her throat. "Someone sent me just this part."

He stepped closer, his eyes narrowing. And his scent hit her hard, with a woodsy bite to it that felt like the bayou itself after a clean, hard rain.

She wanted to put her hands to his chest and lean in to let the energy connect that was flowing between them so strongly.

"Who sent these pages to you?" Intensity filled his eyes, turning them into a deep mocha.

"Someone couriered them to me at my hotel in New Orleans." Except for the one yesterday that had been slid underneath her door at the hotel.

The judge looked at her hard for a few moments then turned his attention back to the papers. "They're the Romeo and Juliet of the Cajun world here in Eufaula, Louisiana," he said quietly in a husky voice, its emotional timbre reverberating throughout her body.

"They're a legend," he almost whispered, his voice as sultry as a trace of swamp mist. "I've heard their story my whole life."

Intensity bathed his beautiful features.

"Age-old mysteries of love," he said quietly.

Age-old mysteries of love? A man talking that way?

A warm glow spread through her. "Romance and affairs of the heart are good stuff," she added. "You might hold the key to the puzzle somewhere in those stories you've been told."

His expression closed down. "I don't think I can help you, ma'am." Gone was the look of wonder when he'd first seen the pages but he was interested enough to ask, "Could I keep these?"

She nodded. She'd made other copies. "So, you don't think you could help with some details?"

He shook his head, dismissively but something told her he knew more than he was willing to admit. "I didn't really pay attention to the love part of those old stories," he said. "I was a boy. We didn't hang around underneath our mamas like the girls." He laughed slightly. "I was more interested in fishing and guns. If the story didn't involve a shooting, I wasn't interested."

"A shooting?"

He nodded. "You're from the South. You ought to know a lot of the old stories ended in shootings."

How had he known she was from the South? She had little, if any, accent.

"At least the Cajun stories do." He started stepping away now, just polite, slow steps backward.

She couldn't let him go.

She didn't want the contact to end, felt an inexorable desire to touch him, look at him, hear his voice flow over her with its masculine timbre. So, she followed him in a companionable way as though he'd meant for her to.

"Actually," she said, "I was hoping to find they were eventually reunited. They were engaged, or intended, as they said. Apparently when the Cajuns were driven out of Canada, Genevieve and Jean Claude were separated. From what I can glean from the pages of the journal, he searched for her for some time." She smiled up at him. "I was hoping for a happy ending."

"There were a lot more unhappy endings during that time." The judge's eyes shifted doubtfully. "I wouldn't write the piece ahead of time."

"Jean Claude's words are so heartrending." She searched his eyes. "Makes you want to know the outcome. It will make a killer addition to my piece. I just hope it's not bittersweet."

She glanced away but out of the corner of her eye caught the judge studying her, his eyes slowly doing a complete once over of her person. She liked the feel of his gaze on her, intimate, as though he knew her body.

She turned back to the judge and his gaze met hers. A spark of want flickered higher, spiraling heat throughout her body, her veins turning into a conduit of desire. Those dark, sensuous eyes of his ...

Their gazes held for one riveting moment and though he made no physical gesture, she could feel him beckoning her to follow. A deep aching desire to get closer to him nudged her. When they reached the door, he held it for her to precede him outside.

Together they walked down the steps to a sidewalk shaded by moss-draped live oaks. The feeling of having been there long before was overpowering. She savored the familiarity of it all.

Then the judge started walking again and she followed. When they reached the edge of the parking lot, he stopped and looked off at the horizon.

"Could I take you to dinner?" she asked, the words out of her mouth before she'd even thought them. But maybe if they had more time, she could extract more information about Jean Claude and Genevieve.

"Are you asking me out?" The judge's eyes crinkled.

The inappropriate heat flashed through her, again. "To discuss business," she justified, but the flush through her body laughed at her false pretense. "Maybe if you get to talking about those family stories, we can jog some information out of your memory."

Eddie looked at this classy beauty, her words flowing through his brain, the sound of her voice as familiar to him as if they'd had thousands of conversations.

But, probably about a million men looked at her photo in the newspaper and wanted to *know her*. In the biblical sense.

Some primordial, Cajun part of his brain told him to stay away from this inquisitive outsider, to stay away from the Lejeune Woman.

The Lejeune Woman had finally come to town and all the old legends kicked in a primal caution. Reading her articles was one thing. But, this woman would be leaving. Probably sooner than later.

He'd been warned about the Lejeune Woman since he was knee high and though he disregarded the Lejeune Woman legend, the local bayou's boogie woman, he knew his mother would let loose on him if she heard about him seeing her. So would countless others.

"You go out there at night and the Lejeune Woman will get you," his granny had said to keep six-year-old Eddie from wandering into the swamps after dark. The Lejeune Woman apparently lived wherever there were gators that little boys wanted to investigate.

But local legend wasn't the real problem with this outside beauty. He just didn't want to get that kicked in the teeth feeling again when this woman left their backwater town.

Big city girls just couldn't take the slow pace.

But this Lejeune woman and her body. Just damn.

If the first Lejeune woman had looked like her, he could see why Jean Claude was a goner. The intelligent spark in her eye to go with that body. Soft cotton hugged curves that were made for loving. He'd like to take her to a fais do-do, use a slow dance to ease up against her. Slow dances were made for women like her.

But no use striking a match if you didn't want to start no fire, he heard himself falling into Cajun lingo in his mind. He used English grammar in public but when he got around old time Cajuns with all their French grammar, sometimes it was hard to weed it out of his language.

English only had been the rule at school.

This outside Lejeune woman was the kind of woman that could make a man break some rules.

And love doing it.

CHAPTER SEVEN

He should say goodbye to this beauty,
the old voices cautioned. And his common
sense told him not to waste time on a woman
who was just passing through.

But, the memory of all the words he'd
read that came from her mind teased him. She
just seemed to think like him, with a
similarity in points of view that always
made him feel that if they'd met, they'd
have a lot to talk about, and would get
along. How could he let this opportunity to
get to know her go by?

She was just here doing her job. And he
really didn't think he could take the pain
of another poorly thought out love affair.
Like his and Lidia's. Why do that to
himself?

Jenna Lejeune was heartbreak on a
plate.

"I can probably refer you to someone up
in Baton Rouge at the university who might
could help you with your research into the
Cajun immigration into the area."

She nodded blankly. "Okay, that would
be nice. I wonder if they have any more of
the journal up there in their library or
archives."

There, no more reason for her to come
back looking for him, pass her off to the
authorities at the university. Problem
solved. Now, to get rid of her. Like his
common sense said he ought. Like the pain
he'd felt when his ex-wife had stabbed him
with the knife of adultery warned him he
should do.

He touched her lightly on the shoulder,

this Lejeune Woman, to lessen any rejection she might feel when he declined her invitation to dinner.

A flush bloomed from her chest to her face, that pale skin warming to a rose colored blush that made him want to touch her skin, to see if it was as smooth and soft as it looked. The blood in her cheeks was evoked by a mere touch?

How would she look under the influence of a kiss? The image drew him to her. Still, he didn't need any trouble. "I think we'll have to catch some dinner another time." He forced a smile. "Then, you can update me on your research."

She stepped back and Eddie opened his pickup truck's door, got in and turned the key in the ignition. Like a guy who didn't want to order up heartbreak should.

In his side mirror, he could see her walk away. Those long legs determinedly moved her across the parking lot, her hips swinging that skirt. That short, flippy skirt that showed a lot of firm, shapely leg.

Heat flashed through him. And the temptation to follow her.

Odd she would show up here, apparently oblivious to any legends involving her name.

Well, she'd probably hear them soon enough, if she stayed for any length of time.

Something inside of him wished that she would, despite knowing that any involvement with her would only end in heartbreak for him. What was it about those Lejeune women and their heartbreaking ways for Devereaux men?

Eddie put his truck into gear and drove

out of the parking lot, determinedly not looking back. But it was only a block later that he glanced into his rearview mirror and saw Jenna behind him, her open car windows wreaking havoc with that long, honey-blonde hair, whipping it around her face.

Oh hell, what were a few more scars on the old heart? No guy worth his guy card gave up the chance to spend time with the woman who'd inspired so many vagrant thoughts just by looking at her picture and reading her thoughts.

And he wasn't about to have to go through the process of re-qualifying for his guy card. He'd spent too much time swimming in alligator frequented water, jumping off high dives and doing other such idiotic things as a young male to want to have to go back to that proving ground.

At the red light, he stuck his head out the window and yelled back, "You don't give up easily." Yeah, he was flirting with her. That's what it was, open flirting with a hot female.

This was her chance, Jenna realized, as she pulled up beside him. "You better give up now." She laughed with the charm she'd used to seduce information from a thousand others. "I can be terribly persistent."

His chicory colored eyes slid over her face, the glance palpable, like a large hand caressing her skin.

"Pull over," he said in that low, gravelly voice that could have been transplanted straight from Russell Crowe. Did guys learn that voice somewhere? Did they teach them to talk like that, low in their throat, so their voice scraped across every cell of her body, as if to squeeze the estrogen loose into her blood?

If so, they needed to keep on teaching it. The sound rolled over her body, with a drumbeat of seduction.

Anticipation surged through her. The hunt was still on. The dogs were barking just over the horizon. She steered her car to the curb.

Eddie turned his truck in behind her. He got out and strolled toward her car.

He sauntered with a self-possessed nonchalance, all loose limbed and athletic looking, nicely muscled arms showing underneath that short-sleeved shirt. But she sensed he felt the pull, felt the draw of excitement that was nearly impossible to ignore.

He approached her car and leaned against the window, one arm propped casually on the top of her car, his presence overwhelming, the raw energy and vitality he exuded vibrating off her female pheromones. She struggled to keep her face serious and business-like.

"Let's grab us a bite," he said. "I have to meet someone later but I've got some time."

What was the gender of that *someone* he was meeting? Though that didn't matter to her. This was only business. Yeah. She was even lying to herself now.

"I know a place, it's not fancy," he said.

"My treat. It's a write-off," she explained in answer to his raised eyebrow. "We can go in my car, your honor."

"You can dispense with the *your honors* outside of court. Eddie will do," he said with a slow smile that slid straight into her veins, then coursed to her stomach with a shivering jolt.

"I'll drive, Eddie." Jenna attempted her best professional smile. There was an awful lot of smiling going on. A good sign. For her story, of course.

When he slid into the seat only inches from her side, she found herself thinking about the genetic material he shared with the long-dead-Cajun Jean Claude. Genevieve never stood a chance of resisting a man who was anything like Judge Edward Devereaux. Genevieve would have been a goner from the start.

Jenna caught herself up quickly. She had to stop thinking of Edward Devereaux as Jean Claude. It was too deadly, marrying him to the man in her dreams and to the powerful words in the journal of the dead Cajun.

She steered away from the curb and along the moss draped streets of Eufaula, her arm only inches from the judge's where it lay on the armrest, with a feeling of intimacy in the close quarters of the car.

"Go left there." Eddie pointed and as his arm dropped, it brushed across her elbow.

An instant pulse of excitement surged through her.

Finally, Eddie pointed out the restaurant. She pulled into a spot and almost jumped out of her side of the car.

She felt ruffled all over. She checked her blouse, making sure it was still tucked neatly into her skirt. As she walked toward the eatery, she attempted to finger comb her hair back to its former sleek smoothness but that was a lost cause because it had blown into a tangled mess.

Eddie held the restaurant's door, which was badly in need of a coat of paint. She stepped into a room that reverberated with sound, loud wailing Cajun music playing on the jukebox and the rattle of dishes and laughter coming from the kitchen. The most delicious smells Jenna could recall wafted in the air.

"Get ready for some spice and heat," Eddie said close to her ear, his breath stirring the hair on her neck, his voice deep and his masculine scent swirling around her.

Was the closeness a hint that he knew just how much he affected her?

Oh hell.

His nearness was as exciting as his words, with their double entendre about the food, or the possibilities for the two of them.

It had been a long time between men, which did not help things one bit right now. At thirty-two, she ought to be immune to these sorts of impulses, her estrogen level ought to have been depleted a bit. But, these days, it felt like she'd been given estrogen shots, injected straight into her veins.

It'd been at least six months since she'd broken off her engagement when her fiancé had wanted her to move with him to Chicago for an important job. Important for him. It was, apparently, a realization of his life-long dreams, which he hadn't communicated effectively to her. He'd said they would be set for life, if he took that job.

Well, he hadn't been listening to her goals and dreams, because he'd been saying it was the perfect time to start a family and that she could stay home with the kids.

Her lifelong dreams hadn't been any of that, the staying home - at least at this point in her life. Or the moving north. She understood the South, loved writing about it with all its quirks, and loved documenting how the culture and political landscape changed and evolved.

The Atlanta paper had always been her dream job. Now, she'd achieved what she'd never hoped to have, her own column, her own beat, where she kind of called the shots. As long as she could convince Richard and Walt that the public wanted to read what she was writing about.

She looked out the window and bet the public would love reading about this little area of cultural backwater, where the people still talked like they'd just emigrated from some Cajun speaking foreign country with their strange accents and phrasing.

She wouldn't want to live here, but then she thought of Genevieve and how she'd come here when it had been nothing but swamp, moss-drizzled trees, and gators.

She'd given up Charlie so easily, but Eddie Devereaux was a taste of sweetness that might set up a sugar high that could be hard to give up.

Just looking at him had her getting worked up. She had to get a grip on herself.

"It's kind of a hole in the wall but I bet the food is good," she said as she studied the restaurant décor, trying to ignore Eddie's effect on her.

"My brother will be glad to know that," he answered. "This is his place."

Jenna swallowed air in surprise and

coughed.

Eddie chuckled low. "Don't be talking bad about anybody down here, cuz we're all related." He placed a reassuring hand on her elbow. But, his touch was anything but calming. "Paulie would be flattered to have his place called a hole in the wall. That was the effect he was going for. Says you get the best food on the wrong side of town and in places you wouldn't think would pass the health inspection, judging by the décor."

Jenna glanced around at the wooden, ladder-back chairs and mismatched tables. "Then, the food ought to be spectacular."

Eddie belly laughed. "Why don't you pick out a table, chére. I'm gonna go speak to my brother." He walked away chuckling, through swinging doors and out of sight.

She just prayed Paulie didn't come out pointing a finger at her for her snooty ways.

She sat at a Formica table with a red and white checked pattern and a moment later, Eddie and a large man came out, not taller than Eddie but fleshed out more, like he liked his own cooking, a lot.

"I'm Eddie's *big brother*." He chuckled jovially, as Eddie half punched his bicep.

"Younger brother," Eddie corrected, "though he is bigger."

"Cooking'll do that to you." Paulie flexed his chest. "Got to taste your product."

"This is Paulie." Eddie waved a hand at his brother, then at Jenna. "And this is Jenna."

Paulie wiped a giant hand on his apron then stuck it out to her. His grasp was warm and soft, nothing like she would have expected from the big man attached to it.

"Nice to meet you, Miss Jenna. And what is your family name?"

She'd gotten used to that. Everyone down here wanted to know who *your people* were.

"Lejeune," she answered.

Instantly, his eyebrows shot up halfway off his forehead.

He looked at Eddie who met his gaze and smiled blandly. Paulie brought his face back into a semblance of normality. It seemed to require a bit of effort. "So, where you from, chére, over by Saint Thomasville? I know there are a lot of Lejeunes over that way."

"Atlanta," she said almost apologetically, already familiar with the local response to the mention of big cities.

"Oh, I'm so sorry." His face fell. Then, he perked up with a smile. "But you ain't going back there, are ya? You here to stay?"

She smiled noncommittally into his warm eyes.

"So, I'll take that as you're not converted to our ways yet." He laughed a big laugh and pulled a pad from his back pocket. He shot his brother another glance. Eddie just smiled back at him.

"My little brother here says you should get Crawfish Etouffee," Paulie said in a sociable voice as if nothing had just passed between him and his brother. "I will tell you it is stupendous," he almost guffawed.

Big. Loud. Non-threatening.

It would be easy to like Eddie's whole family if they were like Paulie. "Crawfish

Etouffee, then," she agreed.

"Crawfish Etouffee for The Lejeune Woman," Paulie said.

Eddie darted an accusing glance at him.

Paulie laughed and walked away, singing to the Cajun tune playing on the jukebox.

What was that about?

Eddie settled into the chair across from her, his expression bland. He could take away her appetite for food if she let him, inspiring another type of hunger. Earthy, organic, and itching-for-something feelings ran through her.

So quickly, she noted to herself. She'd only just met the guy and already she'd decided he was the man of her dreams, literally.

It wasn't looking good for impartial journalism.

"So, you like the big city, I take it?" he asked, glancing away toward the front door.

"I love the big city," she said. "Atlanta is the capitol of the South. Everyone in the smaller news markets wants to move to Atlanta – it's the big time."

Eddie's mouth turned down.

She smiled. "It's exciting. I love it."

Then, she leaned across the table, and awareness sparked in Eddie's eyes.

"Now let's talk about you," she said.

"Or Jean Claude to be more exact?" Eddie sat back with a congenial expression, his hand resting on his knee.

Eddie knew he'd delved right into the topic of her choice. However, right now, he didn't care what they talked about. He just wanted to watch her lips move. There was something so pleasant about the angles of her face as she spoke. Her voice flowed over his skin and circled around him with a familiar tonal quality.

Yet at the same time exciting.

Why was he doing this? Perhaps because it had been a very long time since any woman had instantly made his hormones sizzle. She'd grabbed his attention long before she'd walked into his courtroom, with the words in her articles.

Her thoughts spread out across the pages of her newspaper and the expression in her eyes on the website photo combined into an intriguing mix, affecting him like a spicy Jambalaya, sending heat spiking out into his veins. And he had been just a bit too bored for just a bit too long to quickly turn away from this offer of excitement.

She raised her clear, Caribbean Sea Blue eyes and their intense hue seemed to see right into his thoughts. A drop of sweat began slipping down the side of her neck and he wanted to lift a hand and slide it across her neck, smoothing out the moisture. But he merely gave her an encouraging look to get her talking.

Anything to keep her talking.

"So, you're going to forward me any more of this journal that happens to show up?" he said as a starting point.

"Sure," she agreed quickly. "I'm not expecting to get any more cause I got it over in New Orleans. But I'd love to see the whole thing."

"How'd you come across the part you have?"

Her eyes flickered away. "Journalists don't reveal their sources."

"Mysterious."

"More like if you saw the way sausage was made, you wouldn't want to eat it."

He laughed. "Chére, Cajuns always want to eat sausage. You'll find sausage is a starting point for a whole lot of our food."

Musical, lilting laughter erupted from her lips, much more than the joke deserved. Was that nervous laughter? The kind you heard on a first date? God, he hoped so.

She pushed that tousled, honey-blonde hair with its wavy long locks back, and he couldn't help wondering how it would look spread across his pillow in the morning. He could imagine rolling her around in his bed, with that hair flowing across both of them.

Damn, his thoughts went there so quickly.

He was getting ahead of himself. They were just grabbing a bite to eat together. She, a journalist chasing a story. He, a hopeless horn dog.

As soon as his people learned a Lejeune woman was hanging around, the real fun would start.

He wasn't scared by the old stories but some would be. That might make for a very interesting visit for Jenna Lejeune.

Should he tell her? It wasn't as if she'd be in any danger. People would just change the subject if she brought up Genevieve and Jean Claude, keeping her uninformed but not in danger.

No, not in danger.

CHAPTER EIGHT

Seven women, all past childbearing years, sat around the ancient oak table. The table was scarred and beaten by time, like the women's faces and bodies.

"I knew she was the one." The oldest, a woman in her mid-eighties, crinkled her eyes with satisfaction.

A single candle flickered its warm glow across her face, easing the wrinkles, showing her more as she looked in her youth, beautiful even now, to all the female eyes that returned her smile.

"Not a Lejeune baby's been stillborn since, so there's the proof," a sixtyish salt-and-pepper brunette nodded in agreement.

"Aaah, but that poor Devereaux baby that died already. If the match between the couple doesn't survive," another gray-haired woman moaned low in her throat, "the loss the Devereaux families will incur will be greater, even."

All the women nodded quietly, each secretly glad it hadn't been their own families' young who'd been touched by death. They glanced around guiltily at each other, wondering if they alone held the selfish thought.

But still, the loss of your own grandchild would cut much deeper than another woman's loss of her child. The threat to the unborn Lejeune babies had driven all of them to do what they had to do – put another woman's child at risk. They'd already lost so many and thus had offered up Devereaux babies to save their own families' babies.

"Perhaps, this time, the Devereaux clan will be lucky," a woman said feebly, to ease their consciences.

"Emm," they all murmured hopefully, although there had been many failures before. Still, this might be the lucky time.

"Celeste, how did you know she was the one?" All six women turned to the eldest.

"How could I not know, her words in the newspaper echoed those in Genevieve's journal. They think alike." She nodded. "We've chosen well. I believe this time we have saved our grandbabies as well as those of the Devereaux families."

"God, please let it be so," murmured the second eldest woman to her right.

And like a chant, it spread around the table until they all prayed in unison, "God, please let it be so."

"And forgive me if I was wrong," Celeste murmured quietly, so low that only her friend to the right heard. Her friend who prayed the same prayer silently.

Who carried the same guilt of deflecting the curse off of the Lejeunes and onto the Devereaux families.

****

Jenna's car coasted to a slow stop when she returned to drop Eddie off at his truck after dinner. Darkness surrounded them. Insects clicked from the nearby undergrowth. Warm, humid air licked her skin and the sweet smell of late summer flowers drifted in the barely there breeze.

Neither she nor Eddie said anything for a long moment, but just sat in companionable silence. The glow from the dashboard, combined with a lone street lamp, cast enough light so she could make out Eddie's features when she glanced sideways.

"So," he said. "Big city reporter comes to town, writing all the news that is fit to print or that fits the print?"

She laughed softly at the old newspaper saying. "Where'd you hear that?" She turned to look him full in the face.

He grinned lazily with a look that coursed through her nerve endings. "I took a journalism class or two at LSU up in Baton Rouge in my early college days."

She tried to picture him as a college guy. Probably a heartbreaker, inciting visions in college girls' minds much the same as in hers now. "So, were you Mr. Party Guy?"

He nodded with a low laugh. "Gotta admit, I was. Until I discovered the law and then it was full guns ahead. Once I got in law school proper, I had to sideline the partying almost altogether."

"Almost," she added.

He gave her a sexy sideways grin.

The closeness of the car and the darkness lent an intimacy to the moment. Not altogether unwelcome. It felt a bit like a college date - spontaneous, just sitting in a car, talking to a guy, getting to know him. It felt great.

"So, this research project of yours," he said. "I'm gonna want regular briefings." He raised an eyebrow. "Am I gonna have to issue a bench warrant to get you to report back to me?"

Was he asking for a date?

"I could keep you abreast."

He tilted his head. "Want to set a date for that? Say, Saturday?"

She nodded. Perfect, because she'd

already planned on something that would be so much better if she had Eddie with her. "There's a fais do-do out at the park I'd hoped to go to. It would be good for the article."

The article made it all so easy, with no pressure.

"For research, of course." His eyes met hers, connecting for a long moment with a sizzle that crackled through the air. Then, as if he'd seen something out of the corner of his eye, he turned to stare intently at his truck. "Ah, damn," he said lightly. "I got a flat tire."

"Oh, no." She peered at the truck's back left tire.

"It's all right," he said matter of factly, sounding like a man who'd changed a lot of tires. He pushed open his door and stepped out.

She opened her door and slid out too. Eddie pulled out an oversized lantern-type flashlight from behind his truck's seat, then cocked his head and walked toward the truck's front driver side tire.

He leaned forward, running a hand across the tire.

She stepped sideways to get a look. "Another flat?"

His face was deadly serious. "Well, I don't have two spares," he said simply.

"Do you think you ran over something?" She leaned closer to inspect the tire and saw what had inspired Eddie's dour expression. A large slash across the rubber that could hardly have happened before he'd parked or the tire would have gone instantly flat.

"Kids." He shrugged. "Or maybe someone

who didn't like the sentence I gave them in court. If this is the worst backlash I ever experience as a judge, I'll count myself lucky."

"I guess judges can make a few people mad," she offered.

"Oh yeah, lock a guy up and it'll tick a few of them off."

Jenna laughed at his casual tone. He had an easy way that said he could handle most any situation.

"Was it you? Hired someone before you knew I was gonna commute your traffic ticket?" He pointed a finger at her, then slid it down to hook into her skirt beltline.

Her pulse jumped and she looked down at his hand, so close, almost touching her stomach. Slowly, he reeled her in, raising her heart rate with each inch nearer.

She looked up at him through her lashes, his face just above hers. "I swear, your honor, I don't know nothing 'bout no tires."

A slight smile spread across his lips, then he tilted his head, aligning his mouth to hers. "We got our ways of finding out the truth, ya know."

"Yeah? Enhanced interrogation?" she murmured. *Show me*, she wanted to say. *Show me now*.

His free hand reached up to the pulse point in her neck, slowly fingering the sensitive skin beneath her jaw. "The heart rate reveals all." His voice slid across her skin like a sensor, testing, assessing.

She arched an eyebrow. "I'm a pretty tough cookie. Conditioned to hide my feelings, with all I've seen on the job."

He met her gaze and raised her one.
"Perhaps we should do a sampling test first,
on your heart rate. Say, something like a
little kiss, to see what's normal for you."

His thumb stroked her cheek, nearing
her mouth as if he just might brush his
finger across her lips.

At least he'd left her pulse point.
Because she was pretty sure it was rocking
like a Cajun accordion.

Because this was anything but normal
for her. Been a long time since any man
raised her heart rate with just a glint of
the eye. What was it about this man?

That proverbial love at first glance
guy, the one who checked all the boxes for
your genetic needs for a mate? She laughed
at herself, acting crazy like some teenaged
girl with her first crush.

But that's how it felt, such an
elevated level of excitement every time she
saw him.

It kinda made living worthwhile.

But, this was ridiculous. She was just
reacting to the journal, the photo. And
those dreams.

Damn those dreams.

She was here to do an article and
falling into bed with some local guy wasn't
going to win her any kudos with the locals.

Surely, some woman had her heart set on
the Honorable Judge Edward Devereaux.
Nothing good could come from messing with
the man a local woman had chosen as her own.

Not to mention the skanky impression it
would give. Because in these small town
situations, everyone eventually knew what
was going on with everyone else.

It was the ultimate reality show. She

stepped back and the judge's hand dropped away from her cheek and his other hand finally let go of her skirt's waistband.

"So, can I give you a ride somewhere?" she asked.

Eddie looked up the road as though weighing the offer.

"Got a woman waiting at the end of the ride?" she countered in as light a manner as she could manage. Might as well get the lay of the land right off.

He lifted a shoulder. "As a matter of fact, there is."

Her heart dropped with a bit of silly disappointment. The guy was just an interview.

Eddie smiled innocently. "My mama. I was meeting my Uncle Joe out there to help her move some furniture around."

She felt a hitch of relief, inappropriate as it might be. She was leaving soon. It was pointless to have these thoughts when nothing was going to happen between the two of them anyway.

"Then, I probably need to get you out there."

"It's not too far, just outside of town," he said pointing straight ahead.

They walked to her car and headed out. It felt good having him in her car again, enjoying a little more time in his presence. They rode out of town and turned left at a couple of cow pastures then pulled up in front of a low-slung, bayou type of house with a large front porch. Sitting outside in rocking chairs were two women and a man.

"That's Mama, Uncle Joe and Granny," Eddie said. He turned to look at her. He always seemed to really look at her, really see her. In spite of the proximity of his family, she felt a rush.

"Want to come up and be introduced?" He tilted his head as the porch trio studied her.

"That'd be great, maybe they know something about the history of Genevieve and Jean Claude."

"Eeeeh," Eddie made a negative sound that was hard to mistake. "I think I'd leave that one be for a while."

Why would they care about an old legend, people long dead? These Cajuns, she couldn't even begin to understand them.

As they approached the group, Eddie's folks assessed her, checking out the new girl, the girl Eddie brought by the house. His mother's eyes narrowed at Jenna.

"Jenna, I'd like to present my granny, my mama and my Uncle Joe." He gestured politely with his hand. "Y'all, this is Jenna. She was so kind as to give me a ride after my truck got a flat."

"What'd you conveniently forget how to change a tire?" Uncle Joe slowed his rocker to a halt, leaning forward to check out Jenna.

Eddie's granny chuckled but his mother steadily watched Jenna with that same look she'd gotten from many of the locals. They seemed a real tight-knit community.

"You got me, Uncle Joe. Did you have to make me look bad in front of the girl?" Eddie said lightly. "Jenna's here to do a story on the hurricane aftermath from Rafael. After the storm, so to speak."

"Ahhh." They all nodded their heads sagely.

"So, where's your truck?" Joe turned

the conversation again. "Do you need a jack or something?"

"I'm just gonna leave it till tomorrow, deal with it in the daylight. I'll help Mama and you move that furniture and then maybe you can drop me home on your way, Uncle Joe."

"Sure, boy. No problem."

"Everything looks better in the daylight," his mama murmured.

Eddie's granny narrowed her eyes at Jenna. "I didn't catch your last name, Jenna. Is your family from around here?"

Eddie stilled, his gaze sliding sideways toward her. Something in that quiet pause in his movement said here it comes, get ready.

What? The interrogation?

"No ma'am, my family lives up in Atlanta. Jenna Lejeune," she said then added jokingly, "of the Atlanta Lejeunes."

Granny and Uncle Joe's eyebrows shot up but his mother's face remained steady, as if she already knew everything she needed to know about Jenna. Atlantan, outsider, enough said.

"Lejeune?" His granny studied her face intently, as if looking for answers. "That's a Cajun name."

Jenna nodded. "Maybe somewhere way back down the line. We're pretty much white bread now, though. No real cultural history going on."

"There's always cultural history going on, dear. Even if we don't know it." His mother arched an eyebrow significantly.

Eddie looked at Jenna then, capturing her attention, and he was all she could think about.

"Thanks for dropping me off," he said. "I'll talk to you this week."

They'd exchanged cell numbers at dinner.

"Nice meeting you folks," she said and headed to her car, feeling their eyes on her back all the way, thinking if she turned they'd be studying her with that same intent gaze.

She was such a fish out of water down here. Her name might be Lejeune but she was all Atlanta, something she became aware of every time she talked to longtime residents of the area. Something about the way they looked at her let her know that.

Outsider might as well have been stamped on her forehead - a scarlet O for Outsider sewn on her chest.

Suddenly, Eddie was beside her, opening her car door, so close, his nearness exciting every female nerve in her body.

Glancing up, she met his eyes with a kick of anticipation, wanting to know what it would be like to kiss him, hardly able to wait until Saturday night. She turned away and got into the car.

He shut the door behind her, patting the metal near the window. "All right, then. Drive safe."

She nodded and tried to concentrate on starting the car. Tried to keep her breathing under control until she'd escaped his unsettling presence.

Just damn.

Eddie watched Jenna drive off. He looked straight ahead but out of the corner of his eye, he detected his family gathering steam to say something. As he walked back to the porch, he kept his eyes averted, having learned long ago not to look crazy people in the eye.

That's kinda what he was about to deal with. Loving crazy people. But crazy people nonetheless.

People who took the old stuff too seriously.

"Eddie," his granny started as soon as he hit the porch steps. As the senior member of the group, she knew she carried the most weight. "You don't need to be bothering with no Lejeune woman."

"Eh eh," Uncle Joe chimed in.

"No, siree," his mama added for emphasis.

Eddie turned to look the beast in the eye. Once it came at ya, you had to face it. "Y'all do not really believe all that old stuff, do you?" He looked at his mama, knowing she'd be the most vulnerable to him. Break 'em up, get 'em disorganized and conquer.

"Look in the phone book," his granny countered. "You will not find one Lejeune in this town." She shook her finger for emphasis. "You done got the bad luck started on you boy. Don't encourage it to move in for good."

"You had a flat tire just about as soon as you met that girl." Uncle Joe shook his head knowingly.

Two flat tires actually. But he didn't need to tell them that and really get them scared.

No bad luck boogieman had cut those tires. Somebody with a knife had. And he'd lay money it was a flesh and blood person. But just who it was and why they'd done it was hard to figure.

Eddie walked inside to speak to his sister, leaving the trio on the front porch.

As one, they all turned to look through the window where Eddie's sister sat, heavy with child.

"Oh, Looord," said Eddie's granny. "She's come for our Eddie."

His mother and Uncle Joe nodded, anxiety crinkling into lines on their faces. "Let's hope she doesn't take your girl's child with her to the grave," Uncle Joe said what they all were thinking.

"Let's hope she doesn't take Eddie," his mother added, her mouth quivering. "She *won't* take our Eddie," she corrected herself with conviction. And a steely hardness locked in her expression.

"She won't take our Eddie or our Celia's baby."

.

CHAPTER NINE

Jenna parked in front of her motel in Eufaula. After the murder of the man outside her hotel in New Orleans, she hadn't been able to vacate the place quick enough.

Pickings were slim for a place to stay in the small, southern Louisiana town of Eufaula. But this motel was clean, and decent people ran it so she was satisfied.

But she was going to have to ask them to do something about lighting in the parking lot. The only lamppost's light bulb needed replacing. So as she walked toward her room, she couldn't help but look over her shoulder.

The judge's slashed tires had her spooked, as if the bad luck of New Orleans had followed her here. But that was just hooliganism, petty crime. Eufaula seemed such a nice town but apparently crime could be anywhere.

When she rounded the last car blocking her path to her room, she saw her door, open about five inches with a dim light shining from the room. She stopped dead. A light sweat broke out under her clothes. She sucked in a deep breath, pushing back the nervousness.

The management must be checking on a problem with the plumbing or something.

Still, cautiously she stepped back and around at an angle where she could see through the gap left by the open door. Slight shuffling sounds came from the room. Stepping closer, she sidestepped to try and see a different part of the room. Still nothing.

She sneaked closer, until she was right

by the door. She tilted her head and saw Zoom.

Zoom. She started to call his name but something about his body posture stopped her.

He was going through the notebooks she'd left strewn across the small desk. Picking one up, he leafed through it.

There was an oddness about his stance.

For a moment, in this strange place with the trailing Spanish moss flickering shadows across the parking lot, and the humid air with buzzing mosquitoes and a chorus of other nocturnal insects, she felt very far from home, and alone.

The urge to dial Eddie's cell phone and summon his comforting presence almost overwhelmed her.

But that was absurd. This was Zoom. Good old Zoom.

"Zoom," she said.

He jumped and turned, his expression like a cat caught on the dining room table. "Oh, you scared me." He took a deep breath and sat down in the chair next to the desk. "Man, I must have looked silly just now."

She laughed slightly. "Kind of."

"Hey man, sorry about going through your things but I was looking for the contact information for that last family we did the story on." He looked sheepishly at her. "I tried your cell phone but couldn't get through. I thought maybe you were out at their place."

Why hadn't he waited until she got back?

As though reading her face, he said, "I was starting to get a little worried about you."

Worried?

"This place is freaking me out, Jenna."

Freaking Zoom out? The man who went into the eye of hurricanes, laughing with exhilaration at the storm's fury, who'd never shied away from any assignment because it was too dangerous?

He tilted his head, as if reading her mind, nodding in acknowledgement that his words were out of character.

"I've been here all day trying to track down some of the people I was supposed to shoot." He raised an eyebrow. "And I gotta say, Jenna, this place is weird. Once people hear your name, they shut up and give me the weirdest looks. What'd you do, Jenna, burn down the town square?"

"Me?" She walked into the room.

"What was it one man said?" Zoom looked off into space. "'We don't need no Lejeune woman coming round here. You tell her to stay off our place.'"

He narrowed his eyes at Jenna, waiting for a logical explanation.

But she didn't have one.

She shook her head. "The worst trouble I've caused is getting a traffic ticket for running a stop sign."

"I guess they take their traffic laws seriously 'cause you are considered big trouble by some of these people." He waved his hand. "Not everybody, though, cause I asked someone else who didn't seem to even blink at your name. The motel owners didn't seem to think anything of it. When I showed them my newspaper ID, they let me in your room so I could try and find that information."

"I got nothing," she said with a shake

of her head. "I've been following up on my story like normal. What could be controversial about hurricane survivors? But, yeah, some people act funny when they hear my name. I need to do some research on that."

"Like you don't have enough to research already." Zoom laughed, knowing how she worked, how she found extensions to her main story whenever she started working on a subject.

"But that's what people like about your articles, they feel like they've been on a journey with you when you write about something."

"Ahh, thanks, Zoom. I think that's the nicest thing you ever said to me." She genuinely smiled. They usually had more of a sibling relationship, with Zoom picking on her and vice versa. They spent so much time traveling around the South together they'd become close.

Then, outside the door, a creaking sounded loudly in the quiet night and they both jumped and turned toward it in unison, as if their nerves were equally shot. They craned their necks to see outside the slightly open door.

Spanish moss melted down from the trees like long fingers reaching toward unsuspecting visitors to the region. The wavy creepy shadows bounced along the walls of the motel room. Jenna walked over and pushed the door shut, locking it.

"It was just a branch," she said, hoping that was true.

"Look." Zoom's face twisted with worry. "I already got a room up in Lafayette but I can get a room down here if you'd feel better having me around."

Some part of her wanted to accept but another part, the grownup part, had to say no. Zoom hated little backwater areas where there were so few choices of places to eat. Lafayette had plenty of good restaurants. Eating was always big on Zoom's agenda when they traveled. Said if he had to be away from his family, he deserved some reward.

Besides, if she started needing someone around whenever she went out on slightly scary stories, she'd have to get out of news. It really wasn't all that safe of a business if you got right down to it.

But this story was a zero on the danger scale. The danger had been right after Hurricane Rafael, going into devastated areas, trees still falling, electrical lines on the ground, food and drink hard to find, not to mention finding a place to stay. One night, she and Zoom had slept in the car, reclining their seats to get some shuteye.

These were just follow-up interviews when people's lives were normal. That's all it was. All.

No reason to worry.

"Not necessary, Zoom. After we both get a good night's sleep, we'll realize it was just back country aversion to big city reporter types nosing around in their business. You know how these small towns can be."

He smiled. "Yeah, we've been kicked out of nicer places than this." That was their often-repeated mantra to each other when someone was particularly nasty to them.

"Yeah, at least no one's shot at us, yet."

Her stomach clenched despite her

bravado. There were so many little things, like the expression on Eddie's family's faces when they heard her last name. An unnatural sensation of fear swam through her body, the same as she'd felt in New Orleans.

"You're right." Zoom smiled, but not quite convincingly. "It's just driving around down here, getting lost on these deserted roads, with all the low hanging moss and swamps that's freaking me out."

She nodded in agreement. "It is the perfect setting for a scary movie."

"You got that right." Zoom stood and lifted the corner of the curtain to peer out the window. "But not as bad as right after the hurricane."

She nodded, remembering that horrible time. "Yeah, Rafael really kicked the area's ass."

"The ass that hadn't yet been kicked by Katrina," Zoom said with a laugh.

Jenna walked to her desk, leafed through a notebook, pulled out a sheet of paper, wrote down some information and handed it to Zoom.

"Here's the address and some directions for that second family we talked about. And I also wrote down the motel's number. Leave me a message if you can't get me on my cell phone and I'll check here regularly, just in case. Cell phone coverage can be pretty spotty around here."

"I know that's right. Kept losing coverage all afternoon." Zoom took the paper, then stopped with his hand on the door. He looked back, meeting her eyes directly, nodding for emphasis, "You be careful and stay in touch so I don't have to worry about you getting snatched up by some swamp monster."

She nodded. "Got it, Dad." Then she smiled brightly, as if she weren't spooked herself. As Zoom walked away, she couldn't help looking out into the parking lot and glancing around carefully. She shut her door, bolted it and put on the safety chain.

Then, dragged an armchair over against the door.

She checked her cell phone for missed calls. There weren't any. Zoom's phone must not have been able to connect with hers because of the bad coverage. All day long, her phone had been losing range, unable to dial out.

The scariness level had gone up with that, knowing she was unable to call for roadside assistance or anything if she needed help, if her car had broken down.

There was definitely something about this lowland swampy area that was spooking her, with the ever-present mist that scooted along the ground, circling trees wherever she went.

On top of someone in New Orleans sending her packets containing Jean Claude's journal and portrait.

And the murder.

Yeah, a murder outside your hotel of a guy who'd earlier tried to get into your room while you occupied it would make anyone a bit skittish.

Then, she looked at her bed and forgot everything but her dreams in which Eddie's look-alike, Jean Claude, held her, tempted her.

A flush of heat swept through her, filling her mind with images of the two of them entwined, flesh against flesh.

Would he come to her again tonight in her dreams? A small part of her hoped so, ached for the moment when he took her in his arms.

God, how pathetic was it that her dreams were so much more exciting than her real life?

Until she'd met Edward Devereaux.

The descendant of the man in her dreams? Saturday night beckoned as brightly as her nighttime moments with Jean Claude.

Eddie and Jean Claude were melding together in her mind into one entity.

And the journal began to feel more real. Almost like a memory.

CHAPTER TEN

Jenna floated in that half space between wakefulness and sleep.

Jean Claude stepped out of the mists and beckoned to her, his hand extended in a sensual welcome.

With that enticement, Jenna allowed herself to sink into her dream.

Cajun music, loud and contagious, ricocheted through the air. "Aiiii," the Cajun call to party reverberated in her head.

Fiddles and singing pulsed into her nerves from all directions. The rhythm caught her and carried her along, guidance from Jean Claude's hands only taking her in the direction she was already inclined to move, dancing in time with his beat and the music.

He swung her, his hands coaxing moves from her she didn't know she possessed. Their bodies melded into one continuous moving force, and Jean Claude's hands tightened as he turned her in a Cajun pirouette.

She laughed and looked up into his smiling, playful hickory nut colored eyes. This was the moment she'd waited for all her life, to be held and touched by this man who understood her so well. Every move of his elicited a response from her. He wasn't so much leading in the dance as anticipating her wishes.

A slight sheen of perspiration bathed her and as he swung her closer, their skin connected with an electrical charge conducted by the moisture across her entire body.

He smelled earthy and she felt alive and feral, exhilarated by the energy of the dance, the music, and the excitement of other moving bodies swirling around them in time to the wild song.

And, yes, by her Cajun lover's closeness, the way he looked into her eyes as they danced as if he saw only her, as if he lived for only her.

But suddenly, from outside the frenetic circle of dancers, she felt a presence, foreboding and dangerous, someone watching them. As she swung with Jean Claude in the dance, she strained to see through the crowd, to discern who was watching.

Finally, frustrated and scared, she pulled away from Jean Claude and turned to look directly into the woods. Who was there? Watching, stalking. Making her feel like prey.

She peered into the darkness, as mist crawled toward the dancing crowd.

No one. She saw no one.

That didn't mean they weren't there. An ominous presence threatened from the woods, beating danger her way.

Her heart clenched and pounded faster as if preparing to fight the threat. What did they want?

Then, suddenly, she knew.

Knew that once again she was being separated from her lover. She turned to look at Jean Claude as he slowly faded. Her heart cried out with the loss.

No, she cried, desperately, angrily. Once again, she'd lost him. Jean Claude, she called into the mist.

Jenna jerked awake, and sat up in bed, instantly alert, wildly looking around for the source of the danger, the danger to her and Jean Claude.

An owl hooted in the distance, the sound mournful, lonely and wild, reminding her of all the untamed swamp surrounding the small town. Eufaula was an isolated patch of civilization in the midst of the deeply tangled undergrowth.

This was ludicrous. *Wilderness* wasn't something to fear.

But, her dream suggested something dangerous lurked out in the swamps. To her, and Jean Claude, or his modern lookalike, Edward Devereaux.

She forced herself to lie back down. But the sound of her own heartbeat, and the pulsing of blood through her ears, acknowledged the terror she'd felt in the instant before she'd awakened.

Terrifying, threatening, stalking. Something had cut off the sensual dream of Jean Claude. It had felt like a warning. Of what?

★★★★

Early the next morning, hazy sunlight filtered into the room, attacking Jenna's tired eyes with a headache-inducing glare.

Had she slept at all last night after the dream?

Her muscles ached as if she'd been running for miles, or on high alert for the last eight hours. Restful? Hardly.

She swung her legs over the side of the bed and shuffled straight to the small coffee pot sitting on the counter. Pouring water into the top, she hit the on button and waited for the coffee to brew.

"This has got to end. I want some answers as to what became of Jean Claude and

Genevieve. Then, I can put them to rest.
Maybe that's why I had the nightmares,
because my mind just wants to know."

She often dreamed about intense stories
she was working on, her mind becoming
obsessed with them. That's all this was.

Saint Thomasville and the church that
held many records of the area might hold
some clues. Maybe she'd be lucky and find
marriage or death records for Jean Claude
Devereaux and his Genevieve. Perhaps even
some children born to them.

Wouldn't that be lovely?

She poured herself a cup of coffee and
gulped it, anxious for the caffeine kick.
Slowly, as the caffeine hit her veins, an
angry determination steeled inside of her.
She was going to finish this mystery of the
Cajun lovers once and for all.

Then, she'd finish her hurricane
recovery story. And be done with work.

*So you can concentrate on enjoyment and
fun?*

Jenna laughed at the instant thought
that had popped up in her brain.

Refilling her cup, she jumped into the
shower, got ready quickly for her day, and
left.

Driving to Saint Thomasville was like
visiting a foreign country, the vegetation
so unlike north Georgia's. Acre after acre
of sugarcane flowed past the car. The green
leafy plant grew higher than a man's head,
waving in the wind like green flags.

So dense, she could become easily lost
in the vast fields if she were to leave the
road and venture into the mass of greenery.

Why would she even think of something
like that? Why would she envision herself

wandering in cane fields? And why was she checking her rearview mirror to see if she was being followed?

The dreams were making her paranoid, with no basis in fact for these free-floating anxieties.

But, it wasn't paranoia that someone had deliberately sent the journal and the photo of Jean Claude to her hotel in New Orleans. To lure her to Eufaula?

And then that *handyman* who'd tried to get into her room, then later had been found dead in the hotel alley.

Suddenly, she wondered if Eddie's slashed tires had anything to do with her? Sheesh, why wouldn't she be anxious? So many weird things.

She pushed the pedal down and drove, hoping to quickly return to a somewhat populated area. It was so lonely on this road, so isolated.

In her rearview mirror, she spotted a car coming up on her fast. Faster than any normal person would drive. Instantly, an irrational fear began pounding through her veins, warning her to accelerate. She picked up a bit of speed but not too much over the limit because of her recent ticket.

The car, an oversized SUV, sped toward her, and her heart beat faster and faster. She pushed her car even faster, but, still, the SUV gained on her.

Dry gravel filled her mouth as if she'd taken a bite of the dirt alongside the isolated road. She grabbed her cell phone. No bars, no coverage. She was on her own. Damn, she wished for a gun, wished she had a Louisiana carry permit.

Hell, wished she had a gun even if she

didn't have a Louisiana carry permit.

The vehicle zoomed toward her, as if on a mission. As it approached her rear bumper, it didn't slow down but looked almost as if it were targeting her car. She held her breath, readying for impact, gripping the steering wheel in hopes of controlling her car if it went into a skid.

Then, the car whooshed past her, continuing on up the road, as if it had nothing to do with her. Her breath left her chest in one mighty explosion of relief.

"Oh, thank God. Thank God!"

Her arms began to shake and she slowed her car, attempting to get back in control of her emotions. Then, she looked ahead and saw the same SUV coming back toward her.

"Oh my God."

It sped toward her, veering over the dividing line of the two-lane road into her lane. She steered her car toward the opposite side of the road, but, like a heat-seeking missile, the SUV crossed back over into that lane. It could slam head on into her car, and with the size difference, she'd never stand a chance.

She pulled back over onto her side of the road, hoping the other driver had lost their concentration for a minute and would stay in their lane now.

But, she sensed that was false hope. The SUV veered toward her again, this time only slightly over the line. She readied for impact, slowing her car and pulling to the right as much as possible, looking at the side of the road to see if it would support her car, but there was nothing more than a water-filled ditch here. If she slid off into that, she'd be easy pickings for the driver of the other car to get out and …

She didn't know what. But the memory of the handyman's eyes staring vacantly up at the sky seemed very close to her expectations of what might happen.

The car barreled at her. As the hulking SUV approached, she could see the face of a man through the windshield, his face an angry mask, glaring, full of hate.

"Oh God," she shrieked, readying for the crash. Would that twisted face be her last memory?

But the car just sped past her, with a loud swoosh, that sounded like all the air in her body blowing out of her lungs.

She whipped her head around, trying to get a glimpse of a tag. But the car was moving so fast, she couldn't see anything. At least it was moving away.

She pushed down on her accelerator, and drove as fast as her car would go. To hell with the traffic tickets, she just wanted to get back to civilization.

Finally, she reached the small town of Saint Thomasville. She thought about calling the police, even though she had so little to go on. It had been a non-descript white SUV. How many of those were around? She'd been so focused on his angry eyes that she didn't know how much else she could remember.

Sixtyish, brown hair, a white man. With glaring, angry eyes.

"Damn it, just concentrate on your story. These things aren't related." Why would anyone want to hurt her?

Slowly, she drove to the church where she asked to see the marriage, birth, and death records.

"I'll have to get the priest." The

clerk manning the front desk narrowed his
eyes, studied her for a moment, then scooted
his chair back, knocking it over as he did
so.

He fumbled to get it back on its legs,
then almost knocked it over again as he
pushed past it to the door marked *Rectory
Staff Only*.

"Okay, that was definitely weird," she
muttered to herself after the door swung
closed. But his social awkwardness didn't
necessarily have anything to do with her.

She was going nuts. She was starting to
feel as if she'd driven into some *Twilight
Zone* episode.

After a minute, a meek, very normal
seeming priest walked through the doorway.
Slightly hunched over, as if he spent a lot
of time poring over the bible, he looked
somewhere north of seventy. His lined face
relaxed into a sweet smile as he folded his
hands in front of him. "May I ask why you
would like to see the records, ma'am?"

He said it like it was a routine
question, but the clerk who'd returned to
his desk kept glancing back and forth
between Jenna and the priest.

"I'm trying to find out what happened
to a Cajun couple that was separated during
the exodus from Nova Scotia." She did this
sort of thing all the time, as part of her
job. She was a professional. Even if she
were stalking Jean Claude, her dead man
crush, it wasn't like the priest could read
that on her face.

His eyes crinkled at the corners as if
he were used to ferreting out the truth from
people.

You probably didn't get that in

confession often - I'm lusting after a dead man. What sort of a sin did that fall under?

"We don't usually let the public see the records."

She flashed her newspaper ID card, like a cop showing a badge, proving she was a professional, not a ghost stalker.

Maybe she did need counseling. How did that conversation start? I'm in love with a dead man, can you help me? No, I've never actually met him, this isn't a grieving situation. We're just starting a relationship.

Bring in the padded cell guys now.

The priest glanced at her ID, pulling it closer so he could read it, then his eyes shot to her face, his gaze sharpening, and some dawning revelation filled them. "Oh, I see," he drew the last word out. "That's a bit different then."

He hesitated, his mouth opening, words hanging just beyond the diffidence any good priest must learn to exercise with all they hear, then, he shook his head slightly.

He waved her back behind the desk with a soft gesture. "We have to watch out because some people don't like what they find in our little history books." He raised a shoulder. "People have been known to rip out a page if they didn't want to see their family connected to another."

Jenna laughed slightly.

"It's true." He smiled. "They rewrite history in their own way."

He led her down a dim hallway where their footsteps echoed around them. The building was cool despite the already hot day outside, almost like a deserted tomb.

She shivered. A church should evoke

feelings of safety and peace, not this almost palpable sense of combined doom and destiny. As if no matter what occurred, it was meant to be.

Destiny? Why did that come to mind, something she didn't even believe in? Self determination, self made, pulling yourself up by the bootstraps, those were things she believed in. Making your choices. Choosing your path.

Enough. This was research, not a date with destiny.

Still, as they got closer to a door at the end of the hallway, her level of excitement crept up.

The priest pushed open the heavy, oversized door to reveal a room lined with dusty books that smelled of age, of times long ago with the loves and passions of centuries. History pulsed from the books, with the documentation of so many moments in time.

Births, marriages, deaths. So many lives reduced to just the barest facts, yet between the two or three dates about each person, so much life had happened.

Love, loss, passion, hate, grief, joy. She reached out to stroke the spine of one faded binder and almost felt all the emotions of the people whose lives were encapsulated within the pages pulse under her hand.

The nondescript room seemed anticlimactic to what it held, answers to so many questions.

A surge in her blood agitated her, hoping for the answer to what had happened to Jean Claude and Genevieve. God, she hoped they'd found each other and had a long, happy life together.

The priest pulled out a book, opening it to an aging brown paper page. "These books," he waved toward a shelf filled with similar books to the one he held, "are all the deaths, births and marriages in Saint Thomasville since 1756."

He flipped carefully through the pages. "It starts in French. Halfway through, it changes to Spanish. Then later to English when the area became American as part of the Louisiana Purchase under Andrew Jackson."

History wafted off the pages with a timeless ambience as if the words had only been written just moments ago.

Such an important historical document. "It's amazing," she said.

The priest smiled with such gentility, giving her a wink. "I know I can trust you with such valuable pieces of history so I'll leave you to your research." He turned and walked out the door.

Sucking in a deep breath, she steeled herself, then sat down and opened a book. The records were beautiful, with elegant handwriting characteristic of a time gone by, that people now called calligraphy. She combed slowly through the pages, looking for some clue.

Leafing through record after record, the mustiness filling her nostrils, she became impatient that she would ever find what she was looking for.

Then, finally, she saw the name Jean Claude Devereaux.

Shock rolled through her like a tidal wave, adrenaline exciting her senses. A pulsing excitement filled her, much like a homicide cop looking for a body who knew it was out there somewhere but who still experienced human feelings when they found it.

1763. The marriage of a Jean Claude Devereaux with a Genevieve Lejeune.

Lejeune! Another kick of shock hit her stomach.

Jenna's own last name? "What the hell?"

She'd never seen any mention of Genevieve's last name anywhere in the pages she'd received.

"Well, no wonder." No wonder people looked at her strangely when she asked about Jean Claude. Because of the similarity between the names. "Genevieve Lejeune and Jenna Lejeune," she murmured.

Genevieve's last name floated eerily on the page, as though it had been waiting for her arrival, as though finally she'd found what she'd been meant to discover.

"Someone wanted me to know this." Then, she shook her head. This was getting all too surreal. She had to think of Jean Claude and Genevieve's love story as just another subplot to her hurricane story about the survival of the Cajun people, hundreds of years ago, and the present day.

An impartial, journalistic endeavor.

Yeah, right.

She turned over a page and found a birth for a female child, named Evangeline, less than two months after the marriage. Evangeline, like the poem by Henry Wadsworth Longfellow about a Cajun woman separated from her lover during the exodus from Nova Scotia.

But Genevieve's child was born only two months after Jean Claude and Genevieve's marriage.

"You dog, Jean Claude. You were playing around before you got her in front of a priest."

Then, she remembered her dreams with Jean Claude. Playing around wouldn't have described what Genevieve and Jean Claude had done. It would have been more like a force of nature, a powerful explosion of emotion into a physical consummation.

They'd waited so long for each other.

Priests were probably hard to come by for an official marriage, in the isolated swamp region that the area was then.

Just under Jenna's skin simmered the memory of the way the man had touched her in her dreams. "I'm happy for the two of you," she whispered, imagining the joy that would have filled their union.

Finally, she tore her mind away from invading their privacy and returned to her journalistic pursuit for information about their lives.

Leafing through the record book further, she found another child born about a year and a half after that. A boy.

She continued on in the book but found no death records for Genevieve and Jean Claude.

What had happened to the couple?

She raced through the pages, looking for a death date or other information on their children and found a marriage and children born of the male child. That line continued on through the record book.

But there was nothing for the female child.

As though she'd disappeared along with her parents.

"There's got to be more." She leafed

endlessly back and forth over the pages, but there wasn't more.

Another Lejeune woman's marriage record was shortly after the time of Jean Claude and Genevieve's marriage. Was she a sister?

But, still no further mention of Jean Claude, Genevieve or their daughter Evangeline.

She pushed away from the table, frustrated again. She'd only found some of the answers she'd hoped for.

"Damn this," she cursed quietly, aware that she was on church property, looking around, almost expecting a nun to show up with a ruler to rap her knuckles.

She raised her hands silently toward the heavens. "You gotta admit this is frustrating," she said loud enough so that her words vibrated back to her from the thick walls.

"What is?" a voice said from the other side of the door.

She jumped, not having expected any audible acknowledgement of her statement. God had never spoken out loud to her before. Then, she realized it sounded like the priest.

She laughed slightly, stood, and pushed open the door. The priest stood just outside the door, as if waiting for her. She'd assumed he'd left.

"Sorry about the cursing," she said. He merely tilted his head in acceptance of the apology.

"So, you found what you were after, eh?" A knowing glint filled his eyes.

She drew in a steadying breath. Of course he'd waited, figuring she had a personal stake in this. When he'd seen her last name, he'd immediately thought she was researching to find out about her own ancestors.

Why hadn't he said anything though? Like, *Oh and you must be descended from Genevieve Lejeune. Is that why you're here?*

There was nothing normal about the last couple of days. A dizzy sense of unreality hit her and she felt for a moment like she might be sick.

She placed a hand over her stomach, willing down the nausea, concentrating on what she wanted to know.

"Do you know more about this Jean Claude Devereaux and Genevieve Lejeune and their children than is in the book, father?" She searched his face, for expressions that might reveal he knew information he wasn't prepared to divulge.

He glanced quickly down the hall at the clerk who'd turned at the sound of her voice, peering through the door that now stood open. A ferret-like curiosity filled the young clerk's eyes. As if he had propped open the door so he could watch.

The priest tilted his head toward a side door. "I'll walk you to your car."

They exited the doorway and walked a bit away from the building before he placed a hand on her elbow, leaned in and spoke quietly.

"Some people around here are sensitive about the history of this couple." His expression said he knew so much more. "Over in Eufaula, there has never been a Lejeune family. Here in Saint Thomasville, you will find them." He raised an eyebrow, and a wry expression filled his eyes. "But not over there. If you ask a Lejeune person why they don't want to go over there, they'd just say, *No good can come of it.*"

The priest raised a shoulder, dismissively. "People say there's bad history with this couple, and now the Devereaux don't mix with the Lejeune."

"Like the Hatfields and the McCoys?"

"Ehh." He waggled his hand, and shook his head. "Different. You don't find them badmouthing each other, just keeping away from the other family."

"Well, tonight ought to be fun." Nervous anxiety frothed her stomach. "I'm going dancing with a Devereaux man over in Eufaula."

He looked like she'd said she was going swimming in the bayou with fish hanging from her waist. Alligator bait.

He leaned forward to grasp her forearm, a warning wind sparking up in his gaze. "Take this seriously, miss. They do."

A nervous flash shot through her, alerting all her senses. He was saying this wasn't just about gossip, but real danger.

"Someone almost ran me off the road as I was driving over here."

The priest's eyes widened. "We should call the police."

And say what? "I didn't get enough information for them to really go on."

"Still, you should make a report."

She nodded. "I probably will." Or just hurry and finish her story and get the hell out of Dodge?

She met his concerned gaze for a long moment, then, over his shoulder, she noticed a little cemetery behind the church. Ancient wrought iron gates guarded the grounds, giant live oaks sheltered it, with trailing streams of Spanish moss lending an air of sadness.

Again, despite his warning words about the Cajun couple, her desire to know pushed back her fear. The driving urge swept through her. It was what kept people like her in the business.

You had to have that or you would just pack it up and go on the chamber of commerce beat, doing stories about safe things, like new businesses opening in town.

"Father, where would the oldest section of the graveyard be?"

He shook his head knowingly. "You won't find them there. They're nowhere to be found, Genevieve and Jean Claude."

"Any Lejeunes?"

"Many Lejeunes. Genevieve had a sister who traveled with her to this area."

"The marriage record that was just about the same time as Genevieve's?"

The priest nodded. "Then, other family members must have come because there are marriages and births to others later on."

Moss draped the walkway between the church and the old part of the cemetery like the mists of time, softening the view of the ancient stones.

"I'm just going to see what's down there. Thanks for your help, Father."

He took her hand softly in his, shaking it. "You be careful now, child." Deep lines creased around his eyes. He looked at her the way people look at relatives with terminal illnesses, as if it might be the last time they saw them.

Swimming with alligators.

A cold shiver shuddered through her and she wrapped her arms around herself. Despite the heat, she felt chilled to the bone.

Then, she saw a large stone marker at the far end of the graveyard. It read *Lejeune*.

"The Lejeune section? If Genevieve married, then, I wouldn't find her direct line along with the other Lejeunes, would I?"

The priest shrugged. "Anyhow, she is not buried down there."

Then, he narrowed his eyes and looked directly into hers. "Legend or truth, you be careful out among those Devereaux, eh?" He patted her shoulder, then turned and headed back toward the church.

She watched him for a moment, thinking of all the new information, then walked toward the beckoning stone, determination filling her. No old superstitions, nor people who believed in them, were going to stop her from finishing this second part of her articles about the Cajun couple and the exodus story they represented. She'd been in much scarier situations than this.

Like trying to get a comment from the high placed politician who was later sent to prison for taking bribes. He'd actually pulled a gun on her. If she hadn't ducked and run, she might not be here today. Luckily, the guy was overweight and out of shape and hadn't chased her.

On the way to the Lejeune section, something caught her attention.

The number of freshly turned plots of earth, doll size, so small they could only be for a child. She stopped, suddenly remembering what she'd heard in the courtroom.

About the recent deaths of children.

A wave of sadness swept over her as she walked to one of the small temporary placards marking a small grave. The date was only two weeks ago.

Gazing out across the plots, she noticed how many there were, four little graves. Walking along the path, she looked at each of them, noticing the first deaths was only a month ago, and the last death was four days ago.

It was horrifying to realize this many infants had died in such a short period of time in such a sparsely populated parish. Four here, and at least one over in Eufaula to the man who hadn't shown up for court. Were there others?

She yanked out a notebook and began to write down as much information as each marker provided about each baby. Their birth dates were the same as their death dates, all died or were stillborn on the same day of their birth.

Was she the first reporter to hear about this?

"This is a much bigger story than Jean Claude and Genevieve. Much greater significance." Her heart wrenched at all the tiny plots of freshly turned earth. So small - such innocent little bundles of hope that were taken away from so many families.

She had to find the parish priest, to see what he knew about this.

Then, she looked back down at the dates. Each was exactly a week apart. Except for the last one, which was three days after the one before that.

Then, the one that had happened in Eufaula was only three days after the last of the Saint Thomasville deaths.

So odd the pattern of the deaths, the last few coming quicker and quicker, as if whatever was killing the babies was picking up steam, gaining strength.

CHAPTER ELEVEN

Eddie sat in his office poring over legal briefs, weighing a fine legal point. Suddenly, without warning, his door flew open and his ex-wife rode in on her high-heeled horse.

His clerk looked at him from her desk, with her hands raised in the air signaling, *There was nothing I could do.*

He nodded and stood to close the door, giving them what little privacy his ex-wife's high-pitched voice would allow. "Lidia, always good to see you." He kissed her on the cheek.

But that wasn't enough for her. She grabbed him by the neck and pushed her lips against his mouth. Grasping her by the shoulders to prevent her from making full body contact, he quickly pursed back a semblance of a polite ex-husband type of a kiss before stepping back to put his desk between them.

Sitting in his chair, he assessed the woman he'd shared a bed with for seven years, five of them married.

She was in full combat mode, tight skirt and low cut neckline showing plenty of cleavage. The woman was on a mission.

A lipsticked smile spread across her face as she walked around to perch on his side of the desk, crossing her legs so that her skirt hiked up, exposing a long length of well-toned thigh.

Her looks had never been the problem.

"You between men again, Lidia?" he said lightly. She only came to town looking for him when her ego needed a boost, when she needed a shot of *Oh, aren't you hot, babe.*

*So hot I can't resist my better sense and
I'll go to bed with you.*

Leaning over, she ran a finger down his
shirtfront. "Oh, Eddie. I just wanted to see
you. I miss you."

He nodded, with no comment. Lidia
didn't know the difference between missing a
specific man and just missing having a man
in her bed.

"I do miss you, Eddie," she crooned.

He smiled wryly, looking up at his ex-
wife, with that beautiful face he'd
mistakenly thought fronted a beautiful soul.

"I've been thinking we ought to get
back together." Her voice held a trace of
the sweetness that had originally attracted
him back in his law school days in Baton
Rouge.

"For how long this time, Lidia?" He'd
been weak a couple of times in the past,
even believing her when she'd said she'd
been wrong to leave him.

The sting of stupidity still prickled
from the last time he'd come home to find a
note telling him she'd gone back to Baton
Rouge.

She always had a man lined up each time
she left. The grapevine worked the
information quickly back to him.

But that was Lidia. She couldn't exist
very long without a man. Moreover, she
didn't have to.

"Eddie, I've found a great marriage
counselor and I think we should go."

"We're not married anymore, Lidia."

She slid her hand across his shoulder
and leaned forward to look into his eyes. "I
miss what we had when we were married. I
know I was a bi-ach to leave the way I did."

He raised an eyebrow.

"The ways I did," she acknowledged. "I yanked you around. But, Eddie." She leaned closer, running her hand around his shoulder. "We had something special, or you wouldn't have taken me back before." She nodded in concession. "All those times."

He rolled his chair slightly away so it was too awkward for her to keep her hand on his shoulder and she let it drop.

Her eyebrows shot up, her eyes widened and her mouth rounded into a circle. "You've met someone?"

He turned away a bit so she couldn't look directly into his eyes.

"You have." She stood and paced a few steps before whirling and pointing a finger at him. "Not that Lejeune Woman?" Indignation caused her to rise up even higher on her heels as though she'd caught him in an affair.

"The Lejeune Woman?" Eddie stalled.

"Oh, believe me I've already heard about her. It's all the talk at the diner. One of the maids heard her name as the motel manager was taking her reservation over the phone, and word went all around. Sally made sure I knew first thing when I stopped in at the diner." She adjusted her blouse. "Good thing I went in. Can't touch it for catching up on the goings on in this town in five minutes flat."

"So," she placed a hand on her hip, "The Lejeuene Woman!"

He laughed slightly like it was a joke. But she moved a step closer. "Eddie, how can you be so silly?"

"You're the one being silly, Lidia." He pointed his finger at her. "I can't believe you'd even bring up The Lejeune Woman thing. You don't believe that old wives' tale any more than I do. Less even."

"It doesn't matter what you or I think, Eddie. Everyone else believes it." She picked up the purse she'd tossed on the chair when she'd first come in. "*The ways are the ways*. Isn't that what you told me when I used to question all the traditions and kooky beliefs down here?"

She snorted. "Crazy old ways, is what it is. But, it's their ways, right?"

She wagged her finger at him. "Give me a call when you decide this Lejeune Woman isn't for you. 'Cause I'm serious about getting back together this time."

With that, she flung the door open and walked out. Lidia was always flinging something. He'd liked the hot bloodedness when he was younger but it had grown old when they'd grown older. It just seemed unreliable and not the sort of thing you wanted for the mother of your children. Thank God they'd never had any before she'd left the first time.

* * * * * *

Jenna pulled into a parking spot in front of the motel where she was staying. The late afternoon sun cast shadows through the trees. She was pleasantly tired but pleased with the progress of the second part of her story.

Genevieve and Jean Claude had married and had two children. That was some good news. If she never found out what happened after that, she could end her piece on a good note.

Albeit a mysterious one. And not very satisfying for her personally. She'd rather have found their graves side by side, that they'd passed within a few years of each other, with their children and the rest of their descendants around them.

But, it was what it was. Maybe a few more days of chasing the trail would uncover more info.

Zoom had called from Lafayette. He'd found the most important family for their article and she'd driven there to check on their progress. It had been uplifting. Family had pitched in after Hurricane Rafael and they were all together, living outside of Lafayette.

Warm emotion filled her. A catastrophe had occurred but she could report on the better side of human nature. And her Cajun couple had reunited and had a family. She loved her job.

As she approached her door, she saw a note stuck there. From Eddie?

Her blood pressure shot up and nervous excitement fevered through her.

She snatched the note and opened it.

Stay away from him. You're not his type. Leave town now.

The feeling of infatuation died as quickly as it had been born. She looked around, scanning the parking lot for signs of whoever had written this, but no evil or even mischievous eyes stared back. She pulled her keycard out of her purse, opened the door and closed it behind her as rapidly as possible.

She pulled the chain closed, dragged a chair in front of the door then peeked out the window. Who had sent this?

The same person who'd slashed Eddie's tires? The same person who'd tried to run her off the road?

Or even the person who'd killed the handyman in New Orleans?

A shudder ran through her. But, none of that made any sense. The weird things in New Orleans had happened before she'd even met Eddie. Perhaps, it was really about something else. Had the comment about *He's not your type* really been just a comment to distract her from the real reason the person or persons wanted her to leave town?

Was it about the dead babies? Perhaps a toxic dump by some company into the rivers or streams that was killing babies in Saint Thomasville, finally seeping into the waters of Eufaula. She'd need to get out a map and check the waterways of the area, see what flowed through Saint Thomasville and then onto into Eufaula.

And what companies lay north of both of them.

Damn anyone that knew what was causing these deaths and doing nothing about them. Had the company executives heard a reporter was nosing around and overreacted, thinking she was researching them?

The note had appeared after she'd started making notes about the graves in Saint Thomasville.

An angry fire ignited in her gut, chasing back any fear she'd felt a few moments before.

She didn't scare easily. Especially not when the fate of local babies lay at stake.

Opening her laptop, she began a search for any companies that lay upstream and researching what they produced.

A pop in the parking lot shocked her. She got up and walked to stand beside the window, slowly pushing aside the curtain to look outside.

The parking lot was surrounded by dense undergrowth on several sides, the type of tangled mess that could hide a man with a gun. Perhaps that brown-haired man who'd been driving the white SUV?

Nothing was visible, so she dropped the curtain. Then, returned to her online search.

Damn anyone who thought they could scare her off this story. Those poor little babies.

CHAPTER TWELVE

Slowly, he crept around the outskirts of the parking lot, checking to see if her car was there.

Ah, it was.

A light shone from the cracks around the curtains in her room. Was someone else in there with her?

A virulent roiling disgust stirred his stomach. How dare she think she could lie with another?

She was his.

Always had been his, always would be his.

No matter how many had to die.

There was a truck parked in the lot! Was it that dirty Cajun's vehicle?

The fire in his gut began to rise like a spiraling tornado of retribution. Should it happen now? Just charge in there and take care of business now!

No. Wait.

She needed to choose. It needed to be her decision. The victory would be empty if she didn't choose to come to him on her own.

Blood could be shed, and a woman could be taken. Against her will, if necessary. He'd done it before. And would do it again.

But, this time, perhaps, she would make the right choice.

How many lifetimes did the bitch need in order to learn? They were meant for each other.

He sidestepped to get a better look at the truck.

Besides that wasn't even the Cajun's truck. Maybe she was learning, this time.

How many centuries since this had begun? How many times had they lived this out?

Finally, this time, it would happen as it was destined.

She would see the dirty Cajun for what he was, a lower form of life. Sliding back into the dense foliage, he prepared to bide his time a bit more.

His fingers stroked the pistol stuck into his waistband, and he itched to use it. But, he could wait.

The victory would be so much sweeter when Genevieve chooses him, and the Cajun realizes that he's lost.

CHAPTER THIRTEEN

The next morning, Jenna threw back the covers, still tired from her restless night. She might have claimed not to have been frightened by the note or any of the other weird occurrences, but, in the middle of the night, the eerie feeling that she was being stalked crept across her skin.

She walked to the window and peered out. The landscape appeared much the same as it had the many other times she'd checked throughout the night. Except this time, pinks and purples swirled up from the horizon. She'd seen every shade of night through that window during those sleepless hours.

She'd have gotten more rest if she'd gone through the hassle of packing and driving up to Lafayette to get a room. But, she'd been too tired to do all that even though she was unable to sleep. So, she'd spent the night checking and rechecking the parking lot.

There really was nothing to fear. The note hadn't threatened violence.

But Zoom had taken it seriously when she'd called him just before dawn. A light rapping on her door, and she realized he'd violated every speed limit from Lafayette to here.

She opened the door. "Thanks for coming, Zoom," she managed to say just before he stepped in and pulled her in for a tight, reassuring hug. The presence of her longtime colleague felt good. With one final pat on the back, he released her, pulled back and stared at her face, his eyes rounding in amazement.

"Genevieve Lejeune, Jenna Lejeune. So you weren't the first *Lejeune Woman*." The look on his face was as if she'd told him she'd decided to become a nun. Or a Cajun.

Slightly bemused, slightly disbelieving. Underlying it all, ill-concealed worry.

He picked up the note that was lying on the desk beside the front door. He studied it for a moment then looked up at her. "So you think this is connected to *The Lejeune Woman* business?"

She shrugged. "That might make sense. Or not, depending on how you look at it." She didn't want to tell him how spooked she was. They'd always kept it a practice to not verbalize their anxieties too much. It gave weight to passing fears that would derail them from doing their stories. She still hadn't told him about almost being run off the road yesterday. There'd be a long conversation once he heard that.

She'd tell him about the babies dying later, also, and how that might be a possibility for the note as well. There was just so much happening at once. Keeping Zoom caught up was hard to do, since he was always off taking photos somewhere else. They had a job to do and couldn't afford to get distracted from that.

"Let's get out of here and get some food." He smiled comfortingly. "Things always look better over a big plate of eggs or French toast," he added, long familiar with her weakness for sweets.

Jenna picked up her purse and dropped the room key and her cell phone inside. She checked to make sure she had her current notepad tucked inside, added the warning note, and then followed him.

Outside, she looked around. All during the night, the fog and the trailing moss had changed the landscape into the stuff of horror movies.

Now, things seemed a little more normal. Being down here alone, in a strange land, everything so exotic and different, with all the accents and people breaking into Cajun at a moment's notice didn't help her feel secure. Half the things they said, she couldn't understand. When they broke into Cajun, were they saying things they didn't want her to know? Were they talking about her?

"So, that note's a bit strange," she said, looking sideways at Zoom.

"A bit strange?"

"Okay, way over the top strange. If journalists weren't always getting told not to do a story, then maybe it would really get to me," she said.

"*There's no story here*," Zoom mimicked what they'd both heard a thousand times.

"But when they *don't* want you to do the story, that's when you know you're onto something good," she said what they both were thinking.

And that was when her blood really got going.

"But this feels different," she said, thinking out loud.

"How so?" Zoom looked up and down the street, for the source of the breakfast scents that his nose was so good at detecting.

"It feels personal," she finally concluded.

"Personal?" Zoom harrumphed. "Getting

sensitive now, are we?"

She laughed.

"Where is that smell coming from?" He sniffed the air as if the note was of no great significance and as if breakfast was the only thing that really mattered. But, that was his method for dispelling the tension.

"It's probably My Cousin's." She pointed down the street.

"You found yo' people already," Zoom said with an exaggerated Southern accent.

"No, apparently my kind don't come around here." She laughed good-naturedly. "I looked in the phonebook I found in the motel room. Not a single Lejeune in town."

Zoom stopped and put his hand on her elbow. "Okay, let's just lay it on the table for once." He raised an eyebrow and looked directly at her. "Are you fully spooked, yet? Cuz, I gotta admit this is a rare set of circumstances."

"Yeah." She smiled in concession. "I think it's only so unnerving because I'm sleeping down here. If I were going home to my own little bed in Atlanta every night, it would be different."

"Why don't you get a room up in Lafayette where I was planning on staying? Drive down here every day."

It sounded logical when he said it. But...

"I feel like I would miss a lot not staying here, there's information floating around in the air that you pick up by being here."

"Like the note?" He gave her a pointed stare.

"Oh well, not that exactly."

"But you're staying?"

She nodded.

"Then, I'm getting a room down here, too."

She hadn't wanted to ask him to, knowing how he liked a good selection of restaurants when they were out on the road and this little town didn't offer nearly as much as Lafayette. "Let's go get something to eat," she said.

"Food, glorious food," Zoom sing-songed. He wasn't someone to stay serious for very long. Or at least, act serious. She knew underneath it all that he was still thinking about the situation.

Joking was his way of dealing with trouble.

"My Cousin's is only about a block this way." She led the way. "It's an all purpose diner where I grabbed something to go the other day."

"Diner food, my favorite," Zoom said as they entered to the smell of breakfast wafting through the air and morning conversation between townsfolk.

A noisy ruckus filled the small space.

Then silence. As quickly as if a director had yelled, "Cut."

Everyone turned to stare. A couple dozen curious faces peered at them.

"Morning," she said to the room in general, and people nodded and pretended to turn back to their breakfast but the level of conversation was muted.

Almost as if people were whispering about them. She could swear she heard a few folks switch to Cajun who had previously been speaking in English.

"The counter?" Zoom said, tilting his

head toward two empty stools. They sat down, putting their back to all those darting glances. Jenna settled her purse on her lap.

A large man with an apron wrapped around his ample middle and an order pad tucked into the waistband leaned forward across the counter in an amiable way. "So, you're The Lejeune Woman?"

Zoom barked out a laugh.

Jenna smiled. The way he'd expressed it just sounded like a normal morning greeting.

"That would be me," she answered. "Jenna Lejeune."

"Well, people are a' buzzing."

"I can tell." She looked for a nametag but saw none.

"Sam's the name." He extended a large paw, which Jenna shook, grateful for the normalcy of the gesture.

She lowered her voice. "So, what is it about *The Lejeune Woman* that gets everyone so … excited?"

"Well, there's the legend," he said simply with a shrug as though she knew all about it.

"Legend?" She glanced at Zoom who returned a deadpan look, carefully honed from years of journalistic work to show no expression.

"The doomsday prediction for any Devereaux man who gets involved with a Lejeune woman." He raised an eyebrow and waggled his head side to side. "Word has it, it happens every couple of generations. A Lejeune woman comes to town and brings destruction to a Devereaux man."

"Destruction?" Zoom's voice slid an octave higher to a tone she'd never heard from him before. "How so?"

"Stabbings, shootings. They end up dead. I think one got drowned. I've heard so many variations of the story that I'm not sure what the truth is." Sam shrugged and leaned back against the counter behind him, settling in for a real storytelling session.

Jenna sat forward, anxious to catch every word. More and more, the mystery of the stories about what might have been her forebears sucked her in. If you went by the name alone, Genevieve Lejeune, how could you not get a little bit excited?

And then there was Edward Devereaux. Looking just like what had to be his ancestor, Jean Claude.

Or just looking the way he looked. And the feelings he inspired in her.

She shook her head and focused on Sam again, big, genial, non-threatening Sam.

"One time, about fifty years ago," he said in a traditional storytelling voice, with just the right mix of sense of truth with a trace of fantasy, "a Lejeune woman and her Devereaux lover ran away." His voice darkened, "Only to be found shot dead." He leaned forward, speaking low in a whispery tone as he concluded, "And nobody ever knew who shot them."

Jenna sucked in a lungful of air, realizing she'd been listening so intently she'd stopped breathing. Zoom exhaled loudly. She braced her hands on the counter, grounding herself to reality.

"You don't believe all that heebie jeebie stuff, do you, Sam?" He seemed such a reasonable, down to earth guy, no dark fairy-taleness about him.

"Well, Jenna, there are several sets of tombstones out in the graveyard with the names of a Lejeune woman buried next to a Devereaux man."

"Several sets?"

He nodded. "About every other generation or so." Rubbing a hand across his stubbly chin and raising an eyebrow, he looked intently at her, all joking gone now. "It didn't happen last generation, so people say it's due."

Jenna felt the words deep in her stomach. Was she here to bring doom to Eddie? It could make you nervous, if you had a voodoo state of mind. Which she didn't.

She pushed away the menu. "Maybe just coffee, Sam."

Zoom turned sideways to look full on at her. Through her peripheral vision, she noted the tightening of his jaw, the lines between his bunched up eyebrows.

Then, pulling his face into a smile, determinedly normal, he said to Sam, "I'll take bacon and eggs, grits and a biscuit. With honey, if you got it." His voice loud and jovial, he jerked a thumb at Jenna. "And bring her some French toast and orange juice."

Sam walked away, writing on his pad. Perhaps having accomplished his mission, to scare the bejeebies out of The Lejeune Woman?

She narrowed her eyes, suddenly suspicious of everyone's motives.

Zoom patted her elbow. "Everything looks better on a full stomach, Jenna." He sat up straighter, almost visibly cranking his spinal cord erect. He was so funny when he got into reassuring guy mode, as if he felt it was his duty to remain unaffected by whatever craziness they encountered on stories. And to make her feel safe.

It had gotten her through a few tight spots when she had been almost ready to cave, like the third time their car skidded off the road during Hurricane Rafael.

"We're not buying into these country superstitions. It's a self-fulfilling prophecy. Someone believes doom will follow and then it does because everybody believes it." He nodded firmly. "Really, Jenna."

Her stomach refused to unclench but she smiled. It might be only make believe, but they were on the ride and until they left the haunted mansion, it was hard not to buy into the stories and jump at the ghosts.

Then, she thought of the little newly turned grave plots in Saint Thomasville. And the one that would exist for the baby who'd just died in Eufaula.

"To tell the truth, Zoom. As titillating and putting me at the center of everything as the Jean Claude and Genevieve legend is, there's something much more important going on over in Saint Thomasville, and here now. Much more serious."

Zoom leaned closer.

"Something's been killing babies over there. And now it seems to have moved over here."

"What are you talking about?" His face twisted, lines etching around his eyes.

"There were at least four stillborns or deaths right after birth over in Saint Thomasville over the course of maybe a month. And I was in the courtroom for my ticket the other day and a guy's baby had just died over here. They were all freaked, talking 'bout *it might have moved over here."*

"I can't believe the Centers for Disease Control, isn't all over this," she said. Why hadn't the authorities been called in to investigate? The CDC, EPA, the Environmental Protection Agency, or some other alphabet agency.

A sad little frown hit Zoom's face, probably thinking about his own two little ones at home. "Does anybody know what's causing it?"

"The priest over in Saint Thomasville said the elder women of the town indicated it was genetic, something that came back every other generation or so." He'd given her that information when she'd gone back into the rectory the second time. But, something about his manner when he'd explained the deaths had also been mysterious, as if he were only telling her half-truths.

Zoom shook his head, disdainfully. "I'd be a little less accepting than that."

"Yeaaah," she answered. "It's like they are living in the dark ages down here, with their legends and accepting babies dying. I've been checking into this, trying to trace back the river and streams that run through both of these areas."

"Think somebody might be doing some illegal dumping?"

"Makes the most sense. Although there's a lot that doesn't make sense down here. Like some old legend involving two lost lovers." She tapped the counter with her forefinger.

"Sounds like you're gonna have to open up a bureau here in Cajun country to cover all the stories you keep finding in these parts," Zoom said a bit sardonically.

She raised an eyebrow. "Maybe it's just being in a new area, with all sorts of new inspiration."

"Emm," he murmured noncommittally. "Guess that means I have to stay, too."

"You can jump home for a visit if you want, Zoom. I know you need to see your kids."

His eyes darkened. He never liked to talk about missing them, she knew, said it only made him miss them more. "Really," she urged. "Go home for a bit."

He rubbed his hand over his jaw, which for once was freshly shaven. "I might."

Just then, every voice in the diner stopped. The cutlery stilled and all heads turned toward the front door. Jenna followed their line of sight.

Eddie.

Eddie, Eddie, Eddie, her blood whistled in her ears. *He's here.*

His brown hair was slightly wet like he'd just gotten out of the shower, and shorter as if he'd gotten a haircut since she'd last seen him. He looked clean and alert as if he'd gotten a good night's sleep.

He was wearing a pair of jeans that clung to his thighs. Tall and slim, with a flat stomach and nicely muscled arms underneath his light brown T-shirt, the guy looked damn good. Several waitresses glanced him up and down appreciatively and tried to wave him to their sections.

He nodded politely but his gaze fixed on Jenna. Her pulse responded, followed by the first really good feeling she'd had since yesterday's events with the note and the car on the road. A heightened sense of happiness flowed through her and erased the last ten hours.

Eddie stared at her with such intensity that nothing else mattered. Crazy to have this level of excitement over a guy she hardly knew. But there it was.

Though all eyes followed him as he paced across the room with a sureness of step and a lack of self-consciousness, it was as though they were alone. He never took his gaze off her. When he was a stool away, he stopped.

"Morning," he said in an early morning gravely voice.

A wave of sexiness flowed at her, as though they'd awakened together after a long night of lovemaking.

Suddenly, she could envision it. The two of them locked tight for the entire night with only a few grabbed moments of sleep.

She blushed, sure everyone could see the thoughts written all over her face. Where was that journalistic detachment now?

Eddie smiled as though he'd caught her drift. His gaze swept over her face for a long moment then down across her body before he slid onto the stool next to her.

A responding flash of heat swept through her, as if he'd actually touched her with his hands everywhere his gaze had been.

Jenna heard Zoom's little cough, a demand for attention.

"Oh," she glanced at him. "Eddie, this is my colleague, Zoom, ehh, I mean Michael Mason. One of the best photographers in the business."

"But, you can call me Zoom. Everyone

does eventually."

Eddie half-laughed and stuck out his hand. "Cause you drive fast?"

"Don't answer that," Jenna cut in. "He's a judge."

"Don't judge me, man." Zoom belly laughed. "Nah, cause I like to zoom in on my subjects. Known for my close-ups on faces."

"Gotcha." Eddie smiled. "I actually saw some of your photographs. The ones after Hurricane Rafael caught my attention. The articles were very well done and the photographs compelling."

Zoom sat up a little straighter, the compliments warming him, whether or not that was their purpose.

"So, you read my articles." Jenna looked at Eddie.

He nodded.

"Did you recognize my name when I came into your courtroom?"

He nodded again, with a slight smile, and raised an eyebrow. "How could I not with the whole *Lejeune Woman* thing?"

She laughed a bit, mostly because of his expression. "I've heard about that."

"How could you have not?" He leaned closer, lowering his voice. "You have been in town for a few days now."

She stared back into his eyes, feeling his nearness. She liked that he wasn't pretending about anything. The way he moved closer to her as though he felt their attraction and wasn't afraid to acknowledge it.

This was feeling way too good.

But, she had stories to do. Exciting all this talk in the community about a modern day Lejeune Woman and Devereaux Man wasn't productive.

If only Eddie didn't look the way he looked. And if only he wouldn't lean in the way he did, so she could get a sniff of that aroma that was pure … *him* … mixed with soap and a hint of aftershave.

If only.

She leaned back. "I heard there are tombstones out at the cemetery that have several sets of Lejeune women and Devereaux men's names carved on them. Some deadly legend involved." There, that would surely throw cold water on the fire that was sizzling between them.

He was so near, his breath brushing across her face, his body inches from hers.

So sexy.

Eddie only laughed and leaned in further. "You don't believe all that, do you?" He tilted his head in such an attractive way.

Sam walked up and set a cup of coffee in front of Zoom and another in front of her with a heavy clank.

She stalled for time, turning to take a sip. Sam stood there, fixated on the interaction between her and Eddie, looking back and forth between them. She raised an eyebrow at him and he laughed and walked away.

Three counter stools down, though, a customer raised her hand and Sam stopped and leaned in to hear some comment.

Jenna took another sip of coffee and watched out of the corner of her eye as the lady placed her hand on Sam's elbow and leaned in conspiratorially, speaking in a tone that was disguised by the diner's noise.

Jenna couldn't hear her but the woman's eyes kept darting toward her then back to meet Sam's eyes with a shared understanding.

Oh well.

Eddie traced a finger up her arm and a fire erupted underneath her skin, causing everything else in the diner to disappear, leaving only the two of them. Warmth suffused her, heating her from within until she wanted to find an air conditioning unit.

And stand in front of it for an hour or two.

His finger stopped near her elbow, and she waited, her cup still near her mouth. Unable to move, she waited to see what that finger would do next.

But, he merely left it there, a tortuous distraction from his words.

"Whatcha say we go out to the graveyard and check out those tombstones?" He arched an eyebrow.

Her pulse kicked up and she set the coffee cup down. She didn't need caffeine with her heart ricocheting in her chest the way it was.

"People will talk," she said finally.

"They will anyway," he answered close to her shoulder, his tone sexually inviting. Or maybe that was just how she read that deep, masculine voice.

Damn.

Just then, Sam clattered a plate of French toast down in front of her, with a grin, almost as if he knew he was breaking up a moment.

She was so high strung with the tension of Eddie's nearness that she knew she wouldn't be able to eat a bite. As soon as Sam turned away, she pushed the plate back.

"You're not hungry?" Eddie asked in that same gravelly voice that scraped along her skin.

She shook her head, not wanting to look at him again. "Zoom ordered it for me. I said I only wanted coffee."

Eddie picked up a pitcher of syrup and poured a long stream across the warm, brown crusted bread. Jenna watched his hand, strong and sure as it released the lever to cut off the flow of maple-colored liquid. He took her fork, his arm grazing her shoulder, and cut a bite off. "Sure?" he asked as he held it an inch above the plate.

"I'm sure," she answered then watched as he raised the fork to his mouth.

Suddenly, that French toast looked very appetizing. He chewed and swallowed before saying with a grin, "Now you want it, don't you?"

She laughed and pushed his hand away as he reached for a second bite. "As a matter of fact, I do." She leaned across him, to take a fork off the place setting one seat down from him. As she did, her face came into close proximity to his.

They both stilled, remaining motionless for a long instant, their mouths inches apart. Eddie looked down at her mouth and leaned a millimeter closer.

Quickly, she pulled back, averting her gaze.

He was the kind of man a woman could end up in bed with before she even knew it. The type of guy that things would just feel so right and natural with that her thought processes would go on hold.

And before she even knew it, she'd have given in to - the guy she didn't need to get tangled up in the sheets with.

With all the talk, the craziness surrounding the two of them, she didn't need to stir it up even more, distracting her from her job.

With the fact that she was leaving soon, anyway, it would not be a good idea to get involved with a guy she'd just miss. For a very long time.

She felt his gaze still on her, almost like a large hand stroking her skin, from her neck to her face. She held her breath, waiting.

Finally, he leaned across her and cut himself another bite, swirled it in the buttery syrup mixture and popped it in his mouth with a defiant expression.

He was deliberately tantalizing.

And dangerous.

She turned then. And caught Zoom staring at them as he ate his grits and eggs. She and Eddie were Zoom's dining entertainment.

"Oh," she said, having forgotten he was there. Along with everyone else in the diner. "Sorry," she mouthed, her head turned so Eddie couldn't see.

Zoom slanted his eyes in a reproving fashion, with a bit of pretend jealousy.

Well, he was the one who'd kept telling her she ought to be looking for romance. Now, here it was, sliding all over her, without her having to seek it out, and he gave her that mother hen look.

She slanted her eyes right back at him and he grinned.

"Go for it," he said low under his breath.

"I'm working," she answered back

quietly.

"Working *it,* more like," he said with a devilish grin.

She shot him as dark a look as she could manage, grateful for the diner's background noise.

"Look," Zoom said more loudly, tossing down some money. "I'm gonna head out to get some early morning shots of the mist coming off the swamp." He cut his biscuit into two pieces and stuck his bacon in between, making a sandwich.

Jenna glanced at his empty plate. He'd made quick work of polishing off his grits and eggs while she and Eddie flirted. "Okay," she said.

"Nice to meet you, guy." Eddie stuck out his hand for a quick shake before Zoom walked away. "Guess we scared him off," Eddie said straight-faced.

She whipped her head around to look him full in the face. "This is not happening," she said sternly.

"What?" He stared at her with a deadpan expression, totally innocent.

"You probably give your mama that look, huh? Since back when you were a little boy."

He shrugged and laughed.

"This," she said, pointing her finger back and forth between their chests. "Not happening."

"Nothing going on here." He took a sip of coffee from the cup Sam had dropped off on one of his trips back and forth up the counter.

"But legend does have it that we're destined to be together." Eddie swiveled his stool around to face her, his legs almost straddling her, and her blood pressure spiked. "Can't fight destiny, or so they say."

She touched one finger to his shoulder, which brought him to a dead stop, not a muscle moving. She'd meant it as a joke, for emphasis. But the feel of strong, hard muscle underneath his shirt shocked her with its masculinity.

Sucking in a breath, she forced out, "It also says I bring destruction to you." His eyes met hers, with a connection that made it hard to think. "If we're keeping to the legendary version."

His knee touched hers as he leaned forward.

She glanced away. Had she invited this full force onslaught of masculinity, so close and focused on her?

He ran a finger down her forearm as though tempting her to turn to look at him. She didn't dare, already too aware of him, his presence overwhelming.

"Let's rewrite history then," he said, his voice low and inviting.

CHAPTER FOURTEEN

Steeling herself against his magnetism, Jenna pushed her plate toward him. "It's all yours." Then, she pulled her wallet from her purse.

He laid a hand over hers. "Let me get this. You didn't order it. You didn't eat it. You shouldn't have to pay for it."

She looked at their joined hands, feeling the warmth of his, its slight roughness, its size making her wonder how it would feel sliding across her lower back when they danced this evening at the fais do-do.

She was gonna lose weight at this rate, all the heightened emotions making it impossible to even think of eating.

The Love Diet. They ought to advertise it.

He pulled out some cash and dropped it on the counter then stood. She wanted to look up, to catch the view of him from the new angle but instead stood and turned toward the door. As they walked out, he placed his hand on her lower back in a gentlemanly gesture for her to precede him through the door that he pushed open.

Almost as if they were a couple.

It felt oddly right. As though they really were a couple. She didn't even mind that everyone watched them as they walked out the door and past the large front window.

"Can I give you a lift somewhere?" he asked when they'd gotten out of sight of the diners. They were alone in the parking lot, on the side of the building. "Maybe help you with your research?"

"I'm just a block from here." She stopped and looked up at him. And the sight almost made her change her mind, as his eyes crinkled, an invitation to . . . what?

To what they both wanted?

She shook her head. "I've got to work all day, do some interviews, and I think it would go better if The Lejeune Woman and The Devereaux Man didn't show up together."

He smiled then stepped just an inch closer. But it was too close, because her respiration and heart rate spiked.

"We're still on for tonight?" he asked.

On for what exactly? A few dances, or something more?

She tried to swallow but her throat was dry.

So, she just nodded. Though an evening in his arms was the last thing she needed.

Or the thing she needed most?

"We'll be all the talk," she said, finding it hard to breathe with him so near.

Dancing with him would be torture.

So, why didn't she say no?

Because she couldn't. She was drawn to him, inextricably.

As though it were already written, the outcome.

She didn't believe that.

Not for a minute.

But, the attraction was cataclysmic, as if their connection would be explosive.

Eddie tilted his head, his eyes flashing fire, with a heat that seared to her core, urging her to move closer. He stepped back one pace, his gaze still fastened on her.

And she almost moved toward him, instantly hating the distance between them.

"So, tonight," he said, his voice husky and low.

She pulled in a breath. "Tonight," she acknowledged.

Tonight with all its dangers.

*****

She spent the morning with one family she'd profiled in the initial aftermath of Hurricane Rafael. If her readers felt half of what she'd experienced today, they'd love the article. She only hoped words could capture the joy that had filled her seeing the entire family reunited, from grandma down to the six grandchildren.

Two days after the hurricane, they'd been spread to the winds, not knowing where other family members had gone, communications so bad they'd worried who had survived and who had died.

Luckily, no one had died. And today, she'd found them all living as an extended family at a great aunt's farm, happy to be together.

It was good when she found this sort of outcome to disaster. The day had left her happy and hopeful for the future of the area.

Now, she was free to pursue the deaths of all those babies.

She was driving to the home of an aunt of the Lacroix family, the man who hadn't shown up for his traffic ticket because his baby had died. This was going to be hard.

It was too early to actually talk to the parents themselves since they'd be so deep into the grieving process. So, she'd gone after a more distant family member.

As she drove, she talked on the phone to a contact at the CDC. The Centers for

Disease Control in Atlanta was an incredible resource. "So, there's no record of these deaths?"

"There's a note in here," Joe said, "but nothing about it being disease related which would fit with what you were saying about it being a toxin. Check with the local Health Department and the state EPD folks."

"I guess the Environmental Protection Department might be the best source for toxins. But, I thought I'd check with you guys first, thought it might save me some footwork."

"You know what … " Joe stopped talking for a moment. "There's something in the computer about another spate of baby deaths about fifty years ago."

"What does it say caused them?"

"Doesn't. Just a notation about them. This is crazy."

"Yeah. Can you get back to me if you find anything else out? I'll let you know what I find."

She hung up and kept driving down a long winding road until the blacktop ended and a dirt road continued on into the deep woods. Finally, the road ended up at the aunt's address, which was an old home with a long wraparound porch.

She sucked in a deep breath, and prepared herself for a hard conversation. Then, she opened her car door.

As soon as she got out of her car, a man walked onto the front porch, glaring - a large man with a face like a pit bull. He barreled off the steps, launching himself toward her, as if ready for a fight.

His size would have scared a man.

Every instinct told her to get back in

her car and lock the doors. But she stood her ground. Against her better judgment.

He pointed a finger way too close to her face, with a jabbing motion.

Adrenalin coursed through her, jacking her senses up.

Fight or flight? Fight against him wasn't a winning option for her.

"If you're with that health department, you can get yourself back to the county building and tell 'em we done answered all the questions we're going to answer." The angry, blustery front he presented couldn't hide the signs of recent tears, with swollen eyes, and a red nose.

His hand shook as he pointed it at her.

"I'm not with the health department," she blurted out. Not that a reporter was going to go over much better.

She met his eyes, hoping to make a human connection. He'd be less likely to hit her, maybe?

"I heard about the baby the other day when I was in court. I'm so sorry."

He stopped pointing, his mouth quivering, his hand falling limply to his side. "Oh man, I forgot about that ticket. Wonder how much they'll fine me for that. Like I don't got enough bills with all these hospital charges."

He was the father! The one who'd been issued the traffic ticket. She hadn't expected to come face to face with him.

Her heartbeat double-timed as she absorbed all the pain radiating off him. She infused her gaze with compassion. "They're not gonna fine you for failure to appear for that. Someone knew about your baby and told them. I am so sorry for your loss."

His eyes filled instantly with water, her sympathy apparently harder to take than any accusation would have been, and he dropped his gaze to the ground.

"Oh, I keep expecting someone to show up and arrest me or something the way they acted at the hospital."

"I don't think anyone's gonna try and blame you for the baby's death. There have been quite a few others."

He nodded, then swung his eyes to her face, studying her sharply. "Then who are you if you're not the county people or a court person?"

She'd probably get thrown off the property as soon as she answered. Long as he didn't touch her.

"I'm a reporter."

His head jerked back as if she'd hit him. "So you're doing a story about me killing my kid?"

"Nooo," she drug out the word. "Who's saying anything about you killing your baby?"

"Some lady from the county came up to our room at the hospital and then another government lady came over to our house right after the baby died, asking all sorts of questions, looking at us all funny like." He sucked in air, almost gasping as if it weren't reaching his lungs. "It got my wife real upset. That's what we're doing out here at my aunt's. Trying to avoid those people."

He slung his hand out toward the road. "They act like I did something to him, the way they look at me." His eyes narrowed, as he stared off into the distance.

She nodded conspiratorially, hoping to reassure him that she wasn't out to get him.

"There have been a lot of deaths over in Saint Thomasville, too."

"I know." He shook his head emphatically. "I told them that there is just … *something* that causes these babies to die. They ought to be looking at them factories up on the river north of here."

She nodded vigorously. "I've been thinking the same thing."

He looked at her for a second. "But the county folks seemed suspicious, like maybe my wife had done something to cause our little boy to be stillborn. Asked me if she took drugs."

Tears burst from his eyes and he whirled around, his large shoulders shaking and bent. This was the worst part of the job, participating in other people's grief, feeling the pain that rolled off them.

His shaking slowed after a long moment. Finally he half turned to her, wiping at his face, his voice weak. "That baby was fine on the sonogram. Every time we went to the doctor, his little heart was beating pretty as you please. When he was born, he hollered real loud like he was gonna be a feisty little guy. They put him in my wife's arms, and then let me hold him."

The image of a living baby bloomed full force in her mind, real, not just a story.

"You shoulda seen that little face, the spitting image of me. I thought of all the years to come, all we'd do together." He shook his head, and his face crumpled. "Then, something happened, and he stopped breathing."

Tears began rolling down his face, but he paid them no heed. Just stared off into space, as if seeing the life go out of his son.

This man's child had lived at some point. Just long enough for Mr. Lacroix to meet his son before he had to say goodbye to him.

Sympathetic tears pushed against her eyelids. But she steeled herself. They'd never get anywhere if they both broke down.

And she instinctively knew if she started crying the guy would lose it completely. So, she sucked in her breath and tried not to think about the tiny dead baby and his parents' pain.

Instead she tried to think in conceptual terms. About a trend that needed to be understood.

That's how she could do some good, make a difference in people's lives. If somehow she could bring a better understanding, focus attention on this problem, so authorities took notice and then action, maybe her prying into their private grieving could be justified.

"Mr. Lacroix, I don't think you did anything to cause your child to die. That's why I've come to talk to your family, because of the stillborns over in Saint Thomasville. I didn't expect to find you or your wife here. I am so sorry to bother you."

He nodded silently.

"Maybe they ought to investigate them hospitals. Maybe they're not doing their jobs. So many babies dying over there and over here, too. Seems like somebody could find out why."

His face convulsed in grief and he bent over, his hands on his knees, and sobbed openly, great heaving sounds choking in his chest.

Such sorrow. How do you survive the death of a child?

Sadness and sympathy flooded through her body and tears burned behind her eyes. She placed a hand on his back, feeling his body shaking like a child as they cried. It was too much, too terrible.

She couldn't think of any comforting words that were true so she just patted his back, her hand over her own eyes shielding herself from the vision of his grief, wiping at her eyes, trying to keep her composure to some degree.

"I can't talk anymore, ma'am," he gasped out, standing up, wiping at his face. "I gotta go see about my wife. She's grieving something fierce over her little dead son."

His eyes empty and haunted, he looked at her as if for permission. She drew in a long shuddering breath before she could talk.

"Thanks for speaking to me, Mr. Lacroix." She brushed at the tears on her face then looked away, the agony on the man's face too hard to witness. "I'll let you know if I find anything else out."

As he walked away, she suddenly remembered she didn't know the baby's name. She'd need that for her records. "Mr. Lacroix," she called out. "Is it too much to ask if your son has a name?"

He turned toward her. "Jean Devereaux Lacroix," he said quietly.

"Devereaux?"

"A family name on my wife's side."

Shock rolled through Jenna.

Devereaux. She'd noticed several

Lejeune babies over in Saint Thomasville.
But there had been other names as well. The
priest had said something about the deaths
being genetic, but she hadn't thought about
a family connection to the Devereaux line as
well.

But, it would make sense if they'd
merged when Genevieve Lejeune had married
Jean Claude Devereaux.

Mr. Lacroix lifted his hand over his
shoulder, in a final, sad goodbye as he
walked up the steps. Through the screen
door, a woman peered out. She leaned against
the doorjamb as if it was all that was
holding her up, her face pale and wan.

Mr. Lacroix opened the door and pulled
her into his arms. She leaned against his
chest, wrapping her arms around him. Then,
Mr. Lacroix pushed the door shut, cutting
off Jenna's view of the intensely intimate
and sad moment.

****

Back at the motel, Jenna showered,
letting the warm water wash away the
saltiness left on her face from her tears.
The liquid pounded down across her skin. She
turned, letting it pulse on her neck,
beating at the knots that clutched at her
muscles.

Finally, she stepped out, wrapped a
towel around herself, and shook her hair out
of the shower cap. She dressed quickly,
anxious to get to the dance, to talk to some
locals about the babies, and maybe get some
more insight.

Eddie would be there. But, that wasn't
her main interest. It wasn't.

She wanted to see how many others from
her hurricane story she might run into at

the fais do-do or get leads on.

And follow up on the babies.

The babies. Those sad little deaths. She sucked in a deep breath, determined not to feel the grief of every little baby. She couldn't emotionally live other people's tragedies and still do her job.

She pulled on a flowered, cotton, knee-skimming skirt, and checked herself out from all sides in the full-length mirror, swinging back and forth to see how the material would flow as she danced.

An image of Eddie twirling her and checking out her legs as the skirt swirled around her filled in the picture. Why deny it? She was dressing for him.

Be honest with yourself at least, girl.

Thank goodness she'd thought to bring a couple of skirts, knowing how hot it could still be in South Louisiana in early September.

Someone knocked at the door. Jenna glanced through the peephole to make sure it was Zoom and opened the door.

"Dang, girl," he said. He leered at her legs jokingly, as if seeing them for the first time. "I didn't know you had legs."

She grabbed her purse. "You thought they'd been worn away, chasing to keep up with you on stories?"

She pulled the door closed behind her and they headed to Zoom's car.

"Don't know if I approve of you pulling them out on assignment." He glared down, with pretend disapproval.

"Get your position straight," she said, flippantly. "You want me running around with men or you don't want me running around with men? How can you live vicariously if I'm not doing some running around?"

"Point taken." He nodded with resignation. "I guess I just wanted to hear about it, not witness it, Genevieve."

A whooshing gale force of wind rushed through her at his use of the name. Almost as though it were hers, the name called to her, as if from deep in the mists of time.

Nostalgia filled her, almost a memory - of accordions and fiddles wailing out a Cajun song while honeysuckle wafted through the air.

She closed her eyes as a vision of dancing and laughing filled her mind. And being twirled - by strong, insistent hands.

Then, it faded. She opened her eyes and the present day slammed into her with a harsh force - the motel parking lot with cars on warm asphalt, the blinking neon *Vacancy* sign flickering on and off.

The name Genevieve had felt like she owned it.

But hearing it from Zoom was wrong, like your cousin kissing you. Not that it had ever happened to her.

Zoom was several paces in front of her.

He turned and looked back at her as if only now realizing she'd stopped. She darted him an accusing look, and his eyes widened, then he raised his hands. "Sorry." His face flushed blood red. "Really, I don't know where that came from."

She studied him for a moment, reading his intent. Then, she shook off the strange feeling. "It's okay. Just don't do it again. This whole Lejeune woman curse thing has got me freaked. Like maybe people believe it."

"I got ya." Zoom turned toward the car, and the moment was gone. "It is a bit freaky." He hit the unlock button on his key chain as if nothing had transpired between them. "So, you know where the park is?"

She pointed up the street. "A couple of blocks up here. Turn left by a cow, I think."

Zoom laughed, pulled out his GPS and began programming something into it, and once again, everything felt normal.

Almost.

Several minutes later, they pulled up to the park square and got out. Huge live oaks canopied a grassy area, shading the crowd from the late afternoon sun. Groups milled around, calling to other groups and laughing.

Smoke from barbecue fires wafted through the air with a hickory, tangy fragrance. The zing of fiddles and accordions rose over the noise of the chattering adults and children.

She followed the music, with Zoom several steps behind her, until she found the action - the band and a dance area.

On a packed dirt dance floor, couples of all ages twirled and twined around each other with beautiful complicated steps that looked like a mix of swing dance, Cajun two step and jitterbug, with a little ballroom thrown in.

"I'm gonna take a few shots." Zoom pulled a camera from his ever-present camera bag and took off with the fixated look he got when he saw the makings of good photos.

She found a place under a tree and watched, the music rolling over her, the dancers swinging past her, music and motion assaulting her senses, inducing a pleasant reverie.

From somewhere, the spicy smell of gumbo or jambalaya swirled, with the biting scent of hot sauce.

Only the present existed, not her stories, nor her worries about any complications that had popped up, or sad aspects. She swayed in time to the music, loving the moment.

Then, she felt a presence at her shoulder. Looking up, she saw him. Eddie. Warmth pulsed through her and she leaned ever so slightly away from the tree and toward him.

This hot Cajun had come looking for her. Who knew where the night would take them?

"I'm glad you could make it, sugar." A strong, distinctly Cajun accent flavored his speech, for the first time sounding like all the people around her, people who yelled out exotic sounding words.

"It's like being in a foreign country," she said with a low laugh, "the way people talk down here. We did buy this state during the Louisiana Purchase, am I right?"

"We can't be bought," he said with a sexy grin. "But we can be borrowed." He stuck out a hand. "What about you, chére? Are you available for a dance or two?"

A hot flush ran from her chest up into her face, with a heat that had nothing to do with the temperature or the excitement of the exuberant crowd. "I've been waiting for a dance all day."

"I've been waiting all day too, chére," he murmured in a low sultry voice, taking her hand and pulling her close.

It was just a dance. Just a dance. If that could apply when a man like Eddie held you in his arms.

"We'll start out easy and take it slow," he whispered into her ear as his other hand snaked around her back. Was he talking about the dance or something more?

Deep inside, she hoped it was something more.

The way she felt in his arms was as if they'd done this a thousand times before. She inhaled his scent, woodsy and clean, letting it flow through her to her core. And felt at home, where she belonged.

It was comfortable.

If you didn't count her heart rate. If you didn't count the excitement flaming through her veins.

His eyes narrowed, with a smoky mirroring of the air around them. "Shall we?" he said.

She felt sure the answer was yes. Yes to whatever he was proposing. She smiled, and with that, he brought her just a millimeter closer. Her pulse accelerated to the point of pure mayhem.

She breathed him in, forgetting everything but the roughness of his hands, the closeness of his face, those eyes, that mouth.

He tightened his grip on her hand.

"It's just a one, two, three," he said near her cheek.

It was hard to concentrate on anything besides his arms and how they were a lot more muscled than any judge's had a right to be.

She ran her hand around his shoulder, entranced by the feel of his body. He pulled slightly away, looking into her eyes and she sensed he could read the effect he was having on her. Knew full well that her heart was racketing so powerfully in her chest that it shut out everything beyond the circle of his arms.

"I'm glad you're here, chére," he said softly. And suddenly, she was very glad of the same. In Eufaula, Louisiana. In his arms.

A whole night lay ahead. And the music led so easily through the dance that she didn't have to think, just let Eddie twirl her around the packed dirt floor.

She couldn't imagine anyone felt the moment more, felt the man they danced with more. She wanted the music to continue so she could meld with him, allow him to hold onto her, lead her in a masculine fashion that wasn't threatening.

Instinctively, she knew if she'd suddenly tried to take the lead that Eddie would let her, would go with it. But she just enjoyed letting him set the pace, twirl her and then pull her close again where she could smell his scent.

When the song ended, she stepped back and away from him, breathing hard, grateful for the chance to catch her breath and get her bearings, needing just a minute away from the stimulation of his arms. Being held near to him was too intense.

Eddie let his arm drop from her waist and turned away, his eyes scanning the crowd. Out of the corner of her eye, she studied him. It had been so long since any man had made her feel one tenth of what he did. She couldn't help but wonder what she did for him.

He turned his gaze back to her, as if he'd felt her watching him and his eyes crinkled with that expression that said, *Come to me.*

And God help her, she wanted to. Wanted to move into his sphere, feel the draw and respond to it, without thinking. They hadn't really known each other for very long, but everything inside of her told her she knew all she needed to know about him.

But that was crazy, just hormones inspiring intimacy that her brain ought to tell her she wasn't ready for.

But, really, her brain seemed to be in collusion, finding no reason not to trust this man, who it felt like she'd always known.

Then, a fast-paced jig erupted from the band. Accordions ripped out wailing notes and fiddling fingers flew. The music pulsed through her body demanding motion. Eddie turned to her and extended his hand.

And everything inside of her said, *Yes, finally.*

Let me get close to him, feel his hands on me and his body close to me once again.

She took his hand, the contact sparking flashes of need throughout her. His eyes met hers, as if knowing what she felt, returning it with an answering glint of need of his own.

The fiery music reflected what was going on inside of her, flashes of desire exploding all through her nerve endings.

Eddie clasped her hand tightly, pulling her close, then he drew her into the swinging crowd that knew just what they wanted to do with the music.

The moment was perfect, and Jenna felt happier than she could ever remember. A swirling haze of motion, music and laughter surrounded them.

Then as if from nowhere, a nervous warning sensation shot through the air, prickling her skin with a spiky jabbing alert.

The feeling of being watched overtook her, as it had in New Orleans.

She glanced over her shoulder, attempting to see beyond the couples into the dusk.

A smoky mist spread along the wood line of the dense forested area that lay beyond the park. She could feel someone there, just beyond the mist, staring intently.

Normalcy surrounded the dancing crowd and she tried to shake the odd feeling of a watcher from the woods. But she couldn't. She stopped suddenly. Eddie had kept moving and when she didn't, his right arm broke free of her waist. The hand holding hers, however, held on and he skidded to a halt still grasping her outstretched hand.

His eyes flashed surprise.

"I need to catch my breath," she said to cover the awkwardness.

He smiled in understanding but his eyes said something different, reading her unease. She wasn't even breathing hard. She turned and when she did, he let her hand drop, but he followed close behind her as she left the dance area.

The loss of contact with Eddie unnerved her. She wanted the physical reassurance of his presence again.

She glanced back at him, and he extended his hand. Putting her hand back into his large one felt better and they walked hand in hand to a tree outside of the dancing group. She leaned back against the tree, trying to regain her composure, to regroup.

But the rats kept running through her veins, gnawing on her nerves.

"It can be a little overwhelming the first time you get out there." Eddie stood beside her, making meaningless small talk, looking out at the dancers. But, she got the feeling he was waiting for her to say what was really on her mind.

She was able to read him so well. And apparently vice versa.

She looked toward the dancers but her attention wasn't on the crowd but on the area beyond. She scanned the woods, looking for signs of anyone, with an instinctive animal awareness of being watched.

That feeling had haunted her often since she'd reached Louisiana. It was a warning she'd tried to disregard and write off. But it was getting harder all the time to tell herself that her instincts were wrong.

Women who disregarded their instincts ended up as victims.

She'd interviewed countless victims who said they'd had a funny feeling about a person or situation right before something really bad happened to them.

She strongly supported the theory that you should listen to your instincts. Yet, she'd been telling herself that this tingling down her nerves was silly.

She took a deep breath, for the first time conceptualizing what she'd been doing - disregarding her feelings and the danger she might have been putting herself into.

"Eddie," she said, putting her hand on his arm. He looked down at her hand, making it harder to continue with her train of thought. But she jerked her mind back to the woods and the eyes she'd felt there, watching her.

"Yes," he answered, his gaze fastened on her face, his expression deadly serious.

"What is it, Jenna?" He laid his hand on her shoulder. "What was that look about?"

CHAPTER FIFTEEN

Dusk was falling fast, darkness melting away the edges of the landscape. Jenna furtively studied the woods beyond the park, almost embarrassed, it seemed, to have expressed weakness. He rubbed his thumb along the palm of her hand, seeking to distract her, to bring her out of that place of fear that had taken away the beautiful, light-hearted woman he'd been dancing with a moment ago.

"Tell me," he said. When she didn't answer, he took her by the hand and led her away from the raucous, rowdy dance area.

They walked through the milling crowds, who were oblivious to Jenna's distress, eating from the various food booths, laughing and enjoying the fais do-do. He continued until they got to his truck, where he opened the passenger door, letting her slide in. She did so without a word, her gaze nervously darting around.

He got in, started the truck and drove away from the park. Jenna glanced behind them. What? Was she expecting to be followed?

They drove for five minutes or so. Finally, they reached his Uncle Joe's fishing pier on the river. It was on a secluded piece of river frontage owned by his uncle. Eddie and his cousins had spent countless hours fishing off that pier.

Uncle Joe had gone to pick up Mama and Granny to take them into Lafayette to see a movie. So, Eddie and Jenna would have this area all to themselves.

He opened his door, got out and walked around to her side. She jumped out before he could open the door for her.

He didn't touch her, her skittishness palpable, like a cat who'd just been stepped on. It trusted you hadn't meant it but kept its eyes open to be sure you were watching this time.

She kept glancing up the road.

"Jenna," he said, bringing her gaze back around to him. "This is my uncle's property. No one comes out here but family."

She smiled slightly, glancing away, her cheeks reddening, visible even in this low lighting from a full moon. "I'm fine. I don't know why I'm acting this way."

"What way?" Make her explain it instead of assuming he knew what she was feeling.

"Kinda crazy like," she said with a laugh.

It was good that she could still joke. Most victims in his courtroom didn't end up making humorous comments.

"What's making you crazy, Jenna? The Lejeune Woman thing?" He'd have loved it, under different circumstances, if she'd have said it was him making her crazy.

If they'd been in bed, maybe?

He pushed away the thought. Now wasn't the time.

But, that time would come. He felt it rushing toward them like an avalanche. Ready to sweep them both away with its natural force, a power that was impossible to resist for much longer.

That time was coming. But, not yet.

"Don't think I'm being silly, Eddie." She shrugged her shoulders. "But I keep having this feeling like I'm being watched."

"That doesn't sound so out of touch, Jenna," he said reassuringly. He ran his

hand from her shoulder to her elbow, with
what he'd meant as a friendly gesture, but
changed when she looked down, then back at
him with passion misted eyes.

He wanted to pull her in for a kiss but
knew they needed to get to the heart of her
anxiety before they moved on to anything
else between them. "Everybody in the parish
has been keeping their eye on you since they
learned your last name."

"You're right about that." She laughed
slightly, then looked away from where his
hand still touched her arm.

"But it's more than that." Her eyes
darkened. "Like someone doesn't want me to
know they're watching. And, there was the
note."

Note? She said it so matter of factly.
"What note?"

"Oh, I've talked about it so much with
Zoom, I forgot we're the only ones who
know." She gestured with her hand toward the
truck. "I have it in my purse."

He walked back to the truck, got her
purse and handed it to her.

She accepted it but like someone who
didn't necessarily want to show him what was
in it.

He waved his hand. "If it violates
journalistic practice or something . . ."

She smiled up into his eyes
appreciatively. "Thanks. That's great of you
to say." She raised a shoulder. "But, this
isn't about my story so much. It's not like
I'm divulging sources or private
conversations." She reached in, tentatively,
with two fingers and pulled a folded piece
of paper out with her thumb and forefinger.

She held it by the corner and handed it

to him.

As though she was afraid of the actual paper.

"You don't think they put something on the paper do you?" Damn. He could have kicked himself for saying it. She jerked her gaze back to the folded note, as though she'd never thought of that.

"It isn't like I'm doing some political story, where someone would have a motive to do something so upfront and deadly to me as to put something on it," she said as though trying to convince herself.

He flipped the paper open with a quick flick. "I wasn't thinking, Jenna. That wasn't what I meant."

Stay away from him. You're not his type. Leave town now.

He stared at the block style printing favored by anonymous note senders. Surely his ex-wife wouldn't have done this. Leave an anonymous note? It was more her style to walk up to Jenna in a parking lot and say those things - loudly and in her face.

"I don't know Jenna. I'd be the last to assassinate someone's character and throw aspersions." He raised a shoulder. "And it isn't like her," he continued to add modifiers. "But my ex-wife was in town yesterday. At my office, making noises about getting back together."

Jenna's relieved expression egged him on.

"She did know about you, mentioned you specifically. I'm not saying it was her. But . . ."

Jenna laughed slightly. "Knowing about the legend, she decided to throw a little superstitious scare into me?"

He laughed. "Maybe taking advantage of the whole Lejeune Woman thing."

Jenna laughed outright then in such an attractive fashion that he was glad he'd sacrificed his ex-wife on the altar of Jenna's peace of mind.

It wasn't like Lidia lived here in town. Baton Rouge was a long way away. And Jenna wasn't the type of woman to go around flinging out unfounded gossip.

Then a glow returned to Jenna's face and he forgot all about any other woman. With her softness and assurance back, she was again the woman he could fall in love with.

Love? The thought shook him. He hadn't conceptualized Jenna and love together before.

Lust and Jenna, yes.

Love?

That was another whole ballpark.

The light hanging on the end of the pier shimmered its reflection on the water below, laying a creamy sheen on the river. "Want to see something pretty?" He tilted his head toward the river.

She smiled and looked up at him in a way that took his breath away, and made it hard to remember that he'd planned to distract himself.

He stretched his hand to her, sliding it around her waist and pulling her toward him. She didn't resist, but melted into him, her body molding itself to his as though that were exactly where she wanted to be.

He sucked in air, trying to get oxygen to his brain. But the blood wasn't flowing there. How long could a man's brain survive oxygen deprivation?

He cupped his hand to her cheek, caressing skin so silky and smooth it must be stored in a bottle of skin softener overnight.

She looked up at him expectantly and he forgot everything but her mouth. Slowly, knowing the powerful kick her kiss would bring, he leaned into it.

And forgot everything but the softness of her in his arms and the way her mouth responded to him. She wanted it as much as he did.

Her mouth molded to his, opening, inviting him in. He gladly accepted the invite, sliding into her warmth, her wetness, feeling like one being as they sent sensations shooting back and forth between them.

Finally, she pulled back, breaking free, leaving him unable to breath, unable to think about anything but where the closest bed was. The kiss lasted less than a minute, but it could have been hours for the difference it had made in how he felt about her.

Suddenly, all professional distance was gone. He wanted her in his bed. And he wanted her there now.

She ran her hand down his chest and looked up at him with passion-hazed eyes that promised hours of naked skin against naked skin. Of a night full of touching, kissing and connecting on every level.

God, he wanted her. Wanted her bad.
*****

Jenna looked up at Eddie and thought she ought to be thinking about her research but all she really wanted right now was to pull him down to the ground and make love underneath the moonlight.

But, this force of nature attraction was even scarier than the note had been. She could get in a car and drive away from Louisiana, and whoever had written that note.

But something told her distance wouldn't dispel the need she felt to wrap her arms around Eddie's neck and pull his face to hers.

She broke free of his chest and its gravitational pull, and turned away so Eddie wouldn't see the powerful effect he had on her.

It was crazy to get involved with him.

On an irrational side, there was the curse. Although she didn't believe in it, a niggling little voice kept asking, what if? What if it were true and something bad happened to Eddie.

On the rational side, he was geographically undesirable. She was going to leave this area and go back to Atlanta and her life. And Eddie would stay here. She'd done the long distance relationship before. It hadn't ended well.

When she was younger, there had been the times she hadn't listened to her brain but only her impulses. And those had ended badly, distracting her from her work, causing needless pain. For herself and others.

Why ask for a prescription for heartache?

"Let's get back to the fais do-do," she said determinedly before she could change her mind.

She steeled her hormones then turned and looked at him.

"Uh, sure." He sorta patted his chest, straightening his shirt. "Sure."

"I really would like the opportunity to meet more of the locals in a non-threatening situation. Maybe they'll decide they like this Lejeune Woman."

He turned toward the car, putting his hand on her lower back. "And how could they not?"

The touch of his hand tensed all her nerves, again. She pushed that feeling back into the closet, the very back of the closet. With all those bags of stuff she kept meaning to get rid of.

Did the Salvation Army accept an inconveniently lusty desire for one hot Cajun?

She glanced up at him from underneath her eyelashes. A simple, meaningless roll in the hay with him would be impossible. There'd be no going to bed with this man just to get him out of her system.

A roll in the hay would turn into one long night of lovemaking, with a morning after lust that would last a lifetime.

She wasn't ready to turn her entire life upside down just because a hot guy turned her hormone producing glands into a pharmacy, a cornucopia of desire and heat.

CHAPTER SIXTEEN

Back at the fais do-do, Jenna spooned up a bite of bread pudding, savoring the caramel sauce, its sweetness melting on her tongue. Then Eddie's family descended en mass. Cousins, uncles, aunts. Second cousins.

And a sister. A very pregnant sister.

"I'm Celia." His sister stuck out her hand, her eyes direct, honest, warm.

"Jenna Lejeune." Jenna liked her on sight.

"So, how does it feel to be The Lejeune Woman?" Celia asked, straight faced.

Jenna smiled. No wondering what this woman thought. She just said it. "I've been one all my life and never really thought much about it till I got to Eufaula, Louisiana."

"Being the bearer of doom must start to weigh on you after a while," Celia said with a whimsically upturned eyebrow.

Jenna laughed out loud. Celia had managed to diffuse the tension she'd felt when Eddie's whole family started sneaking looks at her.

"Thanks," she said, touching Celia on the arm. "I needed that."

"No problem." Celia's face crinkled with humor. "It's just an old story that has grown with time. No real truth to it, I'm sure."

Jenna couldn't help but remember Eddie's slashed tires, the note at her motel, the guy who'd almost run her off the road and the feeling of being watched. Somebody felt there was some truth to it. If all of that was connected.

"Everybody talks about it, though." She shot Celia a sideways look. "It's got to make you wonder."

Celia turned to look her full in the face, laying her hand on Jenna's forearm. It felt so good, the comforting human connection. "Does it have you spooked?"

Jenna nodded. "Little bit." She nodded again. "Gotta say, a little bit."

Celia's face softened. "Don't let it." She patted Jenna's arm. "You're a visitor here to Eufaula and I hate that being your impression of us, a crazy superstitious lot."

Jenna smiled. "Well, those wouldn't have been the words I'd have used."

"But yeah," Celia said with a humorous nod. "Wooo," she made a ghostly imitation. "Crazy Cajuns, with their kooky beliefs."

Jenna's approval rating for Celia was climbing. First Eddie's brother Paulie, now his sister turned out to be so nice, too. Eddie came from good stock. Too bad there was the whole voodoo curse thing on her and Eddie as a couple.

Figured he was too good to be true. Cute, check. Smart, check. Evil curse, check.

It was always something.

"Honey, you need to sit down." A man with a lawn chair opened it and motioned to Celia.

"That's my husband, Larry," Celia nodded at the man with the anxious look on his face who lifted his head in acknowledgement of Jenna. "They're all worried about me and my baby."

Celia smiled like she wasn't worried, but a sudden spike of fear for her shot through Jenna. All of those little dead babies and now, Celia looked only a couple of weeks away from giving birth …

Just then, the band struck up a waltz and Eddie extended his hand. "They're playing our song."

"We've got a song." Jenna smiled apologetically at Celia who replied, "Don't worry about the curse. But do watch out for the effects of a Cajun waltz." She patted her round belly. "I believe I got pregnant with this one the night after a really great fais do-do."

Jenna smiled as Eddie pulled her away. It was better when people came right out and talked about it. Curses preferred secretive whispering. Muttering and behind the back glances were good also. Shine the sun on a curse and it lost its power.

Eddie, however, was losing none of his power over her.

If anything, his hold on her was strengthening. He inundated her senses, with his scent and his visual appeal.

As he took her hand, a shiver ran through her. He pulled her close and they swung out into the crowd, moving to the music.

Night had descended fully and darkness lent an air of intimacy, despite the family flavor of the group. His shoulder felt secure and taut as she locked onto it so they became one in the dance.

Twirling and moving to the three-beat song, they covered a lot of ground, both literally and figuratively. Physical closeness and how they connected so well couldn't help but bring to mind another way they could connect.

Jenna tried not to let her mind go there but it was hard not to feel his body under her hands and want to bring him even closer. Celia was right in her warning about the effects of a good Cajun waltz.

When the music died, Eddie looked at her as though reading her mind. "Let's get out of here," he said in a low, husky voice.

A low heat skimmed across her skin, and a quick drumbeat began in her blood, insistent and demanding.

She nodded then looked around for Zoom. She'd forgotten about him earlier but if she were going to leave entirely, she needed to let him know so he wouldn't worry. They had come together.

As they walked toward Eddie's truck, she scanned the crowd. Finally, she pulled out her phone. There was a missed call and a message.

She pressed the button to listen and put the phone to her ear.

"Hey Jenna. Saw you leave with Eddie. I'm leaving too. Take care."

She smiled. Zoom was so reliably easy-going. That's why she'd always loved working with him. That and his great photographs.

"All set?" Eddie looked at her and a shivery pulse of excitement shot straight to her stomach, fanning out from there to points south, filling her entire body with a nervous shimmer.

The drive to the motel would be quick. And she wasn't quite sure what she wanted to happen once they got there. A kiss at the door. More?

The nervous excitement in her veins begged for more, wanted to be close to Eddie, wanted him to kiss the pulse points in her neck, wanted to run her hands across his skin.

Dangerous impulses began voicing their needs.

When they got into the truck, Eddie pulled her by her hand over to sit in the middle of the bench seat. It had been a long time since such a simple gesture had held so much excitement.

He leaned across her to pull out the seat belt, which had become tucked into the bend of the car seat, as if it had been a while since anyone had sat in that middle seat. Secretly, she was happy to see that he had to untangle it before he pulled it back across her.

His scent, musky and male, swirled around her and his closeness allowed her to inhale it, luxuriate in it.

When he finally clicked the seat belt closed, his eyes were inches from hers and the expression in them was full of want, need, and heat. For just a second he hesitated, looking down at her mouth.

Then, he turned and started the truck.

A kick of disappointment hit her in the stomach, followed by a bit of relief. Because, kissing Eddie was bound to lead to places she wasn't sure she was ready to go, yet.

Despite the rushing in her veins that begged her to step on the accelerator and to rush down that road with him.

Eddie tried to keep his eyes on the road as he drove away from the park but he was on autopilot.

All he wanted to do was stare at Jenna, at her beautiful face with the sky blue eyes, that long honey-blonde hair, that body with the curves and the long legs

It was becoming impossible to concentrate on anything but her.

When they'd left the park, he wasn't quite sure where he was going. Just away. Away from all the people.

When he saw the side road coming up ahead, he knew where. He turned the wheel hard to the right, directing his truck down a road that ended at a lonely stretch by the river.

She looked around, obviously realizing they'd diverted from the path toward the motel, but didn't say anything. He tightened his grip on her hand and felt a responding reply.

The truck coasted to a stop and he cut the engine, leaving the key turned so it would power the radio. He tuned it to a station that played his favorites like the Harry Connick, Jr. song on now, a homeboy perfect for his mood.

A full moon floated lazily along the river, shimmering light along the banks with almost as much luminescence as if it had been lit for a play.

Mood lighting.

He un-clicked his seat belt, then half turned, extending his arm along the seatback. Jenna fit into the crook of his elbow but he didn't tighten his arm around her just yet.

She looked out toward the river, almost purposefully not meeting his eyes. Her skin glowed cream colored, her blonde hair shimmering with highlights of moon.

He fingered a strand, letting the silkiness slip across his hand. Leaning in, he inhaled her clean, powdery scent, his face only inches from her neck.

With a miniscule turn of her face toward him, she invited him to kiss her.

The first touch was feathery soft, just enough to excite him to want to kiss her deeper. He wanted that mouth to open to him, wanted to possess her.

Slowly, with his hand at the nape of her neck, he coaxed her to do what he sensed she already wanted. To trust him, to go with him, deeper and further.

She ran her hand across his chest, taking the fabric of his shirt between two fingers to pull him to her. He hit the button to release her seat belt, letting the fastener uncoil itself from her body.

She laughed huskily, deep in her chest with a wanton whiskey tone. That sound undid him, and he lost all hesitation. He slipped one hand around her waist as he leaned in, one hand still on her neck and joined her mouth in a hungry exploration.

He'd been thinking about that mouth all evening.

If he were honest with himself, he'd admit tonight had been coming for some time now. Hell, he'd wanted it since she'd walked into his courtroom. Since he'd first started reading her newspaper articles with the connection it brought to her, with how she seemed to think so much like him. And that staff photo of her, though it didn't do the real Jenna Lejeune justice, still had provided a spike of heat that had foreshadowed this kiss.

The way she kissed him back said she'd been anticipating it too. With a hungry heat, her mouth connected with his, her hands skimmed across his arms and she scooted just a bit closer to him, as if she too couldn't get enough.

The kiss reached a fevered pitch, then a shrill ringing made its way into his consciousness. What the hell?

Jenna started and pulled back. "Oh." She looked as if she'd been woken up, her heavily lidded eyes dazed and unfocused. "I think it's my phone."

He'd already realized that but the heck if he'd been about to cut the kiss off for a phone call.

A cell phone stuck out of the front pocket of her purse, lighting up, vibrating and trilling. Obviously, she didn't like to miss calls.

She pulled the small phone out, looked at the number and gave him an apologetic smile before answering. "Hey Richard, what's up?"

Who the hell was Richard and why did she feel the need to take his call right now? On a Saturday night. While he was kissing her.

He ran one finger along her cheek, her smooth and soft cheek, the skin like satin beneath his hand. She smiled at him, eyes warm, and he almost leaned into her neck.

But her face changed from soft and kissable to concerned professionalism. "No, Richard. It's really not that serious." She pushed the truck's heavy door open and got out.

Walking a few paces, she turned away. But he could still hear her clearly through the open window when she said, "Richard, Zoom shouldn't have told you about that. It's nothing really. I can handle things and if I really think I'm in danger, I'll leave." She shrugged. "It is just superstition and some people maybe reacting a bit too strongly. I'll know when I need to take action."

She listened for a while then said, "Did you read my email about the children's deaths in the area?"

A moment of listening to her boss.

"It's huge, Richard. I'll finish up the story about the Hurricane Rafael evacuees, and the other story we talked about on the Cajun couple. Then, I really want to concentrate on what's killing these children. I've already made some phone calls. This is huge, Richard. I could win a Pulitzer prize for the paper," she said in a wheedling tone.

She listened to his reaction again for a long few moments. The guy seemed to talk a lot.

"I'll keep you informed. And, I promise to be careful." She hung up, inhaled deeply and stared off into the distance for a long moment before turning back to the truck.

She opened the door and got in.

"Danger?" he said, studying her face in the moonlight.

"Oh, it's just my editor overreacting. Zoom probably mentioned the note in passing. Now my editor's all freaked." She waved a hand in the air, dismissively but not convincingly enough.

She'd been worrying more than she wanted to let on.

He leaned across to pat her reassuringly on the back. He'd done it more for her but left it there for himself, keeping the contact to feel her safe and close to him.

But an almost indiscernible change occurred in her expression, a bit of heat sparked in her eyes, and she moistened her lips as she looked at his mouth.

He started to lean in but a small shadow chased the want from her eyes.

"Is there more?" he prompted.

She shook her head, dismissively, but not quite convincingly. "It's just being in a strange place. Then adding stuff like your tire, the note and this legend thing. Makes for spooky moments." She laughed then as though she'd jumped at a scary scene in a film.

Almost embarrassed to react so strongly.

But it seemed like she was still holding back information. What wasn't she telling him?

He pulled her to him, wrapping his arms around her, holding her close. He'd kill anyone if they hurt her. Stroking her back, feeling her safe here with him, he didn't want to let go.

But then she pulled away. "I have to get back. Will you take me home?"

"To my home?" he ventured with a slight laugh. Nothing ventured, nothing gained.

She laughed low in her throat, a sexy movie star sound, and pushed at his chest. "The motel. My home for now."

Release her from this close embrace? It was the last thing he wanted to do.

He leaned in for a kiss, softly, with none of the passion of earlier. This time it was for comfort. For her? Or for him?

It lasted only an instant but it kicked him in the stomach more than any passionate kiss could have. She'd accepted comfort from him.

Suddenly, he worried more about the situation than ever before. Suddenly, there was a great deal at stake.

Her safety was at risk.

She patted his arm. "I'll be okay, Eddie. Really. We're both overreacting now."

She tilted her head, assuming an assured, in control expression. "Come on, take me home. Let's not let these people, with their silly superstitions spook us." She stuck out her jaw. "We're reasonable, modern, scientific minded folk."

He couldn't help but laugh at her tone, fake spunky. It broke the spell of suspense that had descended on them.

"You're right. We're modern-minded folk." He pulled himself away from her and turned the key to start the truck.

Reluctantly.

He hated cutting the moment short, with the intimacy of the truck's cabin and the moonlight setting the stage for further kisses.

The drive to the motel was quick, too quick. When they pulled up, he got out and walked with her to the door. She opened it then turned back to him, giving him a quick peck on the cheek, the closeness allowing him a quick whiff of her scent, clean and sweet, with a bit of wood smoke floating in her hair from the cooking fires at the fais do-do.

He stood there for a moment longer, reluctant to leave, but her body language said she wasn't going to invite him in.

She hesitated so he leaned back against the doorjamb and she imitated his move, propping herself against the other side of the doorway. The night air brushed coolly across their faces. Inside the darkened room, a little red light on the phone blinked a message alert. She followed his gaze.

"A message." She walked into the room, leaving the door open. "Maybe my cell phone wasn't picking up. The reception's crazy around here."

"Mm," he murmured.

Lifting the receiver, she punched a number. She listened and as she did so her face lost all color, glowing white in the dusky room.

Eddie flipped on the room light and walked to her side. He held out his hand for the receiver and she handed it to him, horror rippling across her face.

He punched the number to replay the message. A garbled, mechanical sounding voice came out. "You've been given a warning."

It was impossible to tell if it was male or female, or to distinguish any identifying characteristics. Someone had gone to a lot of trouble to disguise their voice.

"Choose now," it intoned. "Stay away from the Cajun. Or die. Every time you've chosen before, you've made the wrong decision. Choose to live this time."

A fierce, burning rage flashed through his body. He wanted to beat the living hell out of whoever had sent this damned message.

Who did they think they were?

Pulling out his cell phone, he hit the video button to record, played the message again with his phone close to the cradle, then checked that it was there on his cell phone in case it somehow got erased from the motel phone.

Then, he slammed the room phone down. Putting his hand on Jenna's shoulder, he looked into her eyes, willing as much of his strength into her as possible.

"I'll find out who did this, Jenna. They won't get away with it."

Jenna looked at Eddie, fire erupting in his eyes, all manly fury and righteousness. Then, she shrugged. "And, to tell the truth, there's been more."

"Tell me."

"Yesterday, when I was driving over to Saint Thomasville, some car came roaring up on my rear bumper. I really thought he was gonna hit me, and in the big SUV he was in, I would have lost big time. Then, he raced around me, on up the road."

She sucked in a deep breath, feeling all the adrenalin and fear from yesterday. "Then, he came racing back again. That time, he seemed to be targeting me, veering over the middle line, until I almost ran my car off the road, I was so terrified." She gulped in air. "It almost seemed like it was what he wanted me to do."

"What happened then?"

"He left. I didn't get a tag number or anything, so I didn't call the police."

He looked at her with no expression. No judgment. "Anything else you're not telling me?"

She nodded. "Yeah, in New Orleans. Some guy tried to get into my room while I was in the shower. Turned out he wasn't the usual handyman. Then, he was killed that evening right outside the back of my hotel."

Eddie's eyes got big. "Killed?"

She nodded and raised both hands. "It's not clear it had anything to do with me."

He tilted his head. "New Orleans is pretty far from Eufaula. I get it." Then, his expression hardened. "You can't sleep here tonight."

She'd already decided that. Suddenly, the room seemed vulnerable and open to attack. A man could probably kick that door in easily.

She wanted a real hotel, with a front desk someone would have to pass by in order to reach her room. Not this door that fronted onto a parking lot, where no one would see someone approaching her room. "I'll go on up to Lafayette and get a room."

He shook his head firmly. "That's not a good idea. Someone could run you off the road between here or there, or find your hotel up there. You'd be totally unprotected." He gripped her shoulder in a reassuring manner. "You're coming to my house."

That wasn't exactly the way she'd envisioned her first invitation to his place.

"I can't Eddie." This was getting way too crazy. "I'll be okay up in Lafayette."

"This guy found where you're staying here in Eufaula. What's to stop him from following you, finding you up there?"

She loved the manly, determined protective flare on his face. But she couldn't start letting herself be taken care of. When she started that, she'd lose all ability to do her job.

A shrill ringing from the motel phone startled both of them. They jumped and looked at it. She glanced back up to make eye contact with Eddie. It couldn't be the same person.

Eddie motioned toward the face of the phone. It was a newer phone with caller identifier flashing the number of the incoming call. "Write down the number," he said tersely. She grabbed the pad and pencil lying on the desk and noted the number as Eddie hit record on his cell phone again, then nodded for her to take the call.

She lifted the receiver and listened. Eddie leaned closer, his hand on hers to keep the handset between them, the contact reassuring. When she heard the voice, she was glad to have Eddie's hand on hers.

Eddie had positioned his other hand with his cell phone to record the call.

The metallic, disguised voice rang through the phone line. "I told you to choose, the Cajun or life."

Shock vibrated through her. Eddie's eyes flamed with fury.

"Who the hell are you?" he yelled into the phone.

"Your destroyer."

"Why don't you come and try it now?" The anger in Eddie's voice almost scared her. His face changed from the pleasant one she'd always seen to this warrior-like visage she couldn't even have imagined from him.

"You're a cowardly loser. Scaring a woman this way," Eddie said, his voice dropping several octaves lower into a deep, manly growl. "I notice I haven't been getting phone calls from you. What's the matter, you afraid to take on a man?"

If that guy could see Eddie's face right now, he'd be scared.

"My only message for you is going to be a bullet, if she chooses you. She decides, not you. You're insignificant."

"Show yourself, you bastard. You'll see who's insignificant. I'll kill you myself."

Jenna stared at Eddie. She couldn't say anything, caught between the horrifying person on the phone and Eddie's towering force of protective rage.

Eddie set the phone down, without breaking the connection, and pulled Jenna outside, then used his cell phone to dial a number. "John, Edward Devereaux. Can you get over to the Creekside Motel? We've got a situation that requires immediate action. Gonna need a phone record search. Whatever it takes. Yeah, thanks."

He hung up, then looked at Jenna. Shaking his head, he reached for her.

She went into his arms, grateful for the contact. It wasn't like her to turn to a man for protection. But, hell he was the closest human being.

That's all it was, human contact.

"You're staying with me tonight." He tightened his arms around her and she leaned into his solid muscular body.

"I'll be okay up in Lafayette." She mumbled into his shoulder. "Besides, how am I gonna be any safer with you?"

"Because I've got guns." He laughed huskily.

He tightened his arms around her and the embrace changed, from one meant to comfort to something more intimate. One between a man and the woman he wanted.

She might be safer with him in one way. But in another way?

CHAPTER SEVENTEEN

Blue lights flashed through the motel parking lot strobing across a myriad of cops walking around, taking notes and talking to other visitors of the motel. An FBI special agent stood outside the office, talking to Eddie and the manager.

A crime scene investigator tried to collect evidence, brushing for prints around the doorframe after Jenna had mentioned the note.

Jenna walked two doors down to Zoom's room. She wasn't surprised he hadn't come out already, as heavy a sleeper as he was. He'd slept through ferocious rainstorms that had kept her awake all night, showing up for breakfast with questions about where all the downed limbs had come from.

She knocked on his door twice then waited. After a couple of minutes, she knocked again. Still nothing.

"Ma'am." The motel manager walked toward her, holding out an envelope. "He left this for you, was running out in a hurry, scribbled it real quick like in the lobby. Asked me to put it under your door but I forgot."

She took it and slipped her thumb under the flap. *Jen, I tried your phone but didn't reach you. My wife called. My kid broke her arm and is crying for Daddy. Richard okayed a few days off. I'm flying out and will be back soon as I deal with things at home. Maybe you should take a few days off, too. See you soon.*

Time off was a good suggestion really. But she'd be damned if she'd let herself be scared off a story. It hadn't happened yet.

More importantly, if she let herself be scared away, other children could die. Time was of the essence in that investigation.

Eddie walked toward her, blue lights shimmering around his outline. He tilted his head, studying her closely.

She smiled at him, trying for some type of normalcy.

"Where's your buddy?" He motioned to Zoom's room with his hand.

"Emm. He left."

"Really?" He looked mystified. "Before any of this happened?"

"Yeah. His kid broke her arm and wanted Daddy." She shrugged.

"Maybe you should head home for a couple of days, too?" He looked at her, his eyes intense, narrowed.

He pulled her into his arms, in a brotherly, reassuring manner, holding her for a long moment before pulling back to look her in the eye. "What say? You gonna go back to Atlanta?"

"I don't think so," she said firmly. "I don't cut and run."

"Admirable." He laughed quietly. "That's admirable. But I don't know how smart it is."

She tightened her grip on his upper arm. "What do you suggest I do, Eddie? Run away? Some kook prank calls me and I go running willy-nilly with my tail between my legs?"

"Well, nobody said it had to be willy-nilly," he answered. "That would be plumb silly."

She pulled away, starting to feel a fit of laughter coming on. Gallows humor. He was good at it. Dark humor had kept her sane many times on horrible stories that would get you institutionalized if you thought too much about them. It was a mainstay of her relationship with Zoom, as well.

"I'm staying," she said firmly.

"I thought you might." He nodded his head. "Then, how 'bout coming to my house, where I have big guns? You do know how to shoot, don't you?"

"I'm from the South." She shrugged as if that said it all.

"Tough, I like it. This could be the start of a great friendship." Then, his face turned serious. "Really, just for a night or so, no funny business, I'd appreciate it if you stayed at my place."

"Right kind of you." He could go from drop dead sexy to down home decent in two bats of an eyelash, becoming a guy who'd look out for her and not take advantage of the situation.

To go to his house was what she wanted more than anything. With Zoom gone, she was all by herself here. The idea of a *big, strong man* in the next room was very comforting. Even though she'd never admit it. And a big guy with guns was even better.

So Jenna went inside her room to get enough things together to go to Eddie's, just for a night. She'd be back before Zoom returned, would just give the cops time to check out a few leads.

And let her anxieties settle.

She grabbed a nightgown, stuffed it in her bag and walked toward the bathroom. As she passed the open door, she saw Eddie by the curb talking to a motorcycle cop.

She took a second look. It was the cop who'd given her a ticket, sending her to

Eddie's courtroom in the first place. They were talking and laughing as though they knew each other well.

The female crime scene tech was hooking up a device to the motel room phone in case of callbacks.

"Who's that guy talking to Eddie?" Jenna motioned out the door.

The tech stepped over and looked. "Oh, that's the judge's cousin. They're real close, grew up together. Less than a year apart in age." She turned back to her job.

His cousin. He'd known exactly what he was doing when he'd given her the ticket. Probably thought it was a real joke, sending The Lejeune Woman to see Judge Devereaux.

By the time she got her stuff together, the crime scene tech had left as had most of the other cops. As Jenna pulled her door closed, the police chief drove out the driveway, with a goodbye wave out his window, the final official leaving the scene.

The guests at the motel had gotten bored with things when they'd learned it was only a crank call and had gone back to bed. It was just her and Eddie.

He opened the passenger door of his truck and she got in. Almost as if they were an established couple, she with a few overnight things packed.

It felt odd. They'd only had a few kisses - knock you dead kisses - but still. And now she was sleeping over?

He patted her shoulder in a brotherly fashion, as if reading her thoughts. "This is for safety's sake. When you *really* spend the night at my house." He paused dramatically, his eyes shadowed in the dark so she could only sense their expression. "It will be for a lot more of a romantic reason than some kook's scary call."

When you spend the night, not if. Because that was how it felt, as if it were only a matter of time.

He leaned over and unlocked the pocket of the car and pulled out a revolver, setting it underneath the front seat on his side of the car. "Just in case." He tilted his head and started the truck.

They drove through the night, leaving town and traveling along an isolated, rural road that paralleled the river shimmering under the full moon.

Finally, a typical bayou house emerged from the mist, its wraparound porch complete with rocking chairs.

They crunched to a stop in the gravel circle drive and Eddie leaned across her to open her door, his arm brushing across her stomach. A million sensations shot through her, excitement, nervousness, anticipation.

And want.

Heavy, wanting-him need.

They'd be sleeping under the same roof.

His eyes flickered to hers, shadows racing through them, responding to the feelings she felt sure he could read in hers.

Then, he grabbed her overnight bag from the floorboard and got out of his side of the truck, walking around to hers.

She slipped out her side of the truck and met Eddie, his hand extended, his eyes flashing heat at her.

She took his hand, the warmth coursing through her skin straight to her stomach. How would she ever make it through the night without him in her bed?

She didn't want their first night to be tinged with desperation, and the having-to-spend-the-night-together thing.

She wanted him to invite her, entice her, ask her. Not to be there because she needed protection.

She wanted the option to leave or to stay.

Not that there was much doubt in her mind which option she would take. Still, she wanted it to be an option.

Together, they walked up the front steps to a heavy wooden door with side panels of stained glass.

He swung the front door open. A set of black and white photographs spread along the entryway walls. Swamps and bayous spread out, reflecting back an idealized version of what lay outside the town limits of Eufaula, Louisiana.

One photograph in particular drew her to it, with an eerie sense of familiarity. She could have sworn she'd been there before. Not someplace like it, but that exact place.

As Jenna walked down the line of photographs, a cold sheen of perspiration spread across her skin. All of them felt too familiar.

A sick feeling wormed through her veins, and for an instant she wanted to leave and get as far from Eufaula as possible, as far from these superstitious people with their legends as she could.

"Where'd you get these?" She turned to find Eddie watching her, a speculative expression flickering across his face.

"Oh, all over the area," he said, with

a dismissive wave that didn't fit with his
expression.

"Who's the photographer?"

He hesitated then said, "I took them."

She looked at the photographs then back
at him. "They're beautiful. It's like I've
been there before."

He raised a shoulder. "A swamp's a
swamp?"

"Emm," she murmured. "But it's more
than that."

"Are you letting all this get to you,
get into your psyche?" He raised an eyebrow
wryly.

She smiled in acknowledgement. "Guess I
am."

Eddie smiled back at her in a
comfortable manner, then his smile changed
and suddenly she became aware again of the
intimacy of the moment as they stood alone
in his living room, the river rippling just
outside, the watery rushing sounds forming a
white noise that locked out the world.

Eddie studied her face. It was a moment
of luck for any guy to get a woman like
Jenna home to his place. He wanted to move
in, enclose her in his arms and . . .

*Damn. Don't think like that buddy or
you'll be violating some type of duty.*

He might not be a police officer but he
was an officer of the court, which demanded
a certain protocol to victims, even if he
had been planning to try and get her into
bed before the crime had occurred.

She was spooked enough as it was.

"So." He turned and waved toward the
back of the house. "There's an empty bedroom
back here." He led the way, past his bedroom
with the door open and the bed luckily half-

ass made, to a bedroom just down the hall from his.

"It's got clean sheets. I keep it that way in case I have to bring home a pretty crime victim."

She laughed lightly. If she knew how much effort it really was taking not to throw her on that bed and climb in with her.

"I'll be just over there." He pointed at his room. "With the guns." Then he walked away and came back with a pistol in his hand.

"Were you serious about knowing how to operate one of these?"

She nodded.

"This type?" He turned the semi-automatic gun back and forth.

"Actually, my brother had one just like it. We used to go to the firing range, 'cause that's what he likes to do." She shrugged. "I'm the only one in my family who doesn't have a gun. They're always trying to convince me I need one."

She laughed. "I even have a carry permit because I did a story on them just recently, and applied at the time. Still have it in my purse, as a matter of fact."

"That permit's not honored in Louisiana anymore, but if you keep the gun in your car, I think you'll be fine. We'll see what we can do about getting you a Louisiana carry permit, pretty quickly. Maybe we can bend the rules a little bit to get you one. I know a guy," he said with a wink.

She seemed confident and relaxed when he handed it to her. Some women would have treated it like a snake. "I'll just put it in here." She took it and opened up a bureau drawer. "But, when that guy with the SUV was harassing me on the road to Saint Thomasville yesterday, I was wishing for a gun, valid carry permit or not."

"I know that's right." He nodded.

She closed the drawer as if she thought she'd never be opening it again. He hoped to God she didn't ever need that gun, that the phone call was just a crank call. And all the other stuff too. But a murder in New Orleans with a connection to her? Hardly a prank.

He felt a hell of a lot better with her here, where he could watch over her. At least until he could get the calls checked out.

Then, he'd enjoy having her here for a very different reason.

"So, I'll just leave you." Her expression flickered with invitation. Or was that what he wanted to read into it? He'd be damned if he'd take advantage of the situation and have her regretting it tomorrow.

The "morning after" he had in mind for them didn't include any doubts on her part that she'd gotten in bed with him just to be close to a large protective male.

Their first morning after would be a hell of a thing.

CHAPTER EIGHTEEN

As Eddie pulled her bedroom door closed behind him, Jenna stood quietly, listening as he walked down the hall to his room. He didn't close his door.

Only her door separated them.

She could hear him walking around, making rustling noises that might have been him undressing and then sliding between the sheets. She fought against it but still the images of sliding into bed with him, her skin against his flooded through her mind. He would pull her tightly against him. He would . . .

"Oh stop it," she murmured to herself. "You're not going to get any sleep at all if you keep this up."

She walked to the window and looked out at the river flowing below the stilted backside of the house, and inhaled deeply, letting the fresh, watery scent fill her lungs. Gentle night noises formed a cacophony of crickets and owl calls over the rustling water.

She turned away to get ready for bed. Opening her bag, she pulled out her nightgown, shook it out and laid it on the bed, unzipped her skirt and shimmied out of it then pulled her shirt over her head.

Eddie's footsteps approached her door. She stood in her bra and panties, and waited breathlessly, her lungs tightening with the need for oxygen.

"Jenna?"

"Yes?" An incredibly sexy guy stood just on the other side of the door. What was he wearing? His underwear? Or jeans with no shirt?

Damn.

"The bathroom's down the hall. I'll leave you some towels on the sink."

"Okay," she forced out past the knot in her chest and the tightness in her lungs. All she had to do was open the door. The floor creaked under his weight, reinforcing the fact that he was only inches away.

She found it impossible not to imagine his mouth on her neck, his arms pulling her closer. A swirling heat flushed her skin, pooling between her thighs, wanting him.

In her bed, inside of her. There was no denying it.

Only that door separated them and what they could do if she just turned the knob.

"Thanks," she finally said, hating the decision she'd been forced to make. She wasn't getting into bed with him without seduction, without a decision being made on his part that was more than just, *Hey, we're both here, why not*?

Of course that wasn't how things were. But, still, she wanted seduction.

After another moment, he walked down the hall to his own room, each step taking him away from her, further away from the night they could have together.

Jenna unhooked her bra, took it off and let the cool night air blow across her naked skin for a long moment. Then, she drew in a breath and slipped her nightgown over her head.

She needed to go brush her teeth and wash her face but didn't trust herself to go out that door. If she encountered Eddie in the hallway, with all the gravitational pull he exerted on her, who knew where it would lead?

That was the problem. She instinctively knew where it would lead.

She pulled back the sheet and got in. One night wouldn't kill her to skip the teeth brushing and face washing.

She settled into the soft cotton nest and began imagining getting in Eddie's bed. She'd love to feign fear, use it as an excuse.

Or hell, just flat out acknowledge that she wanted him.

But, she couldn't go get into his bed tonight no matter how badly she was tempted.

Instead, she needed to think about her story and what still needed doing. Both her authorized story about the exodus caused by Hurricane Rafael and the side story of the Cajun exodus from Nova Scotia, as exemplified by Genevieve and Jean Claude. And then, the story about the babies' deaths.

There were always secondary stories. You started one report, then always found more.

To tie up the loose ends on her Cajun couple story, she wanted to find the gravesite for Jean Claude and Genevieve. Everyone said some of the other Devereaux and Lejeune couples lay in the Eufaula town cemetery but that Genevieve and Jean Claude weren't there.

Tomorrow, she'd ask Eddie if he knew of any clues to where they might be buried.

If she were alert enough to remember after a long night with no sleep.

She turned off the bedside light, determined to not think about him. This was just a beautiful bed and breakfast alongside a river. That river flowed to the sea and then all across the world, to be sucked up into the atmosphere and fall somewhere else as rain.

As rain on Eddie's bare chest?

Damn it. She laughed softly at her one-track mind.

Across the hall, Eddie heard her tossing and turning in his spare bedroom. He ought to go in there and reassure her.

Was he joking? The last place he needed to go was anywhere near that door.

He wasn't gonna get a lick of sleep.

＊＊＊＊＊＊

The early morning sun filtered through the curtains in a yellow haze. Jenna lay in bed for a moment, luxuriating in the soft, comfortable bed. Then she picked up her cell phone and glanced at it. Eight o'clock. She had gotten some sleep after all.

Swinging her legs off the bed, she grabbed a pair of jeans and a T-shirt out of her bag and dressed, and pulled her hair back into a ponytail. She'd shower later but right now the smell of coffee swirled through the air like a siren's call.

She ducked into the bathroom and brushed her teeth, and touched up her makeup, then headed toward that coffee aroma.

Eddie was leaning against the kitchen sink, drinking from a mug. She didn't know which was more appealing, the smell of that coffee or the sight of him, sleepy with a night's growth of beard, wearing worn jeans and a soft cotton T-shirt that hugged his body.

His eyes met hers with a spark of awareness and then slid down to take in her jeans and T-shirt. Early mornings with Eddie

Devereaux - she could get used to this.

"Want some?" He tilted his head toward the coffee maker.

"You bet." She turned away from those eyes that could inspire all sorts of distracting thoughts, and grabbed a mug that was sitting beside the pot and poured it to the brim.

"Get any sleep?" he asked in a gravely, deep voice. The sound filtered into her veins, feeling almost like a shot of caffeine, waking every cell in her body.

"Surprisingly so. You?"

"I was fine. It was you I was worried about."

"Well don't." She pointed a finger at him. "Don't ever worry about me. Cause I can take care of myself."

He grinned. "How'd I know you'd say that?"

She smiled back. "Playing the role of the plucky heroine will be Jenna Lejeune."

"Right about now, the audience will be yelling, 'Get out of there'." He arched an eyebrow.

"Too stupid to live?" she quipped.

Their eyes met for a moment in a mutual smile.

If she'd been under oath, forced to tell the truth, she could say she didn't cut and run, since she'd been in scarier situations than this.

But, if she had to tell the whole truth and nothing but the truth - she'd have to admit that much of her decision to stay had to do with him - the attraction she felt, an almost supernatural pull in his direction.

"Eddie, I can't tell you how many times I've been driving toward a story and on the other side of the road, I see the evacuation. Cops aren't letting anybody through because it's too dangerous, but they pull the barriers aside to let me pass."

She smiled into his eyes, his gorgeous eyes that made her want to violate journalistic ethics. "It's not all that safe of a job, Eddie."

"Kinda like being in law enforcement." He shrugged noncommittally. "What do you want to do today?"

"I should work on my hurricane or Cajun couple story but what I really want to do is go back into town and start checking around on why so many babies are dying." Her stomach clenched. "The other stories pale in comparison. Why aren't people up in arms, incensed, calling the TV stations, and the newspapers?"

Eddie glanced away, toward the deck outside the sliding door, avoiding her eyes. "Want to see the river?" He pulled the sliding door aside.

Why did people avoid the subject of the babies' deaths? Even him. Avoiding the subject didn't seem like him.

But, she didn't call him on his avoidance, just followed him outside into paradise. The river ran below the deck, a soft mist rising from the water's surface.

"Isn't it asking to be flooded living so close to the river?"

"It's never gotten up past that mark." He pointed to a red slash on the side of one of the deck supports. A date was written beside it.

Various other red slashes and dates marked the wood beam. "You take your flooding seriously."

"It's a fact of life 'round these parts." He took a sip of coffee. "So, today?"

The river flowed by in a steady crystalline stream, low and clear because there hadn't been rain for a while. She gazed at the almost hypnotizing water for a few moments before answering. "I'm gonna take some time and research the infant deaths. It's eating at me."

He glanced away.

"Later, maybe I'll go out to the cemetery. I've heard other Devereaux and Lejeune couples are buried out there. But people say that Jean Claude and Genevieve aren't. What's up with that?"

He tilted his head, a whisper of mystery in his eyes. "It was a long time ago, Jenna."

"You don't believe the whole curse thing, do you Eddie?" She fixed her gaze on him, trying to read the truth in his expression.

He gazed into her eyes for a moment before shrugging. "Jenna, some things, it's better not to think too much about. I don't believe in curses. I don't believe in predestination." He looked intently back at her. "But anyone would have to admit it is strange that Devereaux men and Lejeune women keep dying every time they match up."

"You're afraid of me." That thought kicked her in the stomach, taking her breath away.

He set his coffee cup down on the railing and reached for her. Pulling her close, up against his stomach, he wrapped his arms around her tightly.

Fire raced through her, whipped into a

fury by the sensation of his skin against her bare arms, his stomach against her stomach, and his mouth so close to hers.

She glanced away and casually draped her hands over his upper arms, hoping to disguise the insane feelings inspired by his nearness.

"Maybe those other Devereaux men just weren't as strong and tough as me." His bragging was softened by a smile.

Then his eyes turned serious and he leaned down to her lips and her breath caught in her chest, every cell in her body concentrating on nothing but him. Electrical sparks disrupted any rational thinking, working her into a haze of expectation.

His kiss started gently, just a soft brushing across her mouth, but it quickly took on a life of its own, growing from tentative to possessive.

His tongue delved into her mouth, taking and giving all at once, sending her body into a whirl of desire. She spread her palms against his chest, and his muscles tensed.

She wanted him, wanted his naked skin against hers, wanted to feel every inch of him against every inch of her.

It was impossible to get close enough to him.

As if sensing her reaction, he deepened the kiss until she gasped with need, murmuring beneath his lips wordless sounds of want.

After a long moment, he pulled back, his eyes misted with passion. She thought he was going to sweep her up and take her to the bedroom – hoped he was going to do that.

Instead, he said something that cut

through her desire.

"I know where Jean Claude and Genevieve's resting place is."

A gasp escaped from her lips. She jerked back far enough to get a good look at his face.

"Why didn't you say anything before?"

She stepped back, putting space between their bodies, reaching behind her for the railing to steady herself.

Fire and passion still sparked around his eyes then cooled behind a mist that covered them entirely. Gone was the passionate moment they'd just shared.

"It hasn't come up."

Hadn't come up?

She sucked in a few breaths, letting the sensations of need and want sink away inside of her, and concentrated on the intellectual, the reasons she'd come here in the first place.

The couple was all she'd talked about since she'd met him. A hint of deception danced around his expression.

What was he keeping from her?

"I guess I hadn't asked about their grave site specifically," she conceded. "But you knew I was doing this whole story."

He nodded and crossed his arms.

Those arms needed to be around her. Instantly, she wanted to be back in them. But, she grasped the railing behind her, anchoring herself in place.

It felt so wrong not to be in his arms, such a waste of passion. But the fact that he'd waited until now to tell her about the gravesite was disturbing.

"So where is this burial place?" She forced the words out, trying for as natural a tone as possible, not one that breathed of her leftover desire for him.

Something changed in his eyes, relented and gave up information that he'd been withholding since she'd met him. "It's at my place down the river."

So casual, yet underneath it so much unsaid.

"You have another house on the river? Isn't that a bit odd?"

He shrugged. "It belonged to my great grandfather then my grandfather. Been in the family forever. It's part of me."

He laughed gruffly. A man type of softness passed across his face quickly, as if before he could stop it, revealing how much was hidden by that decidedly casual laugh.

"I go down there whenever I can get off. Bought it off my grandfather when he got too old to go by himself anymore." A wistful, sad expression spread across his face, followed by a dismissive shrug as if his face hadn't just revealed the strong emotions evoked by just mentioning his grandfather.

"You really love him, huh?"

He glanced with surprise at her, meeting her gaze directly before glancing away at the river.

"He's dead, now. But, it was his fishing place. Our fishing place." Another flash of sadness passed through his eyes. "Mostly just him and me, but some of the other cousins, aunts and uncles would go, too, sometimes. My granny would never set foot up there, though."

"Too rustic? Too much guy stuff?" She looked at him inquiringly.

"No, Granny likes to fish. Anywhere except there." He shrugged. "She takes this legend very serious and has never wanted to go anywhere near where the last Devereaux-Lejeune couple is buried. Thought it was inviting trouble. But Grandpa liked it down there."

"The gravesite." Finally. The significance awed her. The final answer to what she'd been searching for. "They're buried together?"

He nodded slowly.

Emotion surged through her as if she'd found a relative's final whereabouts. As if she'd known Genevieve and Jean Claude.

Tears flooded toward her eyes, hot and ready. Her throat clogged with them, and her heart clenched with the power of the information.

It was insane how connected to the couple she felt.

"Yes, they're together," he answered, simply, as if the emotions she experienced weren't written across her face. "So, down the river?"

Why had he offered this information now? Was it because they'd kissed? Had it unlocked areas of himself that he was willing to share with her?

What would happen today if they spent the day together, away from all other distractions?

CHAPTER NINETEEN

Eddie's small boat skimmed along the water, blowing spray into a fine mist on their faces. Dense undergrowth tangled the shoreline, long tendrils of Spanish moss trailing in ghostly fingers from ancient live oaks, trees that had taken root many human lifetimes ago.

Light fog drifted along the top of the water, eerily transforming the swampy river into an ancient, timeless place.

The further down the river they went, the further back in time they appeared to go. There were no signs humans had ever touched the land, no electrical lines or telephone poles anywhere.

They traveled for about forty-five minutes down the river, both of them silent, intent on their mission, she lost in thought, Eddie seeming to honor her mood, not disturbing her. Even if he'd tried to speak, she didn't know if she could have heard him over the boat's motor.

Finally, Eddie swooshed in at a little dock. Set back from the water was a cottage someone had taken a lot of trouble to cute up. White gingerbread trim contrasted with the yellow structure. Almost as if it were waiting for the woman of the house to come home, waiting for Genevieve.

She sucked in a breath, feeling that she was invading another woman's territory. But, slowly, the feeling slipped away, until she felt more like she was coming home.

Eddie tied off the boat, meeting her eyes with a punch that had her sucking in a deep breath. Today was about Genevieve and Jean Claude, not about her and Eddie.

"Do you want to see the house first? Or go straight back to the gravesite?" he asked as if he already knew the answer.

She merely nodded, reaffirming the answer she was sure he could read in her eyes.

And without a word, Eddie extended a hand to help her off the boat, his grip on her hand lingering just a moment longer than was necessary. Strong, warm, enticing.

His palm was rough, yet he always touched her so gently. He started to release her hand, but she tightened her grip, and hand in hand, they walked up the dock.

The connection between them felt so good, with a current of natural affection, and attraction. So right, as if she'd known him all her life.

He led the way along a dirt path that circled around the house and back up a slope, releasing her hand to push stray branches aside from the well-worn path.

One limb slashed completely across the dirt trail, as if the wilderness could so easily overtake the path again. "This stuff grows back pretty fast." He broke it off, tossing it aside, leading the way, clearing the path of other stray bushes.

She followed him, watching his strong form. She'd planned to distract herself from her attraction to him today by looking for the gravesite. But she hadn't anticipated coming into this intimate, isolated location.

There were no prying eyes to prevent them from falling down right here on a soft bed of grass. And doing what she wanted to do - connect with him as intimately as possible.

The thought of him as close as possible to her body sent heat flushing through her.

It was impossible not to imagine how it would be. Because she knew it would be good.

Distraction. She needed distraction. But it was hard to come by with his strong back right in front of her. Those long legs, those capable hands and well built shoulders.

Damn. Nothing was easy about this assignment. It was almost like more and more roadblocks kept getting in her way of finishing her articles.

The longer she investigated, the more story ideas she encountered. Then, this hot, inconvenient attraction between her and Eddie.

Why should she even want to resist Eddie, that betraying little voice asked? Would a long distance love affair really be such a bad thing?

She'd had long distance relationships in the past. They'd always ended rather quickly. Like this one probably would once she left Eufaula, Louisiana. But, why shouldn't she enjoy it while she could?

Why shouldn't she?

Because once she'd had Eddie Devereaux, losing him might be the hardest thing she'd ever experienced. The emotions he evoked in her with just a touch were so powerful. What would making love be like?

Would she leave her job for a relationship?

Everything in her life had built toward that job.

And, she couldn't imagine Eddie outside of the Cajun environment. The guy seemed as intrinsic to the landscape as the gray

Spanish moss. Bayou water seemed to run through his veins.

A heaviness settled in her stomach just thinking about the situation, with a loss somewhere down the road.

They rounded a bend. Eddie broke off one last, large leafy branch and a small park-like clearing materialized in the middle of the densely overgrown woods. Manicured grass covered a circle of ground and perennial flowers edged the border, which was defined with river rocks.

"This is so out of place." She waved a hand at the tangled undergrowth surrounding the tidy clearing. "Someone went to a lot of trouble here in the middle of the wilderness."

Eddie arched an eyebrow, and glanced away.

"You did this."

He looked back at her and nodded. Why had he done this for such long dead ancestors?

He pointed toward the center of the clearing. An ancient granite slab, worn with age, sat isolated and alone in the middle of the wilderness. No family members lay in repose beside the couple, keeping them company in death. Such a lonely final resting spot.

She walked slowly toward it, drawn by an almost overwhelming pull. She leaned down to trace the names and dates etched into the stone, commemorating the birth and death of Genevieve Lejeune Devereaux and Jean Claude Devereaux. An eerie feeling of déjà vu and closure floated up from the stone as she touched it. As if the couple had been waiting for her.

Sadness filled her. She'd wanted to imagine Jean Claude still lived. She'd needed to see this to realize that he was gone for good and she would never find her long lost Cajun lover.

The dreams and the words in the journal had melded together into an experience, almost as though she'd known him. Grief spiraled through her, accompanied by a deep sense of loss.

Eddie took her hand in his, his warm flesh pulling her back into the world of the living. She glanced at him and his eyes were serious and thoughtful pools of coffee-colored empathy.

"Feels like they're still here," he said softly, his voice reverently lowered to a funereal level. "After I read the part of the journal you gave me, I needed to come up here myself."

Jenna nodded. "It feels like such a personal loss although I never even knew either of them."

He murmured in agreement. It was good to know someone else understood the crazy emotions that filled her. Just sharing it made it easier.

"After reading his journal, I felt I knew him, wanted to talk to him." The sadness was a physical weight, leaden and heavy.

Eddie touched her on the shoulder, and strangely, it felt like the touch of a long lost lover, finally found. "You wanted to kiss him."

She laughed softly, her vision clouded by an emotional mist. "Kinda," she admitted.

Eddie slipped an arm around her, his hand in the small of her back, pulling her to him. "Kiss me," he urged in a voice deepened by desire. "Touch me. I'm here."

He waited for her to move first but when she did, he pulled her to him in a fiery passionate embrace, their mouths seeking connection, their hands touching skin.

This was the dream she'd had many nights since she'd received the journal. An explosion of sensation jolted her, with want, with need, desire swirling through her veins. For Eddie? For Jean Claude?

It was almost as if they were one. That was what he was offering, a connection to a long lost love, an impossible love.

She broke away, sucking air into her lungs. "Eddie."

"Yes," he whispered close to her ear, passion simmering in his voice.

"It's like you're him." The words came out before she could filter them. "Do you think I'm crazy?" She searched his eyes for understanding.

"Maybe he's in here somewhere." He tilted his head. "Some scientists say we have genetic memory. Certain animals are born with a knowledge of their breed, their species - they act alike."

He shrugged as though he wasn't even sure he believed what he was about to say. "Perhaps hidden in our genetic code is a bit of the memory of Genevieve and Jean Claude."

Their gazes locked as he continued, "The moment I saw you, it was as if I knew you." Intensity etched his face, desire glowing in his eyes.

That passion sparked a fire in her veins that burned away all caution. "I saw Jean Claude's portrait," she whispered, "then later your face, and it was almost like I was primed, as if I'd known you before."

Irony played about his eyes. "The old folks would say we're reincarnated." He continued in a lower tone, his voice caressing her skin, "If you believe that."

She wanted to believe it, already almost did. "So our DNA remembers each other."

She glanced at the grave marker and again the pain of losing someone surged through her, a powerful churning grief spinning in her stomach. "I miss him. Jean Claude's words have gotten into my head. I can't think of him as dead."

Eddie ran his hand tenderly around the back of her neck, under her hair, stroking her skin, so close, so naked, so intimate. Her last defense unraveled and only want remained, want for Jean Claude, want for Eddie. They'd melded into one being in her mind. She looked into his eyes and an answering fiery need glowed back.

"Maybe he's right here," he said, his voice low and husky. He pulled her close, wrapping his arms around her, his mouth nuzzling the skin just below her jaw.

A need as ancient as the mists that crept along the waters of the bayou flowed through her, urging her to take what Jean Claude and Genevieve had shared.

"I want you," she said, loving the instant, answering reaction in his eyes. "Edward Devereaux, Jean Claude, or some strange mixture of the two, it doesn't matter." She wanted this man in front of her.

She'd waited eons, it seemed, to

consummate this relationship. Had she
returned over and over again attempting to
right an ancient wrong? It didn't matter.

"Now is all we have," Eddie said,
mimicking her thoughts.

"God, it's like you can read my mind."

"It's because we want the same thing,"
he murmured, mouthing along the sensitive
skin where her neck met her shoulder.

His touch soothed her skin like a
healing balm.

His mouth slipped lower, pushing down
her top so that he teased the top of her
breast, and a gasp slipped from her throat
that seemed to unleash his masculinity. He
slid one hand to her rear to cup her and
pull her into him in the oldest male gesture
known to any society.

She lost all ability to stop. His shirt
was a hindrance to their connection. Tugging
his soft, cotton T-shirt loose from his
jeans, she slipped her hands underneath,
desperately sliding over his skin, feeling
his muscles rippling just below the surface.

He pulled her shirt over her head and
she ducked to make it easier. Eddie's skin
against hers was all she could think about,
all she wanted.

He released her long enough to pull his
shirt off and throw it onto the cushioning
grass. Reaching for her low-slung jeans'
waistline, he undid the button then pulled
the zipper down. He inhaled raggedly at the
sight of her panties.

Softly, he fingered the edge before
looking up again. When their eyes met, he
dipped his hand inside the cotton bikini
underwear.

She sucked a breath in deeply, trying

to get oxygen to her brain. Eddie's hand slid lower and lower until finally it found what ached to be discovered.

His hand slipped into her center, and she leaned against his chest, needing his support to stand as all strength faded from her legs. Everything about her revolved around that hand and what Eddie was doing to her with it.

Her head fell back, her eyes closed and she felt Eddie's mouth on the soft pulse exposed at her neck.

CHAPTER TWENTY

Jenna stood underneath the outdoor shower on the cabin's back porch. A wooden screen shielded her from ankle to neck height.

Beyond the porch, a tangle of vines, trees and bushes visually soothed her into a meditative closeness with nature. Sun-warmed water sprinkled over her body. A wooden water tank sat nearby on stilts, with stored rainwater. A smaller tank on top of the shower itself allowed water to heat in the sun.

Eddie and his grandfather and his great grandfather had put a lot of effort into the place, with a water filtration system so river water could be piped into the house. A septic tank lay somewhere off in the woods, allowing the cabin to have a flush toilet.

It was a freak'n bed and breakfast in the middle of the swamp.

The calm and peaceful ambience seeped into her bones and a bone deep feeling of belonging swept through her. For just a brief flash, she imagined living here with Eddie. And their children.

She smiled at that romantic image. Where would the kids go to school? Homeschooled? Yeah, teenagers would love that.

Then she turned off the water and wrapped a towel around herself. Walking back into the house, she looked out the front window to see Eddie fishing from the dock.

She took a minute to check out the rest of the house, the bedroom the only room Eddie had officially shown her. After they'd made love on the grass by the gravesite, they'd come back to the house for a second, more comfortable session.

The grass might not have been as soft as a bed, but their passion had more than made up for it.

A little kitchen was tucked into the back of the cabin, simple but with the basics, except, instead of a refrigerator, there was an icebox. Eddie had piled bags of ice into a cooler before they'd left.

She wandered through the living room into a room off its other side, an office. A law book lay open on a small rustic wooden desk that faced a window looking out on the river. Eddie still avidly fished, tossing his line further out into the river.

That man probably did everything he undertook with a passion. She hadn't been disappointed in bed, feeling as though he knew her body, as if it were his most important mission in life to satisfy her needs.

And he had. Every touch, every kiss was seared into her memory. She was tempted to call him in again. But it didn't seem fair to put any guy through that much sexual work in one afternoon.

They'd lain together, stroking, touching and loving for hours, it had seemed. She couldn't possibly want more.

But she did.

She wanted to make love to him nonstop. Was that The Lejeune Woman curse, how they killed their men?

If so, the Lejeune women didn't hold all the blame. The Devereaux men had to take some of the responsibility for how they looked, acted, touched - imbuing a sensory overload that would be seared into a woman's intrinsic being, becoming a part of her DNA.

The genetic memory connection somehow seemed more possible, with a passion a woman could feel in her bones and ache for in another lifetime.

A flowing warmth flushed through her.

But her gaze fell on the book again, bringing her back to the present.

She picked the law book up, keeping a finger inside to hold Eddie's place. She turned it over to see what he was reading.

Something underneath the book caught her eye. Newspaper articles. With her byline and her staff photo above it.

She set the law book aside and rustled through the articles. Carefully clipped, each of her original hurricane stories from the first days after Rafael. Then behind them, other articles she'd written more recently.

A streak of nervousness shot through her, skittering along her nerve endings with an electric shock of pain.

He'd mentioned he'd seen Zoom's photos and read an article or two of hers that went with them. Printing and cutting out articles, then saving them, seemed almost obsessive. She riffled through them. Underneath the articles lay a photograph of herself, the one on the paper's website. Blown up in size and printed out.

A flash of fear shot through her. Okay, she'd developed a bit of an obsession with Jean Claude, and then transferred it over to Eddie. So, why was this so weird? Why should she feel frightened?

Because she just did. If he'd admitted he'd loved her work, had followed it diligently, then maybe it wouldn't have caught her so by surprise.

What else was the guy hiding?

Glancing out the window, she checked to see that Eddie was still fishing, then she opened the top desk drawer. A small, worn, clothbound book lay inside.

Lifting it carefully, she opened the first page to see antiquated, elegant writing that spoke of a different time, much like some of the writing she'd seen in the parish record books in the church in Saint Thomasville.

I walked the settlement today, asking for news of Jean Claude. Several folk said he had passed this way but had gone on down the river. Will this be the pattern of my days for all of my life? Always a tantalizing piece of information but never finding Jean Claude. Oh, Jean Claude, are you aching for me as I ache for you?

Her knees lost all strength and Jenna collapsed into the wooden, ladder-back chair beside the desk. Genevieve's journal. How long had Eddie had it, and why had he never told her about it?

With one eye on Eddie out on the dock, she quickly flipped through the book. There was talk about Savannah and an English officer who said he would escort her safely back there, said he'd heard Jean Claude had returned to Savannah looking for her.

I tire of the wilds with all of its hardships. I will be safe in Savannah. It is what I ought to do. I shall go to Savannah and wait for Jean Claude to find me.

Then the journal ended.

She flipped through the empty pages, hoping for more. But there was no more.

Eddie had kept this from her! Why?

A movement on the dock caught her attention. Eddie was heading back to the cabin.

A nervous thrumming ran through her veins. Drumming, drumming, drumming with a warning beat. Run, her blood urged. Go now!

Hurriedly, with shaking hands, she straightened the desk. As she picked up the law book, it fell from her hands, landing with a loud thud.

Her gaze jerked to the window. Eddie looked up. Could he see into the house?

She grabbed the book, opening it to an arbitrary page and laying it on top of the papers. Everything looked the same.

She pushed the drawer shut that had held the journal, grabbed the clothbound book and fled to the bedroom, her heart beating powerfully in her ears, and shut the door.

"Jenna, I've got supper," Eddie called as he entered the front door then his footsteps sounded like he was going to the kitchen.

Standing, wrapped only in a towel, Jenna looked desperately for a lock on the bedroom door. There was none. Besides, a man of Eddie's size could easily kick open a flimsy privacy lock.

She was afraid of the man she'd spent the afternoon making love to?

This was crazy. Still, a nervous panic pounded through her, blood spurted from her heart with a crazed insistent desperate message - run!

She pulled on her underwear and bra, then quickly yanked on her jeans, shirt and tennis shoes. Looking around for her purse, she realized she'd left it out in the living room. Inside that bag was the gun Eddie had given her.

She didn't know why she'd slipped it in before they'd left Eddie's house, since she'd felt completely safe with him, knowing he would protect her, and that he had a gun.

Did she need protection from Eddie?

Or was she overreacting? She padded quietly into the living room and over to her purse, slipping the journal into its depths, beside the pistol, sliding her purse strap over her head, letting the purse fall across her chest to her side. She could get to the gun at a moment's notice.

It was insane to think such a loving, gentle man could have ulterior motives. But someone had been threatening her.

The calls? Could he have had an ally, convincing her she needed protection so she would flee with him to his house? Then, to this isolated cabin. Who would help him do that?

His cousin, who'd given her a ticket, sending her to Eddie's courtroom in the first place? Had that been a joke? Or something sinister?

Did Eddie take the curse seriously? Did they all? Everyone she'd met in Eufaula, Louisiana, silently watching her, plotting her demise? Did the entire community have a stake in harming her?

Why? Why would she think such crazy thoughts? But, there was no denying how weirdly everyone reacted when they heard her name.

Now, she was alone with Eddie, in the middle of the swamp, where no one would hear her scream.

The thought of silent, unheard screams

echoing from her mouth was like a childhood nightmare. Running, trying to scream but unable to do so.

She stilled her mind, hoping her subconscious would speak to her as to what the truth was. All of the craziness since she'd gotten to Louisiana was bound to make anyone feel emotionally unstable, unsure who they could trust.

"Jenna, you hungry?" Eddie called from the back porch.

She didn't want to go out there but she had to. Opening the door, she looked to be sure he was outside.

This was Eddie. She knew him. It was hard to believe her perception of someone could be so off that she'd allowed herself to sleep with someone who was dangerous. An ability to read people had always been what had kept her safe in an unsafe profession.

She looked out the front door at the boat and imagined fleeing.

Padding across the front porch and down the dock, looking over her shoulder every step of the way, she would make it to the boat.

She'd never driven a boat before but how hard could it be?

Setting her purse on the front seat, she would turn the key in the ignition. In her fantasy, the engine fired but refused to turn over. Looking up, she saw Eddie coming down the dock.

Desperately, she turned the key again and the engine ignited. She put the boat in drive and pulled back on the accelerator. But in her haste, she'd forgotten to untie the boat from the dock. The line held for a moment before unraveling, allowing the boat to pull away from the dock with the rope trailing behind.

Just before she escaped, Eddie jumped, landing in the back of the boat. She turned the wheel, sending the boat crazily careening away from the dock.

Eddie hadn't regained his footing and the motion sent him crashing around the back of the boat. Letting the wheel go, she would reach for her gun just before he grabbed her.

"Stop it," she said, willing away the images that had felt all too real, causing her adrenaline to surge even further.

"What'd you say?" Eddie called through the back door.

"Nothing," she answered, rejecting the boat scene fantasy.

"Well, come see these guys. I caught a couple of big ones."

She looked through the screen door. Eddie stood on the back deck, a small knife in his hand.

She clutched her purse closer, sliding her hand inside to feel the reassuring metal of the gun. But, this was Eddie. He wasn't going to do anything that would harm her. Not Eddie.

"These'll make some good eating," he said, while scaling the larger of the two. The knife scraped across the skin with a rasp, then with one quick slash, he severed the head.

Some innate sense of self-protection told her not to ask about the articles and her photo. Or about the journal. Not now, while she was this far away from help.

Eddie looked up at her. "What?" he asked, gripping the knife in his hand, a funny expression on his face.

It was a small knife but it had sliced through the fish so easily. The knife held her complete attention, her gaze fixed on it, alert for any move that hinted of aggression. Eddie stared at her for a moment, then set the knife beside the fish.

Relief edged along her nerves. She'd have a second of warning if he went for it.

"I think we ought to get on back to town before it gets dark." She worked to control her voice, keeping it level and casual. Forcing the panic out of it that raced through her body.

He looked at her then back at the fish. "I thought we might spend the night and go back tomorrow."

She glanced away, measuring the distance to the dock from the side steps. Her heart beat a rapid pulse in her temple.

If she broke and ran, would he chase her down?

No one would hear her scream.

Was he also measuring the distance between them?

"Jenna," he said.

She started, every muscle in her body jerking in alarm. But she had to hide it, had to keep her face impassive and casual. Her life could depend on it.

The image of the dead man in New Orleans flashed through her mind.

Could Eddie outrun her?

Of course he could. Bigger, stronger, faster. His loose-limbed, tall, muscled body that had seemed attractive, now looked like a threat.

His gaze lingered on her face for a long moment, like a mist on the bayou before a rainstorm, before all hell broke loose.

"We can put these fellows on ice and cook them up at my house," he said.

Relief washed over her, leaving her weak and shaky. She just had to hold on until they got out of there, until they got back to civilization. She didn't have to say anything about what she'd found. Just wait until they got back to town.

If they got back to town.

She gripped the gun tighter.

******

Eddie kicked the motor, heading up the river. He'd noticed instantly something was different with her. She'd closed off. Gone was her usual expression, with the expectancy and interest she'd shown in getting to know him, with a genuine desire to learn about Genevieve and Jean Claude and everything Cajun really.

Then, suddenly, he realized.

She'd seen the articles. That had to be why she was acting so weird.

Damn. What an idiot he was.

He'd forgotten he'd left them there. How could he have overlooked that? He wouldn't say anything yet. She was too freaked. He'd wait until they got back somewhere that felt safer to her.

He could kick himself. There had been so many bizarre instances since she'd come to Louisiana. She had a right to be a little skittish. Hell, a lot freaked. Didn't help to be way off in the swamps with some guy you'd just figured to be a stalker dude.

It seemed to take forever to get back to his landing. Probably not nearly as long as it felt to her.

They docked and instantly she scrambled

out of the boat.

"Hey, what say we go on into town and get some dinner?" he called after her as she headed up the dock.

She looked over her shoulder and relief flooded her face.

"I'll just put these fish in the freezer and then we'll go."

"We're filthy." She stopped walking and brushed at her jeans.

Maybe she was feeling a bit safer if she could worry about her appearance.

"No problem. We'll go by Paulie's place and we'll fit right in. People will think we're part of the décor."

She laughed a little bit, although her face was still pale.

On the ride to Paulie's, neither of them said a word, she probably out of fear of him, he out of fear of spooking her further.

When they walked into Paulie's, their silence contrasted sharply with the scene inside the restaurant.

Voices, music, laughter. Waitresses dodging around with plates of steaming food. A small dance floor was being used to its ultimate capacity. Groups crowded around tables, eating, drinking and talking. The joint was alive with motion and sound.

She had to feel safe in this large crowd.

Paulie waved them toward a good table, close enough to the dance floor to watch but still far enough away that they could talk.

"Hey big bro," Paulie belted out over the raucous noise, jovially, light-heartedly. "Miss Lejeune, how you are?"

For all his size, no woman had ever

claimed to be afraid of Paulie. It just
wasn't possible. The man didn't have a fear
inducing bone in his oversized body. He
placed a large, reassuring, brotherly mitt
on her shoulder, and Jenna visibly relaxed,
her shoulders falling from the hunched-up
position she'd favored in his truck, as if
protecting her jugular vein.

"Hey, Paulie." She smiled and looked
like the woman Eddie had first been
attracted to.

He felt a release in his chest. It had
pained him to see her angst. It wasn't a
good look on a girl you were romancing. Not
a look he was used to.

But then the circumstances were unusual
and things had moved fast between them.
Memories of their lovemaking flooded his
brain. Skin sliding over skin, passion
flowing between them. A connection so
powerful he would never have believed the
rupture that had hit them once she'd found
his collection of her articles.

He sucked in air, willing away the
distracting images of their lovemaking.

"I'll send your waitress right over,"
Paulie said, then turned and headed toward
the front door and another group needing a
table.

Jenna looked at her menu.

He didn't care what he ate. Anything
would taste like dirt until he got this
situation settled.

"So, Jenna."

She looked up, apprehensive again.

"Something spooked you at the cabin."

She looked at him, her face blank, as
if purposefully hiding her thoughts.

"I'm guessing it was the articles

stacked up on my desk that I forgot to put away," he offered.

She half smiled. That was good. Almost like she believed he might not be crazy.

"I should apologize for scaring you that way. Must have been terrifying way down there in the boondocks."

"Down in the boondocks," she sang softly in tune to the old song. "We listen to an oldies station when I'm in the car with my mom."

He laughed, more out of relief than anything. If she could joke, she had to be feeling more normal. "Yeah, my mom listens to those all the time, too."

Then, he tilted his head, making eye contact with her. "I must have looked pretty stalkerish to you."

She smiled slightly and nodded. "The photograph of me was the kicker."

He closed his eyes and shook his head. Oh man, certified stalker.

"Busted," he conceded, opening his eyes and meeting hers with some of the sheepishness he was feeling. "Kinda high schoolish, huh?"

She twisted her mouth wryly. "Most of my stalker letters come from prison inmates. Guess I'm moving up if I've got a judge cyber-stalking me."

He laughed, then concern flooded through him again, for what she'd experienced, alone on the river, feeling vulnerable.

"I am really sorry, Jenna. It's just that I have had a bit of a crush since I started reading your articles." He leaned in, wanting to touch her. "I was so taken by your writing when an article on Hurricane

Rafael was picked up here by the local paper. I went on the paper's website to see what type person you were."

Heat flashed through him, remembering his first sight of her photo, so beautiful, so intelligent looking. Her eyes had beckoned to him.

"And when I combined that face with your words in your articles, I couldn't stop reading."

Her expression softened and she leaned forward a bit, also.

"Jenna, I was infatuated with you before I ever met you. Not a thing a guy really likes to admit to a woman he's starting to romance."

"Oh, I'm used to it. Like I said, I'm usually real big with guys in prison." She raised an eyebrow. "Get a lot of mail asking for panties I've already worn."

A laugh burst from him, followed by a punch of relief. Okay, she definitely wasn't afraid of him anymore.

She smiled a real smile. Then she leaned back, her face toughening up a bit. Not in fear but more the reporter's façade he'd seen a couple of times when she was working him for her story.

"So, how did I wind up in your courtroom?" She tapped her fingernail on the table. "Was it your cousin helping you out?"

He leaned back, holding up his hands, as if he could push away any involvement in the prank. "Jenna, I had no part in that. That would be a misuse of power." He raised an eyebrow and added, "My cousin, now, that's another story. He legitimately stopped you for running that stop sign. But, probably would have let you go with a verbal warning because that sign was so overgrown. Then he saw your name on the license!"

She laughed in spite of the tough face she'd worn a second before, once again the Jenna he'd seen just before making love to her this afternoon; soft, relaxed and trusting. Open and accepting.

"He's my cousin on my mother's side so we don't have the same last name." He smiled into her eyes. "But as soon as I saw his signature on that ticket, I knew I'd been served payback for a lifetime of childhood jokes."

Jenna laughed outright now. "So, he knew about the articles."

"Oh yeah." Eddie nodded. "We were fishing at the cabin and he saw them. Would not stop ribbing me. *When the Lejeune woman comes to town, you better watch out.* After that, he would poke me at the most unexpected moments and ask, '*You dreaming about The Lejeune Woman*?'"

Jenna smiled broadly before her face turned serious. She reached down and rustled around in her purse. He knew what it was before he even saw it.

He raised a shoulder in admission as she brought the journal to table level.

"What about this?"

He swallowed hard, then took a sip of water, trying to wash the dryness from his throat so he could speak.

"That's another story." He nodded at the journal. "I was planning to show it to you eventually. Been working up to it. Probably would have shown it to you this afternoon if your face hadn't gone pale as a sheet of paper and you got that fight or flight expression in your eyes."

He shook his head remembering. "The way you looked at that knife in my hand."

Suddenly all doubt was gone in Jenna's mind. A man who'd go to all the trouble he had to alleviate her fear was no danger at all.

If he'd wanted to harm her, this afternoon was the perfect chance.

She leaned forward and laid her hand over his. Relief seemed to flow through his body, down into his shoulders and to his hands as he turned them to clasp hers.

He didn't say anything. He didn't have to. His expression said it all.

They stared into each other's eyes for a long moment before finally she broke the contact. It felt way too intimate for this crowded location.

She'd blown the chance to make love all night with this incredible man to the sounds of the river that flowed past Genevieve and Jean Paul's final resting place.

She glanced back at him and knew that if she said the word, he'd get in the boat and drive them all the way back to the cabin.

But she couldn't wait that long. Dinner would be too long to wait.

All she really hungered for right now was him.

CHAPTER TWENTY-ONE

After they'd finished their meal, Jenna and Eddie walked out to his truck. Darkness surrounded them, and a silvery moon cast milky light through the gnarled branches of ancient trees, trees so old they might have looked down on Genevieve and Jean Claude.

An air of timelessness floated in the breeze along with an ambience of romance and expectation.

Jenna felt Eddie moving in before she saw him. The arm that had casually touched her in her lower back as they walked suddenly tightened, swinging her to him.

He turned and brought her up against his chest, both his arms enfolding her in an embrace that felt so good after all the tension of the day.

His mouth descended, touching hers gently then more passionately, intimately connecting with her, drawing her back into that space where only the two of them existed. She lost all sense of time or place, only feeling and wanting him, here, under these trees that had witnessed so much.

Then, a light slashed across the parking lot, shocking her with its brightness. A motorcycle rumbled toward them and its glaring headlight overpowered the soft moonlight.

She and Eddie pulled back from the kiss, glancing toward the motorcycle.

"Your cousin." She laughed low in her throat, immediately recognizing the officer who'd ticketed her. For no other reason, apparently, than his own amusement as a prank on his cousin.

Eddie chuckled in acknowledgement of her laugh but something more serious underlay his expression.

"So, is he here to order me to stay at your house?"

Eddie's smile seemed forced.

"You were expecting your cousin," she said, and he didn't deny it.

The cop glided toward Eddie's truck, his expression all business. This wasn't a couple of cousins meeting up for fun.

Mike killed the engine and pulled off his helmet. "Cuz," he said, then nodded his head at her. "Ma'am."

"Hey Mike." Eddie's tone said get to it.

"Got the records you asked the chief to pull. Thought you might like to see what's on the last page."

Jenna remembered seeing Eddie checking his text messages on his phone during dinner, and sending a quick reply to one, probably telling Mike or the chief where they could find him.

Mike pulled some papers from an inner pocket of his motorcycle jacket and handed them to Eddie. Flipping to the back page, Eddie tilted it toward the glow from Mike's headlight.

"Damn," Eddie said quietly.

"What?" Jenna leaned to see.

He glanced at her, his eyes narrowing, hesitating. What didn't he want her to know?

"What?" she asked insistently.

"The call to your motel room by the jerk, was made from here in Eufaula. It was from a cell phone that was bouncing off cell towers right around here, somewhere."

The phone number she'd written down had

a Louisiana area code so the fact that it had been tracked to this area didn't surprise her. "What would you expect?"

"I don't know. I guess I was hoping it wasn't anybody I might know."

She laid her hand on his arm. These people were all family and long time friends to him. She shrugged dismissively. "Maybe it's a joke, Eddie."

Mike's expression disagreed. Eddie looked at him then back at her. "We don't either of us think it's funny. Now Mike," he pointed a finger, "giving you a ticket and making you come to my courtroom, that's funny."

Mike shook his head. "I can't believe you told her, Cuz."

Eddie laughed slightly. "It slipped out."

Mike nodded knowingly, looking Eddie up and down. "I see how it is."

There was nothing ugly about the comment. More like an acknowledgement of them as a couple.

It felt good.

Then, she looked back at the phone records in Eddie's hands. "Do you know who the cell phone belongs to, that made the call?"

Mike and Eddie's faces both turned grim again. Mike shook his head. "It was a burner, a throw-away phone registered to no one."

They'd called the number afterwards and no one had answered and there'd been no message recording, thus fitting with a burner phone.

Mike glanced at Eddie and gave him a nod, then he looked back at Jenna with a kind expression. "Don't worry about anything. We're gonna find this guy. Everybody's looking out for anybody out of place. He's not gonna get away with it."

A warm feeling swept through her, of being encased in a larger community of people who surrounded her and Eddie in a net of support.

"Thanks." She smiled at him.

"Well, Cuz, ma'am," Mike said. "I'll leave you two be." He put on his helmet and drove away.

"I want to look over those records," Jenna said, reaching for them.

Eddie held onto them for a moment, hesitating.

"They're my phone records," Jenna protested.

"Okay." He handed them to her. "But you didn't get them from me. In fact, you can't quite remember how you got them in the first place."

She raised an eyebrow. "I never reveal my sources. A lot of papers get into my hands that I can't quite remember how I got."

"I forgot who I was dealing with." He laughed slightly, the masculine timbre stroking along her nerve endings with a pleasurable tingle.

She tapped one finger on his shoulder, sternly but with a playful manner, trying not to succumb to the lure of his voice, wanting to concentrate on the phone records. "Don't forget it again."

"Come on." He tilted his head toward his truck.

Where was she gonna spend the night?

A part of her wanted to go and get into

his bed and make love with him all night long.

But the grownup part said she needed some time apart. She was freaking out major earlier in the day and now she wanted to put herself into further intimate contact?

That sort of nervous uncertainty she'd experienced at the cabin came from not really knowing him all that well.

But there was a powerful drive to get to know him, an urge to put logic on hold and let their mutual attraction drive the boat.

But tonight, her logic won out.

"I think I need to stay at my place, tonight."

He arched an eyebrow suggestively.

"Alone," she added. He nodded and opened the truck door, letting her slide in.

When he shut the door, he pulled out his phone and made a quick call, then went around to the driver's side, getting in. "The chief's gonna position a patrol car outside of your motel for the night."

She nodded. "Thanks." Then, Eddie started the truck and drove toward the motel. They were both quiet, letting the shadowy road slip by, live oaks cradling the asphalt strip.

He held her hand tightly in his, driving with his left hand only. She didn't want to break the connection by going back to the motel but she had to. She needed to think. And she sure couldn't do that in his bed.

There was something about this whole situation that wasn't jelling in her mind.

When they pulled up to the motel, there was already a cop car sitting across the street. Eddie raised a hand in greeting as they drove by and she did the same. The cop waved back.

Eddie killed the lights as they slid into a space in the motel's parking lot. "You sure about staying by yourself?" he asked, turning to look at her.

She shook her head negatively. He laughed quietly.

"Me neither," he said. Then he cupped her cheek with his hand and leaned in for a kiss. He barely touched her lips, brushing his mouth across hers, yet it was more powerful than any kiss she'd ever experienced.

She pulled back and looked into his eyes.

Desire crackled in his gaze, ready to spark into a wildfire if she only said the word. But, his understanding nature didn't make it any easier to say what she had to say.

She needed time to work this out in her mind.

"Good night," she said finally.

He nodded and leaned across her to open her door. She slid out of the truck and began the long walk away from him then heard his door opening. He met her at the motel's door, holding out his hand for the key card. When she dropped it into his palm, he opened the door.

Turning the light on, he walked in, checking the bathroom, the closet and under the bed.

She laughed at the under the bed part. No human being could squeeze underneath. She'd already looked.

He slanted her a look and checked the

locks on the window. "Slide that chair in front of the door before you go to bed tonight and keep my cell phone on speed dial in case you need anything."

He'd become very macho. It would be funny if it weren't so damn attractive.

She placed her hand on his chest like *relax, it'll be fine*. But when he glanced down to where she touched him, there was no sweetness or gentleness in his eyes.

Desire. Passionate, wanting-you desire emanated from him.

He pulled her to him, into a searing kiss, a taking your mouth before he took you kiss. A flood of need surged through her, with the desire to be underneath him in the intimacy of sheets and blankets. Her skin warmed and her resistance melted.

His hands stroked down her back, pulling her into him and her body became liquid with the urges he inspired, ancient, primal needs of a woman for her man, lovers meant to be together for all time.

The bed was only feet away, soft and ready.

His mouth moved to her neck, and she knew it was now or never. She pushed him away.

She couldn't, not tonight.

"Go," she forced out the word, "Now, before I change my mind."

He stepped back, breathing deeply, the wanting you look still on him, his gaze holding hers for a long moment, and she almost relented.

But he turned and left.

Thank God. Because she couldn't have resisted much longer. She pushed the motel room door shut and leaned against it, envisioning all they could have done and all that they had done this afternoon.

Her body ached for him, fire burning through her, leaving a misty memory wherever he'd touched her.

And that was everywhere.

She opened her eyes, forcing herself to concentrate on the present. On what needed doing now.

She pushed a chair against the door and set her suitcase on top of it in a makeshift alarm system. She waited until she heard Eddie's truck drive away, then she took off her clothes and got into the shower. Hot water cascaded over her skin, feeling like Eddie's hands.

She washed quickly, then turned the water onto cool for a moment, then shut it off. Wrapping a towel around herself, she walked into the bedroom.

Pulling the curtain aside, she peeked out into the night. Nothing moved in the parking lot or on the street in front of the motel.

The cop car sat reassuringly across the road.

Smiling, she let the curtain drop then pulled a nightgown over her head. The cotton slipped over her sensitized skin.

She closed her eyes for a moment, all the sensations Eddie had evoked haunting her memory. Need for him pulsed through her, insistently, wantonly, as if telling her she would never be free of the desire for him.

She turned up the air conditioner and stood full in the blast of refrigerated air, letting it roll over her heated body.

Finally, she crawled into bed.

With her cell phone by her head, the

cop outside, and the gun sitting on the
night table, she felt secure enough to try
to sleep. But Eddie filled her head, as he'd
filled her body today. She threw off the
sheet, letting the air-conditioned breeze
brush across her skin.

Finally, finally, she drifted into
sleep.

Into a dream in which she and Eddie
danced. Or was it she and Jean Claude? Her
long flowing dress swung behind her as he
led her in a waltz, his hands strong against
her back, pulling her to him then pushing
her away to twirl.

She loved this dream in which she
danced with the man she loved and was
destined to marry and love forever.

The dream continued in some form all
night, Jean Claude kissing her, embracing
her and dancing with her. She woke several
times but drifted back into the land where
she and her love had no questions, no
issues, nothing to keep them apart.

Until a person on the edge of the dream
inserted himself into her consciousness.

He wanted them apart. He wanted her.
And if she didn't want him, no man would
have her. The fury of his anger swirled like
a tornado, ripping branches from trees,
sending leaves slicing toward them like
razor blades.

She broke away from Jean Claude,
looking for the dark presence in the
shadows. Long moments passed, the air in her
lungs contracted until she was gasping for
breath.

Then she saw an image. A man standing
far back in the night, hate blowing from his
eyes.

The man felt familiar.

He would be someone she knew if she could only see his face clearly. But he stepped back and disappeared. Then the sound of a crying baby echoed in the darkness.

She awoke with a start. Sweat dripped off her and her heart raced. Her hands shook as though she'd drunk a million cups of coffee.

She had to remember the dream and try to connect it to the real world.

What was she missing?

She'd tried to dismiss the journal pages and the note on her door as prank-like behavior but there was something very sinister to it.

Then, she remembered the crying baby from her dream.

Like the dying babies in the adjoining parish, and now here in this area.

Throwing back the sheet, she got up and put on coffee. Outside, dawn pearled the sky with dewy pinks.

Life was fresh. If only she could face it as she saw most mornings, as a new chance to investigate and report on things that mattered. Things that made sense.

Pulling on jeans and a T-shirt, she combed her hair and put on a little makeup. She made herself a cup of coffee and paced the room.

What was she missing?

Her purse lay on the dresser, the hotel phone records sticking out. Absent mindedly, she scanned through them. Her cell phone records were also there. Eddie and the local police had been thorough.

She scanned down the calls and her eye stopped at Richard's number. Like a mantra, she repeated it several times, knowing it by heart, having dialed it so many times over the years.

Then she remembered Richard telling her he was descended from a long line of military men that went all the way back to the first Chambers who'd come to this country as a British officer.

And suddenly the man in her dream had a face. Richard's face.

CHAPTER TWENTY-TWO

The realization jerked through her, wrenching her nerves into a fevered pitch. Her stomach roiled and her face felt clammy, with sweat prickling underneath her clothes.

She picked up her phone. Richard always got up early. By now, he would have had several cups of coffee, had checked the news wires, and would be getting ready for work. She called up the contact for his cell phone, her fingers shaking, making it hard to navigate to his programmed number.

Finally, she hit the right key and the phone began to dial. She held it to her ear, needing to get back in touch with reality, to know that Richard was simply the managing editor who'd mentored her, not some soldier who'd marched through time, stalking her, waiting for this moment.

The phone rang and rang. "Pick up, Richard. Damn it."

Finally the phone picked up.

"Thank God," she said, relief flowing through her. "Richard?"

Voice mail. It was just voice mail. Her lip ticked nervously and she raised a hand to still it.

"Richard, it's Jenna." Her voice cracked and she swallowed to steady it. "Call me." She wanted to add more, but reluctantly hit end. That conversation had to be in person, not left on a machine, sounding like a crazy lady.

She shot Richard a quick email from her phone, then glanced at the time again. Was it too early to call Eddie?

A knock sounded on her door and she jumped. "Jesus Christ, get a hold of yourself," she muttered. Stepping around the chair she'd jammed underneath the doorknob, she looked through the peephole.

Eddie. Thank goodness.

With unsteady hands, she pushed aside the chair, turned the deadbolt, slid the safety chain off and pulled opened the door.

"Hey." Eddie's face was lined with stress, fatigue wrinkling around his eyes. He leaned in for a quick hug, his scent surrounding her, reassuring with its familiarity.

So quickly, she'd become attuned to it, with an animal awareness of him. Wanting the contact to last, she hung on just a moment longer than a friendly hug.

He leaned back to look into her eyes, a smoky mist of desire floating there, just before he moved closer for a kiss.

Gently, he brushed his mouth across hers, just a light touch, before he pulled back, looking at her with want in his eyes. "I could so easily forget everything else but you, me and that bed," he said, glancing at the covers that had been tugged up on her bed.

"Yeah." She laughed raggedly, and stepped back, putting space between them. "Yeah." She turned toward the small in-room coffee pot. "Coffee?" she asked, pouring a cup for herself.

"Sure," he said.

She poured a second cup and handed it to him. As their fingers brushed, he smiled. That smile spoke of connection, passion, everything they could have. A million nights together in bed wouldn't be enough.

She pulled her gaze away, and took a sip of coffee.

He took a sip also, coughing afterwards. He wasn't as calm as he seemed either.

"I went through your phone records," he said, his voice gravelly and deep.

"Me, too." She nodded her head affirmatively, messaging that something had clicked with her.

"The chief had people working on them nonstop for me since the call to your motel here." He paced the floor, a great masculine force taking up way too much space in the small room.

Or just enough.

"And?"

"I found something that doesn't look right."

She raised an eyebrow inquiringly, wanting him to come to his own, independent conclusions.

He handed her a sheet of paper, pointing at a number on the list. She knew that number by heart.

"That's Richard's cell phone number. My managing editor."

"He's back in Atlanta right?"

"Right," she answered, even as she said it knowing what was coming, a sickness rising in her throat.

He tilted his head, looked away for an instant before turning his gaze back to look directly in her eyes. "His cell phone has been hitting off the cell phone towers here in the parish."

Her stomach clenched, and she put both hands over it to quiet it. This was worse than a nightmare, it was real. "I had a dream."

His eyes narrowed as he fixed them on

her. "We were dancing."

She stared at him, shock rolling through her. She turned and paced a second then turned to look deep into his eyes, finally accepting his meaning. "You had the same dream?"

"The two of us dancing, then there's a force beyond the circle of dancers, glaring malevolently at us."

Her mind worked to form words. "This can't be happening."

He stuck out his hand but stopped short of touching her, as she glanced down warningly at it.

If he touched her, she might succumb to her most vulnerable feelings, give in to weakness, and collapse into tears. She sucked in a steadying breath. Just because someone big and strong was here, didn't mean she could become dependent and weak.

She needed to remember who she was and all the stories she'd covered before. Real life was often as scary as this fantasy area they'd seemed to enter.

"Whether we're dreaming or remembering, our subconscious is giving us the keys to our survival." His clear voice cut the air as if he didn't want her to miss a single word.

She gasped, sucking in oxygen that seemed never to get to her brain. "What are you saying?"

"You know what I'm saying, Jenna." He reached for her, his hand circling the nape of her neck, pulling her close.

Tears welled up in her eyes and she pushed her face into his chest so he wouldn't see. She wrapped her arms around him, absorbing his strength, his vitality and life force. For a long moment, she just held on, forgetting everything except how he felt in her arms, next to her.

Then, reality pushed back into her consciousness, and she pulled back to look at him. "This can't be real."

His eyes were gentle yet at the same time strong. "I don't understand it so I don't expect you to either. But history is overtaking us."

She wanted to shake her head no, but he was right. "Eddie, how can this be happening?"

"Hell if I know, 'cause I don't even believe it." He gripped her upper arms. "But someone out there sure as hell takes all this legend stuff seriously."

She glanced away, then back to meet his gaze.

"And," he continued, a fierce conviction in his voice. "I'm not going to wait around for history to overtake Genevieve and Jean Claude once again."

She looked at him hard. "You mean Eddie and Jenna, don't you?"

"Whoever. Whoever this guy is coming for." He slid his hand down her arm and clasped her hand firmly. "Get your stuff together. We're getting out of here."

She shook her head. "No. I'm not running. If this is Richard, by some crazy chance, then we're not in danger." They weren't. "I've known him way too long to start thinking he's a crazy, psycho stalker."

The baby's cry from her dream echoed through her memory once again. Her mind had registered that for some reason. An important reason.

"I need to check into some things."

"Check some things?" Eddie stared at her like she was crazy. Okay, that was a pretty good bet.

"There's this guy back in Georgia," she said. "A street person, who panhandles outside of the Fulton County courthouse in downtown Atlanta. Every time I see him, he's full of crazy stories. I always just think oh that's just Crazy Joe." She shrugged. "What if they're not crazy stories? What if Crazy Joe just encountered extraordinary and unbelievable circumstances like this?" She shook her head.

"Wouldn't that be a kick in the pants?" she murmured quietly.

But she wasn't crazy, not yet anyway. But, she was seriously in danger if things didn't go well, of ending up wandering the streets, talking about her lost Cajun lover. Crazy Jenna, people would call her. People who hadn't lived her reality.

"What things do you need to check into?" Eddie's voice was deep and intense, cutting through the fog in her brain.

She thought about it for a moment, something just beyond the edge of her consciousness, something chewing at her nerves, until suddenly she knew.

"I want to go to the cemetery here in Eufaula. I visited the one over in Saint Thomasville and now I need to see the one here."

Eddie shook his head.

"Street crazy, you're thinking, right? Gonna be wandering the streets, muttering."

He cut his eyes at her but didn't grin at her joke. "Sheesh," he blew out a breath. "Okay but I'm going with you. Get your gun."

"Got it," she said, patting her purse as she hung it from her shoulder. "I might be street crazy certifiable. But I'm not stupid."

Eddie watched while she pulled the door behind her then motioned toward his truck. He gave a wave to the cop who sat on the other side of the road. The cop pulled away.

Then, together she and Eddie rode in silence, both probably trying to get a grip on this new, strange turn of events.

Finally, they reached the cemetery, a sheltered acre of ground underneath a canopy of large live oaks. The ever-present Spanish moss seemed even more appropriate in this lonely, granite and marble decorated landscape.

Were the dead trying to speak to them, to tell them what they needed to know? These meadows of the departed held secrets. Important, life-saving secrets?

She got out and began to walk up and down the lanes of family grave plots, stopping to make a note whenever she saw the resting spot for a baby.

Finally she returned to her car and pulled out her laptop, entered the information, then sat back in shock when she saw confirmed what she'd begun to suspect.

"This is unbelievable, Eddie." She turned to find him already peering at the computer page.

"That's a hell of a spread sheet you got going there."

She only nodded. Laid out in black and white it formed an easily read pattern. She'd spent hours walking through the Saint Thomasville cemetery, making notes, then had gone back into the rectory's records room for follow up information.

"Every time, the deaths start in Saint Thomasville, then shortly thereafter they switch over here to Eufaula." She looked at him hard. "And somewhere in the mix a couple dies."

"What do you think it means?"

"I don't know." She'd never seen anything like it. "This pattern jumps across generations. Whatever's causing the babies to die can't be something environmental. Otherwise, you'd have it happening continually."

"You'd think." He nodded. "But, maybe not. It could be something that sweeps down the river or comes in with a storm." His cell rang, and after a quick phone conversation, he turned back to her. "Look, I've got to go to court. There are things that couldn't be rescheduled."

"Sure. Court goes on."

He pulled her to him, holding her in a reassuring, steady manner. "I don't want you by yourself. Come to court with me."

As his arms held her, she wanted to give in, to follow him around. Not for safety as much as just so she could be near him. But she couldn't give in to this rush of emotion. It felt like the first time she'd had a boyfriend and didn't want to be away from him for even a moment.

But, she was a grown woman now, with an adult's responsibilities and obligations.

"I ain't no baby," she said emphatically, with an exaggerated country accent. With a grin, she pushed away the dependence she felt trying to grow inside her, spurred by the need to be with him. "I already told you."

He looked down at her, a frown crinkling his eyes, and sighed. There was a lot that went unsaid between them, which drifted around the edges of their conversations.

They drove back into town in near silence, she thinking about her spreadsheet and he probably thinking about what to do about her.

"It's not like you're in real danger," he finally said, in a tone meant to convince himself as well as her. "You've known that guy Richard for years. Probably just semi-obsessed with you."

She couldn't help laughing. "Yeah, he's semi-stalking me."

"Overly possessive of his employees' time? I've heard of some bad bosses before but this takes the cake."

"It would be like him," she conceded. "I am on the company dime. He's probably thinking, *I'm paying for that room. She better not be having sex in it. That's an extension of the office, since we're paying for it.*"

He half-laughed, then pulled her close for one more hug. It felt like possibly the last time she'd feel his arms around her.

Was this how Genevieve had felt when she'd said goodbye to Jean Claude the last time?

Jenna nosed into Eddie's neck, sniffing his scent. Memorizing it for eternity? She shook her head, pushing the melodramatic thought away.

"See ya," she said casually, trying not to reveal her feelings as she pushed away from him and opened the passenger door. But, she made the mistake of looking back at him.

And saw the smoky, misty passion in his eyes.

"Just damn," she said, with a little laugh, which he responded to with a grin.

"Court shouldn't take long. Keep your cell phone on."

She wanted time to pass quickly, knowing her body would be anticipating his touch every second until they were together again. Now, it hummed with want for him, murmured of the things they'd do together.

She slid out of the car, that simple act taking every bit of strength she had.

He drove away, his gaze returning often to glance at her through in the rear view mirror, only half watching the road.

She stared after him, wanting to go with him. To wait in his chambers until he got a free moment, then they'd … what? Do it in the back office?

That probably wasn't too far from the truth. He made her want to do things that were … unprofessional. To say the least.

But the memory of all those little babies prickled at her consciousness. The baby crying in her dream echoed in her head. Suddenly, passion seemed a distraction from what really mattered.

She'd finally gotten an email from the detective in New Orleans. The man they'd found dead in the hotel's alley was from outside of Eufaula. She got into her car, checked her notes for an address, then headed out of town.

Her throat clenched, nearly closing up. She swallowed hard. The New Orleans death of the *handyman* had nothing to do with her. She'd told herself that over and over since she'd read the email.

But, a little part of her knew. Knew that maybe if she followed the trail he'd left, she might find some answers.

She hadn't told Eddie what she'd planned, because she knew he would freak out.

A little part of her worried the pieces of this puzzle even as she turned her car toward the west outskirts of town to search out the dead man's family.

There were just too many stray parts to her crazy experiences since she'd hit New Orleans.

She'd check out this lead, then she'd get on to the babies and what was killing them. She was going in too many directions, as if she were writing five or six stories. But, experience told her when things happened, they happened for a reason. She had to check out this lead.

She drove down a long, winding dirt road, dodging hanging moss. Again, the perfect setting for a horror film.

That was probably just the city girl in her. Zoom would have seen the photo opportunities. She only felt nervous energy crawling up her spine.

After about five miles, she rounded a bend.

And skidded to avoid a car sitting on the side of the road, its rear end sticking partially out into the right of way.

A woman turned and ran toward Jenna's car, waving her hands, her face desperate, deep lines etching around her mouth. "Help us!"

Jenna stopped and rolled down her window. "What's the matter?"

"My daughter's having her baby and our

car just died."

Panic washed the woman's face although her voice was calm and smooth, as if for her daughter's sake.

The car was an older model that looked like it had been on its last legs for some time now. The side rear view mirror hung loose, the car's paint was worn and rusting through in spots.

Jenna met the woman's eyes with a compassionate gaze. She'd hate to be in labor, trying to get to the hospital in that thing. "Let's get her in my car," Jenna said. "I'll drive to town while you sit in the back with her."

The woman's face strained against the fear that gripped her as she shook her head. "Don't think there's time. We need to get her back to the house. It's just around this corner." She pointed further down the dirt road. "I don't want her delivering by the side of the road."

She glanced at Jenna's cell phone. "You can call for an ambulance to come out and help us." A nervous tic worked around her eyes. "I think they'll get here after the baby comes, though. Baby's coming any minute, now."

A cold wave of nervousness swept over Jenna. Dying babies. Now she was supposed to help with a home birth. If they were lucky, and it didn't happen out here on this lonely, backcountry dirt road.

Jenna nodded and got out, opening the back door of her car. "Thank goodness, I have a Jetta. Lots of room," she said in as cheery a voice as she could muster as she walked toward the other car's open back door.

The young woman probably hadn't heard a word Jenna had said. She moaned, her head back and rolling from side to side, her hands clutching her belly.

If the words weren't doctor, hospital, ambulance, or more importantly painkillers, the woman probably wouldn't hear them.

"Come on, baby," her mother took her hands and pulled her forward.

"It's coming." The girl struggled out of the car, ungainly, as large as if she were having twins.

"Just a few steps," the mother urged the woman who didn't look even twenty years old, long blonde hair hanging limply around her sweaty face. Jenna took the woman's other arm as she stumbled toward Jenna's car.

Grimacing, the pregnant woman struggled to Jenna's car and collapsed into the back seat. The mother ran around to slide in on the other side in the back seat.

Jenna jumped in the driver's seat and put the car in gear.

As she drove, she dialed 911 but got a dead sound. A bad area again. The cell coverage problem was unbelievable. Everything was stacking up against this poor girl. Jenna glanced over her shoulder at a young face that would have been beautiful if not twisted by pain.

Finally, they rounded the corner to the driveway for a typical bayou house, much like Eddie's mother's house or Eddie's house. It looked very similar to a thousand other houses but nothing about it comforted Jenna.

She wanted to see an Emergency sign and hustling nurses. But Jenna pulled in by the

front door and ran around to open the car
door for the pair in the back.

Jenna and the mother positioned
themselves one on each side of the girl to
maneuver the steps. Slowly, painfully, she
took each step as if it were five, panting
and huffing for breath.

"Let's go to the back room, that's me
and my husband's bedroom. There's a bathroom
right off it."

The girl stumbled and almost fell,
pulling her arm away from Jenna to clutch
her belly. "It's coming," she shrieked.

"We gotcha, baby," the mother cooed to
deaf ears.

"It's coming now," the girl moaned. "I
need a doctor."

"I know, baby, I know. We're going to
get you one."

They held her, supporting most of her
weight, as she shuffled one foot in front of
the other until they reached the bed. A
white coverlet topped the bed. Jenna reached
with one hand to yank it off just before the
girl collapsed onto the bed.

"Mama, the baby's coming out."

"I know, sweetie," the older woman
comforted, then turned to Jenna with an
intense nod. "Call the doctor, he's on speed
dial one. Phone's in the kitchen."

Jenna turned toward the door.

"Tell him Casey Broussard's baby is
coming."

Broussard. The same name as the dead
man from New Orleans. Jenna stopped and
glanced back.

"Call the doctor!" the woman hissed,
panic just beneath the surface.

Jenna forced herself toward the other

room. As she got to the phone on the wall by the refrigerator, she noticed stuck to the front of the appliance, a funeral announcement with a photo on its cover.

The face staring back at her was the same as the dead man who'd stared blankly back at her, face-up in the alley behind her hotel in New Orleans.

CHAPTER TWENTY-THREE

The urge to flee the house swept through her, with the desire to run out the back door, and away from this nightmare scenario. Zinging nervous fear screamed through her, shrieking, "Run! Run for your life!"

Her survival instincts told her to get out and far away. But she couldn't. If she left, the girl or her baby might die. They needed all the help they could get.

Even though she felt like she'd entered a drama where the next victim might be herself, she couldn't sacrifice the little baby who was about to be born.

This family didn't deserve two losses. She'd vowed to stop the dying babies.

She'd start with this one.

She pressed the speed dial button for the doctor's office, then spoke briefly to the woman who answered.

"Casey Broussard's baby is coming?" The receptionist's voice rose into a piercing shriek. "Oh Lord, oh Lord," she moaned. "Honey, you get back in there and help Nanette bring her grandbaby into the world. Tell her and Casey we're getting an ambulance out there right away and that the doctor will meet them at the hospital. Ya'll," she yelled away from the phone, "Casey Broussard's baby is coming. Tell the doctor."

"Oh Lord, please Lord, please Lord. Help them Jesus," the receptionist began to chant rhythmically.

When she repeated the plea a second time without speaking directly to Jenna again, Jenna hung up.

"Oh God," she muttered to herself, taking heaving breaths. If that receptionist had freaked out like she did, it wasn't good.

Jenna looked around the kitchen. "Hot water, they always ask for hot water." She rummaged underneath the counter until she found a large pot, filled it with water and placed it on the stove to boil.

The other thing they always did was wash up. She turned to the sink and lathered up her hands with dish soap, rinsed well and dried her hands with paper towels.

Steeling herself, she headed back to the bedroom, the sounds of moans drawing her quickly.

The white-faced young woman's head lolled back against the pillow as she heaved with pain.

"Casey, I want you to listen to me. I need your help now," Nanette coached her daughter.

The girl opened her eyes a slit and nodded almost imperceptibly.

"Good girl," the woman crooned. "One more push."

Jenna ran into the bathroom and grabbed a towel. When she returned to the bed, the girl's mother cut the cord with a pair of scissors, handing Jenna a small body roughly the size of a small cat. It was covered with fluids and blood.

And not breathing! The skin around the mouth was bluish, the tiny hands and feet also tinted an unpromising color.

It wasn't alive.

"She's not breathing," wailed the baby's grandmother.

"I know." Jenna looked up and realized

Nanette wasn't looking at the newborn but at Casey whose eyes were lifeless. "Neither is the baby," Jenna said.

The mother glanced briefly at the baby then back at her girl. "Help me get her off the bed so I can do CPR."

"I'm gonna give the baby CPR, just grab Casey by the shoulders and pull her off the bed," Jenna said as she checked the baby's airways the way she'd learned on a story about first responders.

"Forget the baby. I never expected it to live. Help me with my daughter."

She didn't care about the baby.

Horror rolled through Jenna. She wouldn't forsake this infant. She had to save him.

She turned the baby's tiny body over and tilted its head downward so anything stuck in its nose and throat would drain out, then she grabbed the unconscious mother's legs under one arm and helped the grandmother maneuver her to the floor.

"I'll talk you through CPR if you don't know it," Jenna said as calmly as she could muster.

The grandmother started CPR on her daughter as Jenna flipped the baby carefully back over and opened its mouth. It looked clear so Jenna placed her mouth over the tiny face, covering the nose and mouth and puffed air into the little creature.

Nanette continued pumping on her daughter's chest then blowing into her mouth.

Jenna concentrated on the little life that depended on her. She wished she'd paid closer attention to the infant CPR instruction she'd gotten as she'd participated in a class for a story about EMT medical training.

The EMT guys had joked that with her job she might need the training at some point.

And here it was.

Jenna puffed and lightly pushed on the little chest for what felt like forever. Her pulse beat in her own head, taunting her with the life force flowing through her body that she could only will into the tiny baby.

Breathe, she prayed, breathe. Finally the little chest moved. The little boy was breathing on his own. A weak whimper came from the mouth. Jenna almost collapsed with relief. Tears filled her eyes.

"Ambulance," someone yelled and banged on the front door.

"Back here," yelled Nanette.

EMT's pushed through the open front door, walking in a confident, reassuring manner with packs slung over their shoulders.

"My girl's not breathing," Nanette wailed. "Help her."

One man leaned to place two fingers to Casey's throat as the other man unfolded his pack. "She's not breathing. No pulse," the first EMT announced.

The second guy began attaching a defibrillator in a quick efficient manner.

While he did that, the first EMT took the baby and began inspecting him. "He looks stable."

"Come on, baby," Nanette said close to her daughter's ear.

"Clear," the EMT yelled and Nanette leaned back. Then, he pressed a button.

"Hold him," the EMT handed the baby to

Jenna and she looked down into the baby's blurry blue eyes. Could he see her? Did he know how important it was to her that he survived?

He seemed to look straight into her heart, as if understanding her emotions. She'd heard babies couldn't see clearly at birth.

But, she believed he sensed just how important his survival was to her. And would be to his mother, if she lived.

"Nothing, I got nothing," the second EMT said, kneeling beside Casey.

"Clear," the first EMT said, pushing the button again.

A second later, Casey suddenly gasped deeply.

"Oh, thank you Jesus, thank you God," Nanette said, raising her hands to the sky. "Thank you."

She took Casey's hand. "I'm here, baby. I'm here. You're going to be just fine."

"And so is your baby," Jenna said over Nanette's shoulder. Even if Nanette seemed unconcerned, Casey had to care, want to know. It was probably uppermost in her struggling consciousness.

One EMT ran to the ambulance, coming back with a gurney.

Quickly, they packed Casey onto the stretcher and took her to the truck. Nanette ran alongside them, never once looking back to check on the baby.

Jenna followed behind the EMT's, cradling the newest little Broussard. She'd never carried anything so precious and so young in her arms before.

Even her niece and nephew had been days old before she'd dared hold them.

"Whose car is that?" the driver motioned toward Jenna's car that sat in the driveway, the back door still open.

"Mine."

"Why don't you follow us in your car. Ma'am, you get in the front." He motioned to Nanette.

"I'm going in the back," Nanette burst out angrily, her face twisted with indignation.

"Ma'am, you'll have to ride in the front. There's not room for you and the baby seat we have to put the baby in. And the baby needs to be back there so the technician can get to the baby if he develops any problems."

Nanette glanced dismissively at the infant and got into the back anyway.

"Mrs. Broussard." The driver watched as she pulled the door closed behind her then he looked at Jenna, his eyes wide, questioning. She shook her head, like it was no use to argue with Nanette, and he weakly motioned Jenna to get into the front with him.

"If anything happens with the baby, we'll have to stop, slowing us getting the mama to the hospital," he said.

"The grandma's pretty worried about her own baby," Jenna said, making excuses for Nanette, since she knew Nanette had been Casey's champion since she looked like the little baby Jenna held in her arms now. Nanette's first loyalty was to her own baby.

"I know just how she feels," Jenna cooed to baby boy Broussard. "I'd do anything for you, now, too."

The EMT smiled at her. "Let me know if his breathing sounds labored or his color changes. He pulled out a metallic type wrapper and folded it around the towel that still swaddled him. "That'll keep his body heat in." He carefully tucked in the ends.

Then, the EMT pulled out an infant safety seat, buckled it into the front seat, and transferred the baby into it. He waved Jenna into the front seat beside the seat. "You'll be cramped but we have to do it this way. This'll slow us down too, since I can't drive fast with you not buckled in like that."

Jenna nodded and got into the front seat. As he closed the door after her, she gazed down into the baby's sweet, sleeping face. After the experience of seeing him come into the world, and breathing life into him, she felt responsible for him. She'd be this baby's champion for life.

If the Broussards ever called her and said the baby needed anything, she knew she'd be on a plane or at FEDEX sending it whatever it needed. A kidney, bone marrow, you name it.

The EMT went around to his side of the ambulance. Then they began the long drive back into town, through the deep, swampy undergrowth that crowded close to the dirt road. Mist swirled up over the road, at times almost making the route invisible.

"Man, never seen the fog this bad at this time of day," the driver muttered. He picked up his radio and called to dispatch, "We're heading in with baby Broussard and Casey Broussard."

A crackling hiss was all that answered back. The driver's face wrinkled into a deep frown. "What else can go wrong today? We had a flat tire earlier and had taken it in to get repaired when your call came in. Ours was the only available ambulance. When it rains, it pours," he finished with a weak laugh.

What else could go wrong? Jenna pulled her purse up into her lap, feeling into its depths, grasping the gun.

She looked down at the newest Broussard and touched the tiny, beautiful little boy, so exquisite, with hands the size of one of Jenna's finger pads.

"He must be premature?" Jenna looked questioningly at the driver.

"Only about a month, I think. I remember at the funeral home, the other day, talking about him being on the way and folks saying they were going to name him after Casey's daddy."

Only then did Jenna remember the dead man. "So, that was her father?"

"Yeah, really weird thing. He got killed down in New Orleans." The driver, who looked like he was only in his late twenties, shook his head. "I don't like to go to the city. Too much trouble. Go for a weekend of fun and end up dead."

Jenna looked at the baby whose granddaddy had shown up dead outside her hotel. That couldn't be a coincidence, her newfound superstition whispered.

"So, the baby was okay when he was born?" The EMT drove with one hand and fiddled with the dispatch radio with the other hand.

"No, he was born not breathing."

"Really. And how'd he get to breathing?"

"Me," she said softly, looking at the little child who might be dead now if not for her.

The EMT eyed her respectfully. "Good work. I've seen too many of these emergency home births go wrong. Babies dead when we get there and someone trying to CPR the mother. Don't know what it is lately with the luck around here."

He shook his head. "Our company services this whole parish. We've had three dead babies over in Saint Thomasville last month, one over here, now this one almost died. Our bosses are freaked we're gonna get sued."

Today wasn't about lawsuits. Today was about this little baby who'd survived. Warmth crept through her, thinking of the future this little boy could have.

"Think they'll call him little Bobby?" She stroked one feather soft little hand that looked the size of a squirrel's paw.

"Probably so, named after a grandpa he never met."

She shut her eyes tightly to guard against crying but tears squeezed between her lids. So, she opened her eyes and stared through the tears at the little blessing in the infant safety seat.

"They'll be right glad to see him when they calm down and stop worrying about his mama," the young man beside her reassured. "They'll be real grateful to ya."

She looked at the sweet, innocent eyes of the EMT, so young but the hero for so many when he showed up at the worst moment of their life.

She smiled weakly back at him.

"So many of these little fellas don't make it 'cause something goes wrong with the mama and everybody forgets about the baby, just trying to save their own daughters."

He shook his head. "They can't be blamed really for caring more about their own children than some baby they've never met," he said with a sad smile that held just a trace of the disbelief that Jenna had felt when Nanette had so quickly disregarded tiny, newborn Bobby Broussard.

"People talk about it being a curse, the trouble with the babies," he said, distracted, concentrating on his driving.

She jerked around to look at him. "A curse?"

"Crazy, huh?"

"Seems there are all sorts of curses round these parts." It became hard to catch her breath, as if it had been knocked out of her from a fall from a tree.

"Yeah. Lots of superstitions down here."

She waited for more.

He glanced t her. "People think some disease or something comes from the Lejeune folks over in Saint Thomasville. That's why people avoid them."

Another curse connecting the two families.

But, this baby was fine. This precious, little Broussard proved the curse could be broken.

The thought jolted her as strongly as if she'd been hooked up to a defibrillator. She was thinking about curses like they could be real.

Well, to hell with curses. She'd defy any ages old curse trying to steal the breath from this tiny little baby boy.

***

The low beeping of machines and the

smell of antiseptic could lull someone into believing they were assured of a positive outcome, here at the hospital, surrounded by modern medicine and well trained doctors and nurses.

But, Jenna had seen how fragile and uncertain the future was for everyone, even tiny newborns.

A purplish glow illuminated little Bobby Broussard in his bassinet, cosseted in the neonatal intensive care unit, cared for by nurses intent on securing a future for him as well as the other tiny preemies.

Only a thin piece of glass separated Jenna from him. How long had she stood here, watching him, studying him?

It took all her strength not to go in and beg to hold him. Beyond him, was the section where preemies were attached to all sorts of machines.

So much sweet innocence supported by such complicated technology.

Luckily none of that technology was needed for little Bobby Broussard. Besides the slight jaundice that an ultraviolet light was intended for, he looked great, sleeping peacefully as if he hadn't just almost died.

The day's events had left Jenna as emotionally exhausted as Bobby was physically exhausted.

It wasn't every day that she participated in an impromptu birthing session.

Here, in the well-lit corridors of the hospital, with nurses, doctors, and the best technology that modern minds could develop, the misty terror of the lonely country birth seemed far away.

But, when she'd been fighting to get Bobby breathing again as his mother lay dying, she'd felt alone and terrified about the possible outcome for the newborn, wondering would help ever arrive.

An assured outcome had seemed very far away.

A door creaked open and Nanette walked out into the hallway from the staircase. She didn't make eye contact with Jenna but walked to the window, keeping several feet between them, and stared at her grandson.

She breathed deep, heaving breaths. Then, her shoulders began to shake.

Jenna was afraid to say anything to her, remembering the vicious expression on her face when Jenna had helped the baby rather than aiding in the CPR for Casey. Although Nanette had done just fine, keeping her daughter alive until the EMT's had been able to restart her heart with the defibrillator.

Long moments passed, both of them staring at little Bobby. Finally, Nanette said, her voice quavering, breaking on the first word so that she had to start again, "I want to thank you for saving my grandbaby."

Tears stung Jenna's eyes and she started to reply but Nanette stopped her with an outstretched hand. "I know he wouldn't be here if it wasn't for you."

Jenna waited a moment to be sure Nanette wasn't going to stop her again, then said, quietly, "You had your daughter to worry about."

Nanette turned her head slightly away, and tears streamed down her cheeks. She wiped at them quickly, then turned back to

Jenna with a hard look in her eye, despite the tears that still filled them. "I know who you are."

Jenna straightened, and thought about backing away, her survival instincts warning her. Nanette's words felt like a challenge, a threat. But, Nanette didn't move forward so Jenna just waited.

"You're the one what makes the babies die."

Shock jolted through Jenna. "Me? What do you mean?"

"The curse. When the Lejeune woman comes, the babies will die," she stated flatly and definitively as if it were common knowledge.

Jenna's heart beat in her temples and suddenly all the various threads of the occurrences since she'd gotten to New Orleans and then to Eufaula seemed to pull together into one connected piece of fabric, with a single explanation. "Is that why your husband came to find me in New Orleans?"

Nanette's eyes rounded, her cheeks flushed, and she looked away. "I didn't know he'd gone," she said, defensively.

"Do you think he came to kill me or hurt me?"

"Oh no, honey." She turned and looked straight into Jenna's eyes. "My Bobby was the kindest man in the whole world." She glanced away then back. "Scare you maybe. But he would never have hurt you."

The open expression on her face, and the way she met Jenna's eyes convinced her she was telling the truth.

Or what she thought was the truth.

No telling what a father might do to protect his daughter.

But, that wasn't Nanette or Casey or little Bobby's fault.

"I'm sorry about your husband." Jenna infused as much sincerity into her tone as possible.

"Thank you, honey." Nanette nodded toward the baby. "That's my daughter's firstborn. It wouldn't have mattered to her if she'd lived if her son had died."

She gulped in a deep breath. "But, when I thought my Casey was dying, all I could think about was her." She wiped at her eyes again.

"It would have lain between us as a grievous thing if she'd found out I let her baby die in order to save her."

She pivoted fully to face Jenna, looking her over, as though wondering if the curse still held any power, now that her daughter and the baby were safely alive in a hospital.

Then, she straightened her shoulders, her mouth tight, and stuck out her hand.

Jenna looked down at it for an instant, part of her still afraid of the tough Cajun woman, then she grasped Nanette's hand between both of hers.

As their hands touched, Nanette pulled Jenna into an embrace, wrapping her free arm around Jenna's shoulders. For a long moment, Nanette held onto her. In that moment Jenna could almost feel all the resentment Nanette had felt toward Jenna, because of her husband's death, float away in a wispy trail.

Finally, with one last pat on Jenna's back, Nanette stepped back. "I have to go tell my daughter that Bobby Jr. is just fine. First thing she asked when she came to."

She smiled guiltily. "I'll never tell her what happened while she was unconscious. I hope she never knows."

Jenna smiled back, knowing primal forces had taken over the woman and she'd reacted in a way she'd had no control over. "She'll never hear it from me. I'll never speak of it to anyone."

Nanette smiled, gratitude and guilt equally mixed in her expression. With a little wave, she walked back to the stairwell and disappeared.

Jenna shivered despite the warmth of the hallway, remembering the sight of Bobby Broussard, Senior, lying face up in the alley behind her hotel.

What had been his plan for her?

Someone had killed him. To prevent him from getting to Jenna?

She picked up her cell phone and called Eddie even though he was probably still in court. Just the sound of his voice on the voice mail was reassuring. She left a message to call her as soon as he was free.

She glanced down at her stained clothing and decided to go home and shower and change. She took one more look at little Bobby, sleeping so sweetly and innocently in his hospital bassinette.

That little face emblazoned itself on her memory. So precious and so vital. Suddenly, she could imagine doing almost anything to save him. As Bobby Broussard, Sr. had sought to protect his child?

Had that meant killing the Lejeune woman who brought the danger?

A cold shiver ran through her body, straight to her bones.

* * * *

About an hour later, Eddie showed up at Jenna's motel room. She'd taken a taxi back there in order to clean up.

She told Eddie about the birth, and almost death, of Casey and little Bobby Broussard.

"Nanette said I'm the cause of the deaths of the babies," Jenna finished the story.

"What?"

"When the Lejeune Woman comes, the babies will die," she quoted exactly the words that were stamped on her brain.

The shock on Eddie's face mirrored how she'd felt when the words had originally been said to her. In fact, she could almost swear that was exactly the expression she'd seen on her face, reflected from the glass window between her and Bobby Broussard, Junior.

Then, something changed in his expression, a closing down, and he reached for her hand, taking it firmly in his with a reassuring squeeze. "Let's go talk to my mama and my grandma."

"Consult the old ladies," she murmured. "Birthing babies is women's business," she attempted a much lighter tone than she felt. "Maybe they can shed some light on this curse business."

Eddie narrowed his eyes, a lot going on behind that curtain he'd pulled shut after he'd heard Nanette's words.

They got in Eddie's truck and Eddie turned the key and backed out of his parking spot in front of Jenna's motel room.

His grandmother and mother were not going to be happy to see them together. He flipped open his cell phone and dialed his mom's house. When she didn't answer, he tried her cell phone.

"Hey, where you at, Mama?"

"We're at the hospital."

"Grandma got something wrong with her?"

His mother didn't answer, the silence hurting his ears.

"What is it, Mama?" he made himself ask.

"It's Celia. She's in labor."

Early labor. His chest compressed as if someone were squeezing his heart, and suddenly it became hard to breathe. A chilly clamminess spread across his skin and he could see himself as if from above, looking down on his truck.

He was driving to the hospital where his sister was in early labor.

And he was bringing The Lejeune Woman.

CHAPTER TWENTY-FOUR

"In labor? She's not due for almost another two months, yet," Eddie said, as though if he repeated it, she might say something different.

"I know." She sighed heavily. "I guess the baby might could be all right. They're having them much earlier than they used to and surviving. Two months is hardly anything anymore. And, Celia's due date is less far away than that."

Worry soaked her words.

"We're coming over, Mama."

"We?"

"Me and Jenna. We wanted to talk to you, anyway."

"He's got that Lejeune woman with him," his mother said to someone nearby. "Come on then, we've been wanting to talk with you both, anyway."

He'd never heard such a heavy tone from his mother, who usually laughed off most worries.

"Who's we?"

"Your granny and myself. Got some things we've been thinking of saying to you since your sister got her pains today." She sighed again, infusing the sound with so much despair. "I hope that medicine they give her stops her labor."

"When did she go into labor?"

His mother gave a long sigh. "I didn't tell you but we've been here for two nights already. She went into labor right after the fais do-do. They left the park and went straight to the hospital. They've been trying to hold off the birth, giving her steroids to help the baby's lungs develop a bit more. They say even a few days of the steroids can help at this point."

No one had told him about Celia going into labor! What did that say about what they thought Jenna's influence might have on the situation?

Eddie made a hard right and accelerated. His sister's early labor wasn't good. Then he glanced over at Jenna and he recognized the look on her face.

Babies dying.

And his sister's might be next?

"We'll be there in a few minutes, Mama."

He hung up to concentrate on his driving. His stomach clenched and churned. Celia's early labor could not be connected to all those other dead babies lying in the cemetery. What would it do to Celia if she lost the baby she'd dreamt of her entire life? He couldn't even imagine.

"Damn it all," the curse slipped out. The curse? Was this how it had started, with someone screaming to the heavens to damn the entire line of Devereaux and Lejeunes?

But, you didn't call a curse down from heaven. That sort of damnation and spite came from hell.

Who had brought this sorrow to his family?

He thought that almost as if the curse could be true.

It couldn't. He'd never believed the superstitious nonsense associated with the supposed curse.

But, now that it was his sister and her baby … Suddenly, a creeping fear gave the supposed curse new relevance.

Jenna laid her hand on his arm, patting

in a reassuring manner. But, the look in her eye said she was as worried as he was.

They screeched into a parking spot at the hospital and ran immediately to the Labor and Delivery section. Half his family was there, lining the halls, sitting in the waiting room. If he went to the cafeteria, he'd probably find the other half, eating hospital food and drinking hospital coffee.

It was like a reunion.

Except nobody was happy. The lined faces of the older folk were creased even deeper with worry, aging quicker in the last few days than in the last ten years, their mouths tight, as if to prevent any words from slipping out that might further alarm the younger folk.

When he and Jenna walked through the door, all faces turned to them, all eyes fastened on Jenna. Their eyes all said the same thing, looking at her as if she were the curse incarnate.

None of them had told him about Celia's labor, which said a lot, for his family to keep a secret. Had Mike known last night? No. He instantly knew everyone had kept Mike in the dark as well, knowing he and Eddie had grown up as tight as brothers.

He took Jenna's hand, tucking it underneath his arm, pulling her into his side, and stared everyone in his family down, until they all dropped their blaming gazes away from her.

The shudder that ran through her body told him she'd read their messages clearly.

"Where's Mama?" he asked his uncle. The old man raised a shaky hand to point down the hall.

"Come on," Eddie said to Jenna, pulling

her with him as he went to find his mother. He rounded the corner to see her talking to his granny, their heads close, their voices low.

As soon as she saw him, Eddie's mother took his granny by the arm and tilted her head to Eddie to follow them. Eddie pulled Jenna along with him. She was as much a part of this as anyone. She needed to hear what they would say. They went out into a little patio garden outside the labor area.

Greenery surrounded the spot, with a little paved path leading into a more wooded area. Benches were placed every so often along the path. It was perfect for expectant dads to pace off some of their worry when they got a moment to go outside for fresh air.

The four of them walked down the path, Eddie taking his granny's elbow so she wouldn't do the pancake flop she was so famous for, falling unexpectedly.

When they'd achieved a degree of privacy, Eddie's mother stopped and looked around, making sure no one was within earshot.

"We're not supposed to," Eddie's granny blurted out, confirming this conversation had to do with her and Eddie. Though Jenna already knew it.

"The pressure shouldn't make us do what we ought not to," Eddie's granny cautioned.

Jenna smiled reassuringly. "I know that there were many deaths in Saint Thomasville and now they're happening here. And someone told me today that I was involved. A curse?" she said, meeting their eyes, giving them permission to say it. "What's the connection?"

Margeaux hung her head for a moment, then raised it, purpose burning strong in her eyes. "They say we're not supposed to tell you but it has never gone right and how much wronger can it go than our grandbabies dying in the womb?"

Jenna laid her hand on Margeaux's forearm and Margeaux covered it with her own hand. Margeaux reached for Eddie with her other hand, forming a circle of three.

Eddie's granny stood outside the circle. "You shouldn't tell."

"Here it is," Margeaux said, with a wan acknowledging smile toward her mother. "If you do not defeat the British soldier, the Devereaux babies will die. For a year or more, they will be born dead."

Jenna winced. The British soldier?

"That seems to be about the length of the soldier's power, then it fades away until the generation after that is born." Margeaux's eyes darkened. "That generation is born innocent of the past and then he can return again, looking for his Genevieve and his Jean Claude to do battle again."

She stared fiercely into Jenna's eyes. "He wants to steal you away, and to do that he has to kill Eddie."

A shock of realization shattered Jenna. Somehow, she knew it was the truth.

Eddie broke contact with his mother and stepped back, his face pale. "You knew all of this and you didn't tell me."

Tears rushed from Margeaux's eyes, her face crumpling, showing what she'd look like as an old woman, wrinkles shriveling her face.

"I couldn't," she protested. "They say it will give the curse more power." She reached to touch Eddie's arm. "I trusted in your strength. I knew you were the one to defeat him finally."

She glanced at Jenna. "And she knew, already, somehow. Jenna is the wisest of all the Lejeune women who have come. She knew and I only confirmed." She dropped her eyes. "Perhaps that is not breaking the rules."

Jenna smiled reassuringly. "It can't go any worse than it has in the past. It is unbelievable but when I look at the data." She shook her head. "No, when I look at all those little gravestones for all those little angels, I can't help but believe the unbelievable."

Margeaux smiled, sadly.

A deep yawning sense of doom rose up in Jenna's chest. A curse coming for the lives of little babies. The next one, Eddie's little nephew. The fact that the ultrasound had shown it was a boy lent even more credence to Margeaux's words.

Then Eddie's granny stepped forward, a weak smile on her face. "As you say, it cannot go worse than it has before."

Jenna looked into her gray eyes, those knowing eyes looking out from the past with a message from long ago. "You've lived this before, haven't you?" Jenna asked quietly.

Watery emotion filled the old woman's eyes and she gazed off into the past, as if seeing images of long buried babies, men who'd wept with their women, and wailing mothers holding their dead infants.

"I have," she whispered, then she glanced at Margeaux. "Margeaux wasn't my first."

Margeaux looked away, obviously familiar with this bit of family history.

"My cousin was the Devereaux man," Granny said. "I was seven months pregnant when he was killed by the English soldier." She shook her head, grimacing, her eyes haunted with an ancient pain, not yet dead.

"My little boy was born too early." A sob wracked her and Margeaux put her arm around her mother's shoulders, hugging her tightly, their heads placed side to side.

"Now, this thing – this monster - comes to take my grandbaby's child." She looked at Eddie, tears running down her cheeks. "And to take you - to take my Eddie."

Eddie's face hardened into the mask of a warrior, his jaw tight, his eyes burning coals of anger.

"It won't take me and it won't take Celia's baby either, Granny. I promise you that." Determination coated his features, his body tense and strong, appearing to grow larger in size, into a terrifying force. It was easy to believe he could defeat any threat, real or legend.

The old woman stared into his face, as if memorizing it for all time. Eddie reached for her, hugging her tightly. His other arm closed around his mother, encapsulating the two of them in his protective embrace.

"Nobody's causing my mama or my granny any grief, I promise you that," he growled fiercely, his voice a deep rumble in his chest. "Or my sister, or anyone else I love." His eyes met Jenna's with conviction, and the message that she was included in that group of loved ones.

His mother pulled back and looked into his face, a weak grin forming. "I always knew you were extra contentious for a reason."

Eddie laughed low in his chest. "Now aren't you glad you didn't beat it out of me?"

"Your father sure wanted to, as much trouble as you caused as a kid. But I told him it might be the very thing that would save you if you were the next Jean Claude."

The next Jean Claude as if he weren't even really Eddie but a reincarnated version of his Cajun ancestor.

"Do you really believe all this, Mama?"

"How can I not, Eddie?" She shook her head fiercely. "I've heard this from the old folks and now here it is come full blown into real life, just as the old women whispered it would be."

Granny smiled darkly. "I would be one of the old women. You need to have had your firstborn to be included in the knowledge. Our people need to at least understand what is coming for us."

Jenna nodded. "How do we defeat the threat?"

Both Margeaux and Eddie's granny swiveled their heads to look at her hard, with assessing glances. His granny tilted her head in acknowledgement of Jenna.

"You and Eddie must meet him face to face, together as a couple, so that he knows you have rejected him. And you must both survive the encounter."

A chill shot through Jenna, realizing a life or death moment lay ahead of them.

"You must survive him," Eddie's granny said with a hard stare at her grandson. "If that means you kill him before he kills either of you, then so be it."

"I can do that," Eddie bit off.

"And, I," Jenna answered, feeling

strength rising in her, the strength she needed to protect Eddie and all of the Devereaux babies that might be born in the next year.

Eddie still had an arm around his mother and his other arm around his Granny.

"You must meet the British soldier and come out of the encounter alive. This must happen before Celia's baby is born," Margeaux said in a shaky voice, "or it will die."

Even now, that baby was struggling so hard to be born early, as if the curse with its evil force was trying to suck it into the world to meet a sad fate.

Fierce determination fired in Jenna.

She stretched a hand to Margeaux and another to Eddie's granny and they took it. With that touch, she completed the circle, a circle of three women and a man they all loved, joined in a pact against Hell. And whatever Hell had sent forth.

"We will defeat the curse," she vowed, meeting Eddie's gaze, seeing the same granite edged anger in his eyes that filled her.

"We will defeat the British soldier," Eddie clarified. "In whatever form he comes."

CHAPTER TWENTY-FIVE

Jenna and Eddie went to his house to regroup, to make phone calls and to think.

Especially to think.

About the unthinkable.

And to formulate a plan to deal with something that was so hard to believe. But, everything they'd seen and experienced said there was no denying it. Logic be damned.

Jenna went out onto Eddie's deck, leaned against the railing and punched in Zoom's cell phone number for the twentieth time already. "Voice mail." She hit the disconnect button then directed a few curse words at the phone.

Then, she dialed Richard's cell. "Oh, let me guess, voice mail?" His phone went straight to voice mail, as well. She immediately dialed his office number and got a recording.

"Damn the person who made voice mail." She hung up. No use leaving the same voice mail again. Adding curse words to her boss' message probably wouldn't help the situation.

Eddie was inside. He'd said he was, "Gonna cook up some food." Which was probably best so he couldn't hear her. Best not to turn into a cursing nut in front of him so early on in the relationship.

She paced the deck and weighed her options.

Call Zoom at home while he was with his family? She hated to do that. But, she had to.

His wife answered on the third ring. "Vickie, this is Jenna Lejeune," she said in the most pleasant, I'm-not-calling-about-a-curse voice she could muster. Surely, by now, Zoom had told his wife about all the crazy things he and Jenna had encountered since they'd been down in southern Louisiana.

"Jenna, it's so good to hear from you. What are you up to these days?" Vickie's voice rose as if it were a very special occasion, almost a birthday or a Christmas tone of voice.

"Oh, you know," Jenna answered, wondering why she merited that tone, though she hadn't spoken to Vickie in some time. "Still continuing on with the Cajun and New Orleans stories."

"You're back down there? You love those stories, don't you? Any excuse to take you back to that area," she trilled, with a little laugh. "I still follow your work in the paper."

Jenna held the phone by her ear for a moment. Vickie acted as if she didn't know first hand from Zoom what stories she was doing.

A nervous thrumming began along her nerve endings, tattooing anxiety throughout her veins as the blood pumped adrenalin through her.

"How's Marilyn?" Jenna asked about Zoom's little girl. "Was the break very bad?"

Vickie said nothing for a moment and the pace of Jenna's blood accelerated. "What are you talking about?" Vickie finally asked.

Jenna coughed, trying to find her voice, trying to find the right words. When she already sensed what was coming.

"Zoom said he had to go home because

Marilyn broke her arm."

Vickie sputtered. "What? That was months ago."

"I've been trying to get hold of Zoom. Is he around?" Maybe he'd just lied because he needed a break from all the Louisiana drama? God, she prayed that was true.

Vickie sucked in a long breath, then let is out slowly so that Jenna could hear it through the phone. "Jenna, Michael's not here. You know we got a divorce, don't you?"

A divorce?

A loud crashing of cymbals exploded inside her head.

Zoom had never said a word, had pretended things were just the same.

"Vickie, I didn't know." How could she have been so blind to what he was going through? "I guess Zoom just didn't want to talk about it. You know how guys are."

"Emm," Vickie murmured. "Yeah, I do. Even when I told Michael I'd gotten a lawyer, he continued to act as if we'd work everything out. When I got papers telling him he had to leave the home, he acted like it was temporary. The king of denial, that's Michael."

And Jenna had been blind to the whole thing. How could she not have noticed the stress he must have been feeling?

What else was she blind to about him? Suddenly, it began to seem like she didn't know any of the people surrounding her anymore.

But, her life had always been so normal, with things that made sense. If she'd heard a bump in the night, she thought about falling limbs, not someone breaking and entering.

Or at least that's how it had been in her life until now.

Now, an ordinary breaking and entering didn't seem so bad. That was at least *of this world*.

Not some damn curse.

How did you explain the latest happenings to the people back home? *Well, there's this curse, you see?*

Yeah, that'd get her a room at the crazy house.

"Well, sorry to hear about the divorce," Jenna forced out in what she hoped passed for a normal tone. "I wish you and the kids the best."

"Keep on writing. Love the stories," Vickie said. Then they both hung up.

Immediately, Jenna called Walton, the editorial director of the paper, someone who wasn't a usual first contact for her.

"Jenna, so good to hear from you. How them Cajuns treating ya?" Despite his college degrees and his salary, Walton was a good old boy, with no pretensions. One of her favorite things about him.

"Oh, I'm good, they're good. They are Cajuns after all. Laissez les bons temps rouler."

"Let the good times roll," Walton interpreted then belly laughed. "And the story - ya had time to do any work between the food and the music down there?"

She smiled. It was good to talk to a little bit of normal. She gave him a brief update on her story.

She hesitated before launching into the real reason for her call. Because normal was about to go out the window, if she started telling Walton about what had been happening lately.

"Walton," she started out slowly. "I can't get hold of Zoom or Richard. Are they there in the office?"

"Emm," Walton made that same sound as Vickie had, that sound that said, are you crazy or am I? "They're both down there with you, Jenna. Have you lost track of both of 'em?"

Nausea rose in her belly.

Both of them were missing and according to Walton, they were here in Louisiana. She had prayed to hear something different.

Could Richard possibly do something so weird as stalk her? Could Zoom?

Never would she have thought anything so bizarre of either of them.

She put her head back and let the sun soak into her skin, putting some emotional distance between herself and the information, letting the river's watery noises fill her mind.

"Jenna, you still there?" Walton's voice echoed distantly from the phone.

"Just a couple of days ago, Richard and you were on a conference call with me. Was Richard in the office then?"

"Nooo," he said. "Three-way calling. I piped him in, then clicked you onto the call. He said you were still at the hotel, didn't want to bother you. But, I said we all needed to touch base so we could all be on the same page."

"Oh, that's right. I'm losing track of time." She hoped her voice sounded somewhat normal, because her blood pressure was skyrocketing and doing crazy things to her right now. "Listen, do me a favor, if Zoom or Richard call, how about not mentioning this conversation?"

Walton laughed. "Don't want 'em to know you're crazy, huh?"

She forced a laugh. "They both already know that. Let's just not let them know I'm off my meds."

"Done. Hey, how about emailing whatever you've got on your stories already so I can stay in the loop."

"You're apparently more in the loop than I am."

He laughed congenially.

"Gotta go." She hung up and looked out at the river, trying to get a grip on the weirdness. After a few moments, she pushed the sliding glass door open and entered the kitchen.

Eddie sat at the kitchen table, his laptop open, searching the Internet for answers on anything he could find about the British soldier, Jean Claude or Genevieve. He'd been looking for legends surrounding them, or Eufaula. Who knew exactly what would help, he'd said. She walked up behind him and wrapped her arms around him, leaning her chest against his shoulders, her cheek close to his.

He answered with a hand wrapped backward around to grasp her thigh and pull her closer.

She loved the intensity and emotion bathing his face. His protective instincts were so strong, his desire to defend his family and find the person who threatened his sister's baby so fierce.

"Thought you said you were gonna cook." She leaned over his shoulder, checking out what he was looking at on the Internet.

"I'll throw some leftovers in the

microwave. Just wanted to see what I could find out about our friend, Richard."

"What did you find?"

"Nothing specifically interesting about him, just stuff you'd expect, like journalism awards and mentions of his work at the paper." He pointed at the laptop screen. "But I put in our British soldier and look at this."

There was hit after hit on him.

"Somebody's been doing a lot of research and documentation on the soldier."

Jenna studied the list. "Click on that one," she urged.

When Eddie opened the site, a detailed genealogical chart appeared.

"He had a daughter," Jenna said.

"Named Evangeline," Eddie finished her sentence.

"Oh my God." The words slipped from deep within her soul. "That's the same name I found in Saint Thomasville, born to Jean Claude and Genevieve two months after they were married."

Jenna followed the British soldier's genealogical chart down until she saw a name she recognized. "That's my great, great grandma, Beulah Moss Lejeune." Her mouth dried up and she couldn't force any more words out. She leaned over Eddie's shoulder and took a swig of the coke sitting by his computer.

"You're descended from the British soldier." Eddie's voice held wonder and disbelief.

What else did that family line reveal?

She drew her finger down the chart, down another branch of the family tree until she saw Richard's family name. Her gut clenched. This was impossible.

"And if I'm reading this right, I'm related to Richard as well." She heard her voice go quivery and weak. "He's also descended from the British soldier," she forced out over the nausea that rose in her throat.

"The both of you are." He glanced backward at her, making eye contact, with an expression that said he was as rocked by the information as she was.

"I don't understand it. The family name that descends from Evangeline who seems to be the English soldier's daughter is Lejeune. Why would she have that name instead of her father's name?" She looked at the long line of Lejeune's who spread out from Evangeline. Evangeline was married to a man by the name of Spradlin, yet her children are named Lejeune and that name goes on from there."

"This is some crazy-ass shit." Eddie sat back with the same shocked expression on his face that she was sure mirrored her own expression. "Oh, sorry 'bout the language."

She laughed. "If ever there was stuff to curse about, this is it. A curse calls for some cussing."

He leaned forward to scan through the rest of the British soldier's ancestry chart. He married twice and had several children, sending his genes cascading down the line."

"Obviously, the British soldier never connected with a Lejeune woman again since there are no descendants from him that connect to the Lejeune line, either in Louisiana or in Savannah," Eddie said dryly.

"I can't grasp all of this." Jenna put

a hand to her forehead. "It's like we're researching this curse as though it were possible." It couldn't be true.

"Can't it?" Eddie said as if he'd heard her thoughts.

She looked at him hard.

"I could read your face," he said with a laugh, "not your mind." Then, he pulled her around to sit on his lap, wrapping his arms around her tightly. "I don't think we have to believe in this curse or the British soldier."

He shrugged. "But, they apparently believe in us."

"Not funny." She laughed weakly.

"None of this is funny, believe me." His eyes narrowed. "Since you're descended from the British soldier, you carry his DNA."

"And part of his genetic memory?" She nodded, understanding his meaning. "Perhaps I'm The Lejeune Woman who can finally defeat him."

"Because you're battling against a part of yourself that has all the same knowledge that *the British Soldier* possesses."

She laughed harshly. "We've entered into La La Land so completely."

"La is the abbreviation for Louisiana." He squeezed her around the waist, with a reassuring pat.

Jenna laughed darkly. Despite the severity of the circumstances, despite all that was at stake, Eddie could still joke.

She turned in his arms, placing her head against his shoulder, feeling his strength, believing that if anyone could keep her safe, it would be Eddie. And she would do all that she could to protect him too. As well as his sister and his soon-to-be-born nephew.

"Celia's baby could be born at any minute," Eddie said, his face turning serious as he drummed on the table with his fingers. The sound of his fingers was like the seconds ticking by before Celia's baby came onto the planet. "If this curse is real, we have to defeat the British soldier before that happens. We don't have much time."

She nodded. "I know what we have to do." She sat back and looked into his eyes. "We have to lure him to us."

He arched an eyebrow.

"There's something else you don't know yet. Zoom is missing, as is Richard. Neither of them is in Atlanta." She patted his shoulder. "And Zoom has been keeping a lot from me. He's divorced."

"Really?" Eddie's face darkened. "He said he was going home to see his wife and kid."

"I know." She didn't want to believe anything sinister about one of her best friends. "I think he was too hurt to talk about the divorce. It was his way of hiding out in a hole until the pain of the divorce passed. It allowed him to deal with it on his own, then he would tell me later."

God, please let that be true. Please.

Zoom wasn't a stalker. Richard wasn't the British soldier. Denial could get her dead. Like all the other Lejeune women before her?

"So, we think your editor, Richard, is the one we're expecting?" Eddie's face showed all the same doubts that she was trying to push back.

"It doesn't sound good on either count, Richard or Zoom." Tears rushed to her eyes. She was losing a friend or a colleague either way. Richard might not be the bud that Zoom was but she'd always respected him and he'd pushed her to be a better writer.

"If it weren't for Richard, I don't think I would have won half the awards I've received."

Eddie patted her waist reassuringly.

"No matter how annoying some people find him, I owe him a lot. He always asked the questions that made me think, made me look for the extra angle."

Eddie just nodded. They both stood to risk someone they loved. If she didn't discover the truth about her friends, then Eddie stood to lose his sister or her unborn child, or possibly both of them.

"I think we should make our stand down the river at your cabin, where the graves of Genevieve and Jean Claude are," she said, the thought just coming to her. "There's power there. That's where it has to be." Conviction filled her with the knowledge that Genevieve and Jean Claude's essence swirled in the air at their final resting spot and would help them.

"You're right." Eddie pushed her off his lap, stood, then placed his hands on her shoulders and looked intently into her eyes. "Let's pray for all the strength that Jean Claude and Genevieve can give us, for all the power of their knowledge, as well as for the understanding of the devious and evil mind of the British soldier."

"He wasn't evil." Jenna shook her head, realizing she knew more than she should about the way the British soldier thought, as if his thoughts somehow echoed in the recesses of her mind as well as the memory of the love of Genevieve and Jean Claude. "He was just driven to do evil things by the same emotions that were for good when they found the right home. The love that Jean Claude and Genevieve shared was also the same powerful drive that twisted the British soldier into what he was."

Eddie smiled as blackly as a moonless night on the bayou. "Like I said, you may be the one who can defeat him with understanding. Cause I sure as hell have no sympathy for him."

Jenna realized that her empathy for the British soldier had come from her heart. "I do get him," she said. "Sad as he was, or is, I do get where he's coming from. *There but for the grace of God, go I*, as my mother used to say."

And for a blinding instant, she was so grateful she had found Eddie and that he returned her feelings. Fiercely, she wrapped her arms around his waist and pressed herself up against him.

He returned the embrace, pulling her close into him, with such passion that for a moment she almost forgot the danger they faced. But just as quickly, the threat reinserted itself in her consciousness and she pulled back.

Eddie nodded as though steeling himself against a similarly distracting passion. "We have to prepare for what will come."

She laughed weakly at the way he'd phrased the comment. "Your ancient DNA is raising its head. That sounds like something lifted from the bible or a classic novel."

"Or Genevieve or Jean Claude's

journals?" Eddie winked. "Okay, then speaking simply, let's get the guns and get out of here."

"Some food too."

"We can fish," Eddie said but he turned to the cabinets and began pulling out provisions.

A short time later, they were racing down the river in Eddie's boat. The misty spray flashed across her face but did nothing to erase the feeling of disbelief that filled her.

"We'll be safer at the cabin," Edie yelled over the boat's engine. "Have the home court advantage." He roared the motor full tilt.

Water flew by, putting distance between them and civilization. The cabin felt safe this time. Before, she'd felt uncertain. Now, Eddie was safe. Being with him felt reassuring.

She watched Eddie's home retreating behind them and welcomed the sight. Looking forward, she ached for the refuge of the cabin where Genevieve and Jean Claude probably had made their last stand.

Her cell phone rang. "It's Zoom." Eddie slowed the boat to almost a stall. A sick pang wrenched her stomach but she punched the button. "Hey buddy. How's it going?" She forced a natural tone.

"Hey, Jenna. You okay?"

"Yeah, Zoom. How's your kid?"

"Oh, she's okay. It'll just take some time to heal."

She wanted to blurt out questions. But she couldn't.

"I'm so glad your kid's okay. Look, Zoom, I'm going down river with Eddie for a couple of days. I kind of need a break, too."

"No problem, girl. I told you I've been holding out hope you'd get a little romance in your life." He raised his voice comically. "You go, girl."

Something about his joke sounded flat, not his usual naturally funny self. But, she laughed to continue the charade. "So, you're gonna be in Atlanta for a few days?"

"Yeah, just a few days. I really needed a break. Louisiana has lost its bloom for me."

She wanted to say more, to tell him about her fears that Richard was the stalker. And, ask Zoom why he hadn't told her about the divorce and why he'd needed to use his daughter as an excuse to leave Eufaula. But, she couldn't. She had to entice whoever was after her and Eddie down to the cabin.

It probably wasn't Zoom. But she had to put the information out there in case he talked to Richard. And she couldn't tell him what she believed about the whole Cajun curse. Who would believe it? Better to leave Zoom out of it.

Unless, of course, he included himself for nefarious purposes. A pang clenched her heart to even think her good friend could be involved.

"I'll see you soon," Zoom said.

She sensed a distance in his voice. God, she prayed for some normal reason for his behavior.

"Thanks Zoom. I'll talk to you soon." She punched the disconnect button.

Immediately, tears welled up in her eyes. Eddie leaned out a hand and pulled her back to sit by him. "It's gonna be okay."

"Everything is just so out of whack." She swiped at the tears leaking from her eyes. "I feel so betrayed. By people I thought I could trust."

He held her tightly. "It might not even be Richard's fault. He could have some imbalance."

She nodded gratefully. "I hope he doesn't have to die for us to defeat whatever this thing is?" She couldn't bring herself to say *curse* out loud. It sounded too crazy.

"Maybe we could get him some help. If it is him," she finished lamely. They'd already convicted him in their minds.

"Couldn't there be some other explanation for his cell phone being tracked to this area?" She pulled back to search Eddie's face for some sign he might believe that.

"Maybe there's some reason he's in the area he didn't tell you. Coming down to check up on you?" He glanced away. "Anyway, let's not worry about it. The entire police force is looking for anybody they don't know coming through town or on the river. They may get this British soldier before we do. Then, they can bring him to us in a controlled manner to confront him."

"Thank goodness for cousins," she joked. "But, the town's gonna get labeled a speed trap."

He smiled at her half-hearted attempt at humor.

"Anyway," she said. "I have to let Richard know where we are. We have to bring him to us as quickly as possible, if it is him. For your sister's sake." She looked down at her cell phone screen and punched up Richard's number then hit dial.

It instantly went to voice mail so she left a message after the beep. "Richard, it's Jenna. I've been trying to get hold of you. I'm going down the river to a place where my Cajun couple is buried. It's about fifteen miles down there. No way to email any of my story 'cause the reception is so bad. I'll call you when I get back and let you know what else I know. It's turning out to be a pretty good story. Talk to you later."

She hung up, her stomach churning like a rain swept bayou.

Eddie powered up the engine, driving them closer and closer to where it had to happen, where it might have originally occurred since Genevieve and Jean Claude were buried there.

This whole nightmarish thing had to end. For good. Hopefully, in she and Eddie's favor. Or, the babies would die, according to Eddie's mother and granny.

Celia's baby would die.

When they reached the pier, Eddie grabbed their bags and dropped them just inside the cabin's front door.

"Before we leave here, we'll have everything settled, hopefully." He glanced back at her, his eyes giving nothing away as to any anxiety he might be feeling.

Settled? *Settled* could mean both of them dead.

He stood there, in jeans, looking like the best thing she'd never seen in her life.

A man worth dying for?

If that's what it took to finish this curse.

More like a man who'd make life worth living. For the rest of her life?

Damn, she was thinking about the curse as if it were real. What was real for sure? The way that man looked, the intelligence, and warmth in those chocolate-colored eyes.

She walked to him and wrapped her arms around him, leaning her head against his chest. He enclosed her in his arms, and having nothing to do with the stalker thing, or a curse, it felt so right. There was nowhere else she wanted to be.

"Time to put this curse to bed," she said into his chest.

He laughed huskily, and the sound rumbled from deep inside of him, coming through his skin, vibrating against her cheek.

Eddie looked down at the top of her head. That silky honey blonde hair that had been so beautiful when he first met her still made him want to dive his face into it. But he couldn't let his guard down. He needed to be alert to any possibility of danger.

"The police chief has people watching the river, a couple of guys on either side so they'll spot anyone coming up that way," he said, talking to distract himself from what he wanted to do to her right now, as much as to reassure her.

"They've also got somebody watching a little dirt road that comes in the back way. Hardly anybody knows about it. But, just in case."

He shrugged. "They'll get anybody trying to sneak in here. The chances of someone actually making it to the cabin are slim. They'll surround him, make him listen to reason. Make him get help."

He'd kept talking to avoid thinking of the bed that was visible through the open doorway. He was damned if he'd take advantage of the situation.

Sure they'd made love before but now was different.

Now, she was forced into close contact with him. She really ought to leave and get as far away from him as possible. But, she was putting her life on the line for his family.

The thought shook him.

That she was willing to do so much to help his family. Because that's the type of person she was, with her journalistic drive to unearth the truth and to help others.

After all of this was over, she would leave. In a car, on a plane, or in a body bag.

After they'd confronted their apparent joined past. When they'd defeated the British soldier, if they defeated him, after her story was finished, after they'd put this to rest, she'd go back to her life in Atlanta. All he'd have left of her would be articles that he could read online at the paper's website.

He'd yet to meet a woman who wasn't from Eufaula who didn't visibly balk at the idea that the small town was where he wanted to spend his life.

Jenna's blonde silky hair didn't look like it had any part of Cajun in its genetic material. He should have learned his lesson with Lidia, learned to stick with his own kind and choose a nice Cajun girl.

Not another girl from the outside, the exotic.

But, those types of problems were so far down the road. Now, they just needed to concentrate on staying alive.

He tilted his head back, looking at her face.

He wanted to make love to her. But he couldn't with all the pressures she had to be feeling.

"Let's get out of here," he said, pushing her gently away. "Want to go fishing?"

She laughed. "Fishing? We're being hunted by a cursed killer and you want to go fishing."

"Hunted by a cursed killer? Look who's being dramatic." He pulled a face for her sake. They really were safe up here. He'd always felt secure at the cabin, felt it was where he belonged. With all his cousins, brothers and the rest of the police force watching them, they'd probably arrest the supposed *British soldier* long before he'd had a chance to reach them.

Would that satisfy the curse, a prison cell for the stalking nutcase?

Instinctively, he'd fled with Jenna here.

But, despite knowing heartache lay ahead for him, he still wanted to take her to that bedroom and connect with her on every level, physically and emotionally, making the most of whatever time they had left. Before the intense confrontation started.

Instead, he tilted his head toward the river. "Let's go fishing while the fishing's good. You never know when it's going to be your last day on earth anyway. Might as well spend your time doing what you love."

Before he could turn away, something flashed in her eyes, like the flames of a fire that started deep inside her.

Reaching for his shirt, she fisted the material in her hand, tugging him closer.

He allowed her to pull his head down, until only a millimeter of air separated them. A whisper floated from her mouth or was it a sigh?

Either way, there was no mistaking the invitation.

Passionately, hungrily, he took her mouth, and she returned the kiss as if she'd been waiting for this moment for several lifetimes, hot and eager.

Finally she pulled back and looked into his eyes. "If it were my last day on earth, I sure as hell wouldn't spend it fishing when I could be making love with you." A misty passion glazed her eyes, like fog rising off the bayou after a rainstorm. "It will take whoever's coming for us longer than tonight to figure out where this cabin is and then to try to sneak up here. Even then, I'm betting the police or the sheriff will get them first."

She arched an eyebrow, with a hungry glint in her eyes and his self-control relented with a fiery whipping force. Need pulsed through his body, a desire that would not be denied.

He lifted her in his arms and carried her into the bedroom. Tonight might be all they had, whether life pulled them apart or death separated them.

He intended to make the most of the time.

CHAPTER TWENTY-SEVEN

He pushed through the dense underbrush where these damned Cajuns chose to live. Just like them to exist here in this swamp, infested with snakes and gnarled clinging vines.

It was time to finish this. The Cajun was going to die. Genevieve would be his and the Cajun's line would pay. They knew Genevieve was his, yet they always enticed her down here for the dirty savage Cajun. Genevieve had searched out her Jean Claude and now he would be destroyed. Genevieve would come back to Georgia and they would live together as they were destined to.

The Cajun would never see him coming, wouldn't suspect a thing.

Until it was too late.

****

Jenna lay in a post lovemaking haze. It was known the world over as post-coital bliss. But that was way too tacky to describe what she felt.

No one could feel as connected as she felt to Eddie, as right, spooned in against his stomach.

"Eddie," she said, and he softly ran his hand down her back from shoulder to thigh.

"Emmm," he murmured.

"Do you believe we've lived before?"

Nothing.

"That we are Jean Claude and Genevieve?" she prompted.

He laughed low in his throat then lifted her hair to kiss the back of her neck.

"I can certainly see why I'd come back century after century for you," he said in a husky voice.

She laughed, his nuzzling sending sensations through her, warming her almost as much as the flattery. She pulled his arms tighter around her, nestling back into him.

That brought a definite reaction in spite of their recent bout of lovemaking.

She rolled over in his arms and his mouth moved in but just a whisper away, she hesitated. "I would come back looking for you too, Eddie."

His eyes darkened with passion and he kissed her as if it were a pact they were signing for the centuries. Tears came to her eyes as she returned the kiss, squirming to get closer and closer to him.

She couldn't get near enough. She wanted to join with him as tightly as possible.

When he entered her, she looked up into his face, studying it, memorizing it as if she would be searching for him in another lifetime, hoping to recognize him.

The thought of losing him was so wrong.

He built momentum, pushing into her as though he too felt this frenzy of wanting to preserve something that could so easily be lost.

Finally, he called out her name, possessing her with a masculine force.

Physically, it was too much.

Emotionally, it was just enough.

Later, they lay relaxed and lazy again. "I do feel as though I've known you much longer than the time it's been, Eddie."

He nodded.

"The chemistry is so right," she added.

He ran a hand across her cheek, cupping her face with his palm. "You're gonna kill me, baby, if you keep talking like that."

She laughed. "It's a feminine plot to
get as much cuddling as I want."

His jaw tightened. "You can have all
you want any day."

She kissed him lightly. "Next week
then."

He glanced away, not acknowledging that
they might not have a next week.

Then, he looked back at her, meeting
her gaze hard and direct. "I can't say we've
lived before or that we carry their genetic
memory, but there is something so bizarre
about how we click." He shrugged. "As if
we've known each other before."

"So deja vous-ish," she added.

"I don't know about any of this lived-
before stuff." He narrowed his eyes with a
sensuality that connected with her stomach,
sending a passionate swirl through it, and
he moved in close to her mouth. "We just
need to listen to our hearts."

She cuddled closer, soaking in his
pheromones. A lazy air of contentment curled
around them, disturbed only by a slight
breeze of desire. He pulled her tightly
against him again, skin against skin, heart
close to heart.

Then …

Finally, much later, they strolled out
onto the front porch. The sun cast its last
fading haze across the river, the time so
much more precious because it was the last
hour of daylight.

Eddie definitely was going fishing now.
"We gotta eat," he said, with a dramatically
manly gesture, puffing out his chest.

But fishing? Today? After all that
loving? No. "I'm gonna go back to the

gravesite," she said.

"You got your gun?"

She patted her small, cross-body purse she'd slung across her chest. "Got it right here."

He winked. "Smart girl. Keep it close, just to be safe." He downplayed it in his tone but his eyes betrayed his worry. "Can't be too careful. He'll probably wait until dawn to come anyway, so he'll have more hours of daylight. Besides all the cops between him and us."

"Got it." She watched as he walked to the pier, his strong back looking like it could stand between her and any danger.

Then she turned and headed up the path that wound through the peaceful woods behind the cabin, quiet with an aura as though nothing bad could happen there.

When she entered the clearing that held the graves, she circled the area, looking at the flowers, reading the inscription on the tombstones. Were Genevieve and Jean Claude really there?

How could the space feel so peaceful if it were the final resting place for two tortured lovers?

As she reached a far corner of the landscaped garden in the middle of the wilds, she stopped by a gardenia bush, smelling a blossom. As she leaned forward, a glimmer of copper sparkled out from underneath the dirt.

What was that?

She brushed away the earth with her foot, then leaned to smooth away more with her hands to reveal a plaque. It peeked from beneath the dirt, as though long forgotten. *Listen to your heart. Those* words were emblazoned on the metal plate. The same words Eddie had spoken to her in the bedroom. Her stomach clenched. But, it probably had a simple explanation.

Eddie must have seen it at some point. Was that why he'd said those words? Had they become something of a family mantra? Or had the words come from somewhere in his subconscious?

She stared at the plaque, breathing in the air where the lovers lay. A sense of strength and purpose filled her.

She'd worried about the geographical problem with she and Eddie before, about the impact on their careers if one of them moved. But now, she realized those were such insignificant problems.

When you finally found someone you could love as much as she knew she could love Eddie, you couldn't let such a small detail as five hundred miles come between you.

Not these days, with planes and cars. It was a problem that a couple of guys with a moving van could solve. And a lifetime of being married to a career suddenly sounded so pitiful.

She wanted a lifetime of Eddie. And Eddie's babies.

Whether she moved or Eddie moved was inconsequential.

Something told her that neither of them would be able to let the distance come between them.

Looking down at the gravestones reaffirmed that life could be over so quickly. Even a normal lifetime spent loving Eddie wouldn't be enough.

"Are you speaking to me, Jean Claude

and Genevieve?"

She waited, listening to the whispering of the wind through the trees, the birds calling to their mates. All of the sounds blended together into a mysterious voice of the wilderness. Was that Jean Claude or Genevieve whispering to her through time?

Then, the ridiculousness hit her and she laughed. At the crazy woman, standing in the middle of the Louisiana swamps talking to long dead lovers.

****

Eddie played his line, waiting for a bite, when a small sound in the brush caught his attention. He pretended to continue fishing but reached one hand to his waist to take hold of his gun.

A sixth sense played along his skin, telling him it was a human in the bushes, sneaking closer to him. An ancient warning in his DNA said it was the English soldier.

Crazy, to think of the predator that way, but hell, he might as well since that was who the man seemed to think he was.

This guy was smarter than any of them had figured. To find this place, and get past all the police lined along the river, he had to be wily.

Well, his string of luck was about to end. Slowly, Eddie extracted his gun, locking his fingers into place on the handle.

Dropping his fishing pole, he rolled behind one of the wooden pillars that supported the pier, hiding as much of his body from the line of fire as possible.

A man stepped out of the woods.

"Zoom," Eddie whispered in disbelief. He'd expected an unknown person to appear.

Eddie rose to one knee.

"Zoom," he said louder, greeting him as if he'd been waiting for him. "Jenna's been worried about you."

Zoom walked toward the pier, a gun extended, pointing at Eddie. His gaze was intense, feverish almost, glancing all around.

Eddie stayed with half his body hidden, ready to duck fully behind the pillar for cover, his gun behind the pillar where Zoom couldn't see it.

"Where is Jenna?" Zoom advanced, his expression harsh, his eyes narrowing. "What'd you do to her?"

"She's there." He nodded his head toward the path Jenna had taken. "She's up at the cemetery."

"The cemetery?" Zoom stalked toward the pier, taking quick, shallow breaths. "You killed her?"

"Zoom," Eddie said emphatically. "I haven't done anything to her. She's fine."

"Really, where is she? Jenna!" Zoom yelled in a crazed, shrieking tone. "Jenna!"

He listened for a second, then screamed, "Bastard! You killed her." He ran toward Eddie, his gun extended, reaching the foot of the pier.

Eddie had no choice. Zoom was getting too close and from the expression on his face, he wasn't in a reasonable mood.

"Stop!" Eddie yelled, showing his gun. "Drop your weapon."

Zoom's eyes narrowed. He brought the gun higher, aiming. Eddie finally was forced to pull the trigger.

The bullet hit Zoom's shoulder and a burst of red exploded on his shirt. He crumpled against the first pillar of the dock, then collapsed into a heap, the gun sliding out of his grasp.

Eddie jumped up and ran forward to grab Zoom's gun before he recovered. Just then, a gunshot erupted from the woods and a fiery ripping pain tore through Eddie's left side.

He grabbed his side, the pain bringing him to his knees, but he managed to keep hold of his gun and roll so that he was partially protected by another of the large pillars that supported the pier.

From where the gunshot had come, someone emerged, walking from the woods along the bank of the river.

A large man with a gun. And he was holding something in his arms.

Eddie's eyes watered from the pain but he trained his gun on the man while trying to figure out what the guy was holding.

It was a closely wrapped blue bundle, held in front of his body like a shield to block gunshots to his torso.

The man smiled malevolently and turned the bundle so Eddie could see more clearly.

A tiny face was just visible from this distance. There was no mistaking the fact that it was a baby.

A sickening jolt shuddered throughout Eddie's entire body at the juxtaposition of the innocent face of the baby with the evil expression of the man.

The bastard playfully swung his arm, as if at any moment, he might toss the infant into the river. "Rock a bye, baby, in the treetop, when the wind blows the baby will drop."

He laughed. "This is your third cousin, I believe. Little Bobby Broussard."

The baby Jenna had saved that very morning. If this monster threw it into the river, that baby would sink like a stone.

Saved in the morning from the power of the curse, only to die at the hands of this beast in the evening.

This man had somehow managed to get a baby out of the neonatal intensive care unit of a hospital? Suddenly, the curse seemed very real.

"Put him down," Eddie yelled, aiming for the bastard's head.

The guy swung his arm again. "You shoot and I promise you, the last thing I will ever do is throw this baby in the water." Then, he turned the gun toward the baby. "If I don't shoot him first."

He actually placed the gun on the baby's belly.

"Put your gun down if you don't want me to shoot this cute little cousin of yooouurs." He yodeled the last word out as he walked closer, an evil smile on his lips.

If Eddie shot him in the head, would he reflexively fire off his weapon, killing the baby?

*****

A cracking gunshot reverberated through the trees. Jenna jumped and instinctively raised her hands in a protective defense before she realized the noise had come from some distance.

She sucked in a breath and listened for any further sound.

Yelling filtered through the woods.

She ripped the gun from her purse and flipped back the safety lock.

Who was shooting? Was it Eddie shooting defensively or someone trying to kill him?

She had to help him.

An explosive first step took her past the gravestone and halfway across the clearing. Then she was pounding down the dirt path toward Eddie, the gun ready in her hand.

Moss and branches raked her clothing and arms with a fiery painful clawing. But she couldn't stop. She had to help Eddie.

Loud, angry voices ricocheted from beyond the cabin. She couldn't make out who was yelling.

Finally, she burst from the woods and rounded the cabin, then jerked to a halt, skidding in the dirt she stopped so fast. Near the foot of the dock, were Eddie, Zoom and Richard.

Eddie lay on the pier, propped on an elbow. Blood covered the left side of his shirt in a crazy explosion of red.

Zoom's body lay crumpled and motionless. Richard stood near the foot of the pier, a gun extended toward Eddie.

Hate burned from Eddie's eyes as he seemed to struggle to keep his gun leveled at Richard.

Why didn't he just shoot Richard?

She held her gun straight in front of her as she ran from the woods. "Stay back, Jenna," Eddie yelled then placed his gun on the pier, his gaze connecting with hers.

Richard turned to look at her, a smile spreading across his face as if this were just any other day, an editorial meeting. How could he be so duplicitous? And crazy?

"Eddie," she yelled, keeping her gun trained on Richard. "Are you all right?"

"I'll live," he replied.

Richard grunted like he doubted it.

"Zoom," she called. No answer.

Richard half turned toward her and her attention focused on the blue bundle he held in his arm. It almost looked like … a baby.

"He shot Zoom," Richard barked angrily, his usual indignation and self-righteousness on full display.

"I had no choice." Eddie tried to lift himself up but Richard looked back and pointed his gun menacingly at him.

Despite the danger to her, Eddie, and Zoom, all Jenna could focus on was that tiny bundle held in Richard's arms.

Was it a baby? Oh, God, she prayed, not a baby.

"He lured you down here, Jenna." Richard flashed her a glance. "This has been some kind of insane plot all along. Zoom's kept me informed. He's been following this guy since the start, telling me of his suspicions."

A shock jolted through her. She studied his face. His expression was convincing, almost as though he believed it.

"Cajun Devereaux here has some crazy idea that you are his long lost love from a past time." Richard's voice rose in pitch.

She glanced at Eddie.

Richard motioned with his gun at Eddie. "He has been following you and watching you. Zoom never went to Atlanta. He called me and told me what was going on. He was terrified for you, but was afraid to say anything, said you'd fallen under some sort of spell by this guy. He brought me up the river to find you. And this bastard shot him."

Eddie looked at her, shaking his head. "Ask him what he's holding in that blanket."

Richard turned so that the bundle was

almost completely hidden by his body.

"It's nothing," Richard said, dismissively.

"Show it to me," she said softly, soothingly as she paced closer.

"He has the Broussard baby."

Jenna jerked her gaze back to the half-visible piece of cloth.

"I had to," Richard said simply. "I was afraid someone would kill it. They have some sort of crazy logic going on involving these babies. They kill them if they survive birth."

Jenna glanced at Eddie.

Eddie raised an eyebrow, shaking his head dismissively. "Listen to your heart."

The words written on the copper plaque. Their mantra? The mantra of all the other Genevieves and Jean Claudes?

Such simple words, yet so powerful.

A wave of conviction and certainty of the truth rushed through her, bringing with it a surge of power. This was the moment of their disaster. A moment that had been coming for centuries. And somehow this infant had been brought right into the middle of the conflict.

That bastard had brought him here as a pawn.

She raised her gun a bit, leveling it at Richard's head. Could she hit him square in the head from this distance? She began walking closer.

Richard's eyes widened as if he recognized the decision she'd made, to believe this whole crazy nightmare scenario was real. A split second later, his face exploded in rage.

"Don't you get it," he yelled, his gun

waving wildly toward Eddie. With just a quick movement of his finger, Eddie could be dead. He was already injured and could bleed out as she listened to this idiot spout his foolishness.

"This guy has been luring you to him every time we all are reborn," he growled, his voice taking on an increased air of lunacy, of someone gone over the edge of the rapids of crazy.

She'd heard that tone before, in a man who'd taken hostages in a SWAT standoff in Atlanta, yelling his demands out the window to the cops. They'd provided everything he asked for, but finally the man had killed the woman and two children he'd held at gunpoint anyway.

Negotiating with a madman was a losing enterprise. She had to save Eddie from this lunatic.

"You are mine." The words rumbled from deep inside Richard's chest, fueled by testosterone and an ancient feeling of entitlement, a man unable to accept rejection.

Stalking through time? Couldn't get a restraining order for that.

"Mine," he continued raving, his voice rising higher in tone. "Not his. You promised yourself to me."

"I saw Genevieve's journal, Richard," she pleaded, hoping to lure him back to sanity. "She loved Jean Claude."

"But that bastard disappeared on her." Richard's face glowered with anger and resentment, blustery red blotches splattering across his skin. "He left her alone in the world to fend for herself. That's when she promised herself to me." His eyes narrowed. "She gave herself to me."

A gasp rose from deep inside Jenna, ripping painfully through her body. Genevieve's baby had been his. And instinctively, she knew Genevieve hadn't *given* herself to him. It had been rape.

And that was why when the baby grew older, the child had changed her name back to Lejeune to honor her mother.

She stared at him. They were all sinking into a maelstrom of fantasy, accepting the legend as truth, with herself even going so far as to think she remembered the rape, felt it in her body and soul, the indignity and pain she'd suffered at Richard's hands in the past.

A vengeful anger swirled up in her stomach.

But, the past was gone. With all the times Genevieve's descendants had failed.

Now was all that mattered, with her, Eddie, and the little baby that Richard held in his hands. This was their life, their chance.

"Richard, you're not him," she implored. "That was a long time ago. You can live your life differently."

"No." His eyes fixed on her, alligator eyes, cold, hard, focused on their next meal – Jenna as a sacrifice to his twisted desire. "I've always known you were her come back. From the moment I saw you."

The longer she kept him talking the more chance they had to get the baby safely away from him. The more chance to overpower Richard, or for help to come. She was making conversation but her thoughts were on that little baby she'd held in her arms this morning.

She had to save that baby.

Shivers ran through her. The enormity of the moment almost overwhelmed her but she sucked in a deep breath. "When I applied for the job at the paper?" How long ago was that?

"No." Richard's face twisted in a laughing, ugly, pompous grimace. "I saw you before that. A long time before that. At a news conference in Savannah, when you worked for that little paper."

"Oh my God."

"Exactly." He nodded and moved closer to her, his eyes narrowing with intensity into little beady points of passionate lunacy. "In this time and many others, I've searched you out." He closed the distance between them by half. "I've waited so long for you."

"Stay away from her!" Eddie yelled, struggling to get up.

"You stay out of it, you inconsequential bastard." Richard menaced Eddie with the gun.

"Don't," Jenna said quietly to Eddie, reading his intention to reach the gun lying on the dock. She stepped closer to Richard, to draw his attention back to herself. "Richard, you told my editor in Savannah about the opening at the paper in Atlanta?" It all fit together so perfectly now, Richard stalking her when she'd been a rookie reporter.

She inched closer to him. If she could get her hands on the baby, maybe Eddie could leap on Richard or get the gun and subdue Richard.

She had to get Bobbie Broussard away from this lunatic.

"I brought you to me," Richard taunted with a smarmy sense of power and entitlement, with a right to own whatever woman he chose. "Finally, finally, we can be together. It's taken multiple lifetimes but finally you will be mine."

"What about the journal sent to my hotel?"

"Me," he said, with self-satisfaction. "You needed to find him. I wouldn't know who he was. Only you would recognize the Cajun loser."

He continued on in that self-satisfied tone, "You had to reject him yourself. I had to bring you back to him, to see that he was nothing and then you would realize, finally, that you were mine."

She sucked in a harsh breath that scraped down her windpipe, all the way to her lungs, with the realization of the enormity of his confession, all that it meant.

"You killed that man near my hotel in New Orleans."

His eyes flickered away then returned to look intently into her eyes. "He would have killed you to keep you away from the Cajun. I saved your life."

"Oh, Richard." He'd killed once, he could do it again.

"And the copy of the portrait?" she prompted. "Someone slipped it under my door at the hotel."

"I have no idea where that came from. Some of these damned Cajuns maybe, the Lejeune side that wanted you to come, to deflect the curse off onto the Devereaux line."

She reached her hand out as if to touch

Richard's arm but really she was reaching for the baby.

With a wicked twist to his mouth, he turned sideways, putting more distance between her and the bundle. "This will be our child. He will replace the child you left behind when I took you back to Savannah." He shook his head apologetically. "I never should have made you leave your little boy behind in Lafayette, even if it was his." He leveled a hate-filled glare at Eddie.

He was deep into his delusional fantasy. If she could only shake him loose from his psychosis, bring him back to himself, as Richard, the managing editor.

"None of this ever happened before," she said pleadingly. Although, it all seemed too real to her, as though she'd fought this battle many times. "We aren't *them*."

"Yes." He nodded savagely. "We are *them*. I have to kill him so he can't pursue us and hurt you. He will never rest until he has you. He will chase us forever."

"I love him, Richard." She stared deeply into his crazed eyes, willing back the sane man she'd thought she'd known before.

Rage flooded his eyes, hate erupting from his pores, with a sheen of crazy that covered his face. "No," he spit at her, his mouth twisting. "You must choose me." He turned the gun toward her and an explosion rent the air.

The sound waves ricocheted along her nerves, jangling her senses, making her unsure of who had just fired. She stumbled but still kept her gun toward Richard.

Zoom groaned, his arm extended. He'd

shot Richard but that seemed to use all the energy he could muster because he fell backwards again, his face sagging with pain and weakness.

Richard clutched his side and turned toward Zoom pointing his gun. But Eddie lunged forward to grab Richard's leg, pulling him off balance.

Little Bobby Broussard wailed in a high pitched baby's cry of distress.

With a vicious grunt, Richard tossed the blanketed bundle into the river.

"No!" Jenna screamed as the baby disappeared. Instinctively, she dove into the dark water.

Blackness swirled before her face. She couldn't see anything, didn't know which way to swim. Then, suddenly a beam of the last evening sun broke through the water and illuminated a small bundle sinking to the river bottom.

She had only a second before the darkness would swallow him again.

Kicking powerfully, Jenna propelled herself forward and latched onto the swaddled baby. She pulled it to her chest, holding it there.

Thank God. Now, if she could get him out of this murky nightmare of a river. Just to the edge of her vision, she saw something move. Maybe an alligator coming for her or the baby?

Her heart rocketed into her chest, and she kicked away from the dark, moving form, ready to jab into the face of a watery onslaught of death. No damned gator would take this baby. She'd die before she let that happen.

With her free hand, she swam for the

surface, breaking into the air with a gasp
of relief.

Pulling toward the dock, she grabbed
the side and lifted the baby onto the wooden
surface. Then, she struggled to pull herself
up onto the dock, wanting to shriek with
fear that at any moment, a gator could latch
onto her legs and pull her under.

Her water-soaked clothes pulled her
back toward the dark water with a sucking
draw that felt almost like death trying to
pull her back into the realm of the gator.

A scream formed deep in her gut, but
she held it in, knowing it would use energy
she needed to reach the infant. To make sure
it was breathing.

Zoom lifted himself onto one arm and
worm crawled toward the blanketed baby.

"Get away from him!" she screamed,
still not completely convinced that Zoom
hadn't played a willing part in Richard's
plan. A shot of adrenalin gave her the
strength she needed to pull herself onto the
dock.

Once she was level with Zoom, she could
see the expression in his eyes. He wasn't
going to hurt the baby.

Zoom pulled open the blanket, tilting
the little boy to the side.

Jenna crawled across the few feet to
Zoom and little Bobby. She squinted at his
tiny face. "Breathe, Bobby, breathe," she
pleaded. Suddenly, as if in response to her
voice, the baby gurgled out a mouthful of
water.

Then, miraculously, the little guy let
out a wail that sounded better than anything
Jenna had ever heard in her life.

"He's okay," she sobbed. "He's okay."

Lifting him in her arms, she listened to his breathing and watched to be sure his chest was lifting in a natural rise and fall.

Zoom smiled back at her as if in agreement that the baby seemed to have survived the ordeal unharmed. Twice today, the baby had beaten the curse.

Where were Eddie and Richard? She scanned the shoreline for them, then looked toward the cabin. "Where are they?" she screeched.

"They went up there." Zoom pointed weakly.

Toward the dirt trail that led to the burial site of Jean Claude and Genevieve. Would another body lay there tonight?

Eddie's?

Oh, hell no! She scrabbled to her feet and grabbed the gun that lay a few feet away.

Yelling and then two gunshots echoed from the woods. She gripped the pistol tightly. Could she leave the baby here with Zoom? No. Zoom was so weak he could lose consciousness again, then the baby might tumble into the river.

Carefully, she picked up the newborn and held him with one arm. If Richard came back for her and this baby, he wouldn't find her defenseless. She walked slowly toward the wood line, pointing the gun toward the path, ready if danger burst from those woods again.

Which man had survived?

Because she knew, instinctively, that only one man would walk away from this epic clash.

CHAPTER TWENTY-SEVEN

She gasped for air, her heart beating a thousand times a minute, the blood rushing in her ears. It seemed to take forever until finally she saw the branches waving with a man's form pushing through the brush.

But which man?

Then she saw him and air exploded in her lungs.

"Eddie," she called. "Eddie." She ran toward him, still clutching the baby in her arms.

Eddie stumbled haltingly to her, enclosing her and the baby in his arms in an embrace, pulling them into his chest where she inhaled his scent, warm, breathing, alive.

He held her for a long moment before he crumpled slowly to his knees. She went with him, one arm supporting him under his arm and around his back, suspecting she was the only thing that kept him from collapsing completely in a dead fall.

"We're safe now. He gave me no choice," he whispered in a weak, bloodless voice.

Richard was dead. They were finally free. And all the generations to come after them. Thank God.

An enormous rush of relief blew through her as if released from deep in the portals of time. A fierce maelstrom of emotion flowed out of her, with all of the heartbreak and tears that had been suffered by all of the Genevieve's before her.

Then, a small, impossible knife of grief twisted in her stomach. For the sad role that Richard had played in this event. The man who'd been her managing editor, the

man she'd looked up to, respecting his
intellect and his news sense.

How could a colleague she'd revered so
much when she'd first joined the newspaper
have turned out to be this twisted?

But an eerie felling of destiny
reminded her that maybe he had been
genetically driven to do what he had done.
Much like she and Eddie seemed predetermined
to find each other.

As hard as the legend was to believe,
it seemed to morph into reality, with babies
dying and her boss turning into this
stalking monster, willing to kill in order
to obtain his heart's desire.

It was impossible to justify the
actions of so many different people unless
they were somehow tied to history or fate,
driven by something more powerful than a
mere human will.

She'd always felt this connection to
southern Louisiana, volunteering to cover
the hurricanes, over and over, always
finding story ideas that would bring her
back to the area.

Richard, as well as someone else, had
lured her to Eufaula, Louisiana. Bobby
Broussard Senior had searched her out in New
Orleans to scare her away. Or kill her?

Whatever the explanation, she realized
she'd always known something was off about
Richard, some sense of something not being
right.

She'd never responded to his romantic
advances. Because of something more than a
lack of attraction.

There had been an uneasiness whenever
she was alone with him.

Her subconscious had warned her.

Tears clouded her vision as she pulled back to look into Eddie's eyes. She and Eddie had saved the little Broussard baby. And saved themselves, as well.

"We survived," she whispered, looking into Eddie's eyes, the most beautiful eyes she'd ever seen.

This lifetime, they'd won.

Won a lifetime of love with each other?

"We beat the curse," he answered, pulling her close against his chest. "How many times have we gone through this, until we finally got it right?"

Did he really believe what he was saying or was it an emotional reaction to all that had happened?

Zoom stirred, muttering something. He'd sunk into unconsciousness while she'd waited for Eddie to reappear. She looked back at him. His eyes began to open.

"You're okay, Zoom. Everything's going to be all right."

He nodded weakly.

Then, a large whirring sound became audible and a sheriff's helicopter buzzed down the river toward them. Never had such an annoying sound been so welcome.

The bird lowered, blasting a rush of air over the clearing. There was just enough room to touch down on the opposite side of the cabin. Almost as though it were planned that way.

How many lucky coincidences had they encountered? How many lifetimes had it taken them to get it right?

Eddie looked at her. Did he realize what she was thinking?

His knowing smile said he did.

Jenna cradled the baby in her arms,

using the blanket and her body to shield him from the blast of the helicopter.

Eddie's cousin, Mike, opened the helicopter's side door and ran to them. "Thank God, you're okay," he yelled over the roar of the helicopter. "Where is the British soldier?"

Eddie pointed toward the cemetery. "He's dead."

"Good." Mike nodded vigorously. "That damned British soldier used that baby as leverage all the way up the river. No one would resist him and the photographer when they saw that baby with a gun to his head." He looked like he wanted to throw up.

A similar sickness filled Jenna thinking about how close to death the little baby had come.

He'd called Richard the *British Soldier*. As if the legend were true.

"He tied up cops and left them helpless in the woods. I guess he didn't kill them because that would have totally alienated the photographer."

"He got you too?" Eddie asked.

A huge bruise purpled along Mike's cheek.

"Oh, yeah," Mike said, then glanced down at Eddie's side, drenched with blood. "Not as bad as he got you, apparently. You okay buddy?"

Eddie nodded, leaning against Jenna for support. "Looks a lot worse than it really is."

"We need to package you up and get you out of here."

Eddie tilted his head toward Zoom and Jenna who was holding Bobby, Jr. "Them first."

Jenna shook her head. "No. You go with the baby."

Eddie nodded weakly, unable to argue. So, the EMT and Mike loaded Zoom in one side of the chopper and Eddie with the baby in the other side.

As the helicopter lifted off, Eddie looked down to see Jenna standing so small in the middle of all that wilderness, dwarfed by the trees and the river. But nothing could diminish the power of her expression as she watched them leave.

The strength of her spirit, her soul, had helped to break the curse, the longstanding demonic nightmare that had spread down through the generations.

He'd never doubted that she could.

※※※※※

Jenna watched the helicopter take Eddie away. Soon, they'd be together.

She turned to Mike. "What about Celia's baby?"

Mike raised his shoulders. "She was still in early labor, last I heard."

Then, the sound of engines rumbled from deep in the woods.

"The cavalry," Mike said. A pair of ATVs erupted from the path leading from the gravesite.

"There's an old logging trail back in there," Mike explained as he rubbed at another red spot on the side of his forehead.

"You got hit pretty bad. You okay?" She peered at the angry knot.

"Yeah," Mike said with a rueful nod. "I woke up tied up but determined to get loose and radio for help. The guy didn't find my backup radio. Man, though, he left a string of ticked off, angry cops and deputies all the way from here to town. Gotta give it to him, he was pretty effective for such a crazy guy."

Jenna nodded, wondering just how crazy Richard had been. What was true and what was imagination in this whole unbelievable situation?

Mike walked away to talk to the cops who had ridden in on the four wheelers.

Then, a boat buzzed up the river carrying more deputies. Mike walked back to her. "Our taxi's here," he nodded toward the boat.

A handful of sheriff's deputies got off. Mike spoke to the driver who nodded and then Mike waved her onto the boat.

The dark landing was lit now only by lanterns and flashlights. Would the beauty of the place be forever spoiled for her by the ugly events of this evening?

A deputy sheriff used an oar to push the boat away from the dock. He reached for the controls to the motorboat but stopped at a sound emanating from back in the woods.

A deep moaning sigh of release echoed from far back in the dark. Primordial, almost human, it rumbled through the trees toward them.

The sound wave hit her, pulsing through her body, connecting with her very cells, spiraling through the core of her being until finally the moaning died away, leaving her wrung free of tension, relaxed and content, with a sense that only happiness lay ahead of her and Eddie.

The deputy at the steering wheel looked back at them, with awe and fear tingeing his expression. "What was that?"

"A gator?" Mike said. He glanced at Jenna and even she could see he didn't believe that one bit.

"Never heard a gator sound like that," the deputy said with a nervous laugh. "That sounded almost human. Like some recorded Halloween sound."

It sounded like a final gasping release of tension from centuries of conflict and heartbreak.

It echoed still from the resting spot of Genevieve and Jean Claude.

Jenna and Mike looked in that direction. But they saw nothing and no other sound came from the woods.

She knew instinctively. "It's the death of the curse."

She closed her eyes as a smile spread across her face and for a long moment, she luxuriated in a sense of accomplishment. For Eddie and herself, as well as for Genevieve and Jean Claude.

And for all the Lejeunes and Devereaux that would come after them.

Footsteps brought her back to the present. A deputy ran along the dock.

"Mike, your cousin's baby was born. Eddie's gonna be happy to hear he's got a bouncing new nephew. Mother and child doing fine."

Mike looked at Jenna with the widest smile possible. "I guess you're right about that curse finally being broken. Two babies of our line have survived after the British soldier appeared."

She closed her eyes against the tears that rushed out. The curse had definitely been broken. Leaving the way open to happiness for all the descendants of Jean

Claude and Genevieve.

Leaving the possibility of a future for herself and Eddie. What they decided to do, now, was up to them.

*****

There were almost two days of giving police reports, talking to the press and getting medical treatment.

Despite the blood loss, Eddie's injury hadn't been too serious.

Zoom was still in the hospital but he was going to be okay. His ex-wife flew down from Atlanta to be with him.

There wouldn't be charges against him since he had believed he was saving a hostage. He'd never been implicated in any physical attacks on law enforcement, and had never seen the endangerment of little Bobby Broussard since he'd always stayed with the boat when Richard had gone to confront cops or deputies.

They'd floated downriver with the current when they'd neared checkpoints, with no boat motor to alert cops. Zoom said Richard seemed to have some preternatural ability to detect where deputies lay in wait.

Zoom had no idea Richard was leaving law enforcement officers tied up in the woods, had thought he was just conferring with them about the situation.

Man, he'd felt stupid, to be taken in by Richard like that. But, Richard seemed to have developed a great ability to deceive, one she sensed he'd developed over hundreds of years.

Finally, she and Eddie were able to return to Jean Claude and Genevieve's final resting spot. As they stepped into the small clearing behind the cabin, a warm welcoming sense of happiness swirled around Jenna that seemed to emanate from the gravestone.

"Do you feel their peace?" She looked at Eddie who nodded.

"They've finally escaped the torture of knowing their descendants will face their same tragic end." He stared down into her eyes, a shift in light playing across his face. "That or we've realized their love in this new lifetime." He laughed as if he might be joking.

She studied his face, his beautiful face, with its masculine strength, but also a sensitivity that seemed to have been honed by centuries of suffering. "Do you buy," she asked, "that we've loved each other in another lifetime, that we're Genevieve and Jean Claude reincarnated to finish their mission of reuniting with our one true love?"

He smiled knowingly. "I don't know if I've met you in another lifetime but I do know I've been looking for you for all of this lifetime."

Warmth emanated from him, swirling through her, his words melting her center.

Then, he pulled her into an embrace, his arms closing around her in a circle of love that seemed centuries in the making.

Were they Jean Claude and Genevieve reincarnated?

She didn't know the answer to that one. But with Eddie's arms surrounding her, she knew she was exactly where she'd been trying to get for all of this lifetime.

Where she wanted to be for the rest of her life.

Then, he brushed his lips across hers

softly, with the slightest of touches.

"I can get used to this," she murmured underneath his lips.

"Never," he answered. "A lifetime of this won't even be enough."

Then, he kissed her and she knew they had a love that would last a lifetime.

Fifty or sixty years of Eddie Devereaux's kisses? Maybe that would be enough. For this lifetime.

The End

Dear Reader:

If you enjoyed this book, I hope you will leave a review wherever you bought this book or on Goodreads. That really helps me get the word out to other readers. If you would like to be notified about future books, you can subscribe to my newsletter.
Click here to join: *http://www.rileymckissack.com/contact*
Or visit me at *http://www.rileymckissack.com*
Or on Twitter or Facebook

Other Books by Riley McKissack
Men of the Badge Novels
Targeted to Kill Mick's and Becca's story kicks off the Men of the Badge novels

Tempted To Kill Alisa and Weston's story

Taunted by a Killer Forrester and Cassie's story

No Escape From A Killer Luke and Emmy's story moves Men of the Badge to the North Georgia mountain town of Hawk's Peak

The Killer You Know Grant and Katie reunite in Hawk's Peak

Men of the Badge Novels Set in Chance
The Gravetender's List

About a Girl

Not By Chance

Missed Chances

Men of the Badge Bundle

Storm Warnings - Island Heat

Deadly Undercurrents – Island Heat

www.ingramcontent.com/pod-product-compliance
Lightning Source LLC
Chambersburg PA
CBHW062020170626
46813CB00001B/230